Story Summary

Kansas 1899. Deborah Sutton barely remembers her family's feud with the Van Cleves. Her mother died that summer, and her father was killed. Nothing else mattered to seven-year-old Deborah eighteen years ago. Still, Deborah knows the Van Cleves tried to steal her family's land, and she despises them for it.

Trey Van Cleve does remember the land war. Trey saw bloody bodies hanging from the roof of his home and fled fire in the night. The monster under Trey's boyhood bed had a name, and the name was Sutton.

One night when they both seek solitude in the same shadowy park, Deborah and Trey meet. Each is intrigued by a mysterious stranger who is no more than a friendly voice in the dark. Learning each other's identity is an appalling surprise. How can a Sutton befriend a Van Cleve? How can a Van Cleve love a Sutton? Deborah and Trey are going to find out.

Into the *Light*

BGB

03/08

20/4/23

?)

nnell

Copyright © 2013 by Ellen O'Connell
www.oconnellauthor.com

ISBN-13: 978-1490371016
ISBN-10: 149037101X

DEDICATION

This book is dedicated to my first readers, who have made my romances better books, and who didn't fail with this one.

Bringing Deborah and her sisters back a second time in *Beautiful Bad Man* was the idea of one reader, which in the end inspired the entire story of *Into the Light.* The idea for the setting of the Afterword in this book came from another first reader.

Thanks, ladies.

Into the Light

1

June 24, 1898
Las Guasimas, Cuba

THE FIRST BULLET smashed into Trey's shoulder, spinning him in his tracks. The second knocked him off the narrow trail and sent him tumbling down the steep mountainside into dense jungle below. He landed on his back with a thump that drove the air from his lungs.

Long seconds passed before his lungs inflated again. The first wheezing breath was pure pain. Trey stared at the green canopy of foliage overhead as another shot echoed from above. He almost laughed. A Spanish sharpshooter would boast tonight about picking off an American soldier and slowing the advance on the entrenched Spanish positions.

Someday this would be a fine story to share with friends over a drink in a cool bar. Stripped of the dirt, sweat, and pain, it would be funny. Before seeing action of any kind, Trey Van Cleve, best sharpshooter in his outfit, gets blasted ass over teakettle by the enemy. Trey tried to get up and fell back flat. No part of him wanted to work right yet.

He examined the wound in his shoulder. Not much blood had leaked out of the neat, round hole in his flannel shirt. Of course the navy blue color absorbed and hid the wet stain pretty well.

The crimson pool spreading on the crushed fronds under him told a different story. The numbness had passed. Pain throbbed more and more persistently in his shoulder and radiated down his arm, across his chest, and into his side. After tearing through every muscle in its path, the bullet had exited in a much messier way than it entered.

Still, it was only his shoulder. He should be able to sit up or at least roll over by now.

He couldn't remember hearing a second shot, but something had hit his back and blown him off the trail like a rag doll. He squirmed and explored with the fingers of his good hand. Blood. Not much but enough to lead him to another wound. Right next to his spine.

His fingers trembled as they explored the damage and found another hole in his shirt, in his flesh. One he couldn't feel. The wound was right *there*, angling beside and under the bony column that let a man walk upright, and nothing below his waist moved no matter what he did. Legs, knees, ankles, toes. Nothing.

Fighting panic, he tried to think. The shoulder wound was survivable—if he could slow the bleeding—if once the shooting stopped men started combing through this ungodly tangle of trees and bushes looking for wounded—if he was still conscious and could call out when he heard them—if he passed out and they found him anyway.

Did he want to survive half whole, dependent on others for his most basic needs? He'd treated defying death like a hobby these last years, traveling alone in wild places, seeking adventures like this war, but he'd never considered not dying, but living crippled, unable to so much as sit up on his own.

Considering it now, he didn't find much to recommend it. Then again, paralysis could be a temporary reaction to shock. It had to be. Once the surgeons removed the bullet, everything would work again.

What if it didn't?

Dying would be easy. Do nothing. Pass out from loss of blood and fade away.

Damn it. The letters to his mother and sister he'd kept putting off would never be written. He'd never find a home, find a wife, settle down and have children.

Gambling against death was one thing. Losing another. Dying on this sweltering, humid, pestilence-ridden island would definitely be losing.

Cursing the Spanish, the Cubans, the American Army, and himself, most of all himself, Trey untied the bandana at his throat and shoved it under his shirt, over the top of his shoulder, and into the hole on the other side, muffling most of his moan behind clenched teeth. Fresh sweat popped out on skin already soaked with old.

He fumbled for his knife, pulled his shirt out of his trousers, and began cutting pieces for more bandage material. When he finished doing everything he could, he lay quiet and waited, grateful the blood-sucking insects that swarmed day and night preferred diving into his spilled blood rather than taking more directly out of him, hoping the stories he'd heard about land crabs in these jungles were exaggerated.

THE SEARCH DETAILS found him, although he passed out. The doctor in the tent hospital at Siboney stopped the bleeding Trey's efforts had only slowed.

Medical personnel transported him to an offshore hospital ship where a surgeon used the modern miracle of a radiograph to locate the bullet next to Trey's spine and remove it. No other miracles occurred. His lower body remained paralyzed.

By the time he reached the hospital in Montauk, New York, Trey was close to drowning in an ugly mix of anger and self-pity. No one had forced him to volunteer to fight the Spanish in Cuba. No one except Trey Van Cleve patched his own wounds and gambled on a different outcome.

Reason made no difference. Trey did not want to live in a wheelchair, dependent on others for almost everything except combing his hair and feeding himself.

More of the men of the 1st United States Volunteer Cavalry returned, some wounded, more suffering from pernicious fevers and other diseases. The few ambulatory patients left Trey alone, which was fine with him.

He didn't want pity or even sympathy. He didn't want company, and except for doctors and nurses paid to deal with him, he got what he wanted—until the day a living skeleton plopped down on Trey's bed without invitation.

"I'm Jamie Lenahan," the skeleton said, "and you're Webster Alexander Van Cleve." He paused, then added, "The Third."

Trey said nothing as he studied the man. Lenahan had the dark hair, pale skin, and blue eyes of the black Irish. Even now, what was left of him was a handsome man.

Getting no reaction from his opening gambit, Lenahan tried again. "I hear a Spanish bullet put you in that chair. A bullet in the back."

Trey had heard the rumors whispered about him. Until now, no one had shown the courage to face him with the accusation.

To his own surprise, and probably Lenahan's, Trey laughed out loud. "If you're spoiling for a fight, you'll have to find someone else to oblige, and you're in worse shape than I am. I'll leave this place alive, and I wouldn't bet on your odds."

Lenahan grinned back, blue eyes fever bright. "It's betting that's brought me here. I've wagered some of the men I can get the truth about that wound out of you, and I've a sister who needs all I can leave her."

"If pure quinine doesn't help, have you tried any of the other recipes?"

"Quinine is all they're handing out here, and the chances of snake oil working for me are the same as of you wearing out dancing shoes. What work would I be getting if I went home like this? Now tell the truth, were you running the wrong way when that bullet hit?"

"Surely you know a coward will lie. Why not just ask the doctors?"

"Some of the boyos did, and they were told to mind their own business."

In spite of a certain lilt to his voice, Lenahan had no real accent except from New York's Lower East Side. He also didn't have the problem meeting Trey's eyes that plagued even the doctors and nurses.

Trey settled back in his chair, enjoying himself for the first time in a long while. "Hiring nurses and caretakers for the rest of my life will be expensive, so I can use the money. How much will we win?"

"We?"

"Fifty-fifty."

"Five dollars. It's five dollars."

"Sad for your sister."

The two of them eyed each other a while. Lenahan cracked first. "Devil take it. It's a hundred, and I'll give you ten."

"Forty."

"Twenty-five, and only if you've got more than a story."

"We were marching single file on one of those narrow trails along a ridge, broke through the jungle into a clear spot, and a sharpshooter singled me out. I know the names of men who were behind me and saw it."

"You're making that up. You were the sharpshooter. Everyone knows that."

"Ironic as it is, I was supposed to find a place and set up to pick off some of the Spanish, but I never got that far." Trey wondered if Lenahan knew what ironic meant, knew defining it for him would be a bad idea. He stared into the blue eyes, waiting for the other man to give way again.

"Twenty-five," Lenahan said, "and that's if I can find one of these men you say saw you shot."

"Done. Talk to Horace Findlay. You'll have to find which tent he's in, and I heard he's in no better shape than you, so you better hurry."

Lenahan managed to rise from the bed and walk away without staggering. Cursing someone else's fate instead of his own at least varied Trey's daily routine. He liked the way Lenahan had charged right at him.

When the Irishman returned the next day and handed him twenty-five dollars, Trey decided to take a chance.

"I'll give this back if you'll spend it on whatever quinine formula the doctors think has the best chance of working for you. If it doesn't work, it's one more gamble I took and lost. If it does, you come work for me when we get out of here."

"I'm not taking charity," Lenahan said, his mouth tightening to a slit.

"I'm not offering charity. I'm going to need help. If you can get back on your feet, you can provide it."

"You need a nurse, and I'm not one."

"I'm not asking you to wipe my ass. I'll hire someone else for that."

"You have two arms. Wipe your own arse."

"Only the left arm works worth a damn," Trey pointed out.

"Use that one and work to fix the other instead of sticking your nose where it's not wanted."

Trey nodded and watched Lenahan's retreating back with regret. Leaving the money on the bed, Trey went back to staring down the line of army cots in the tent that was his home in Camp Wikoff.

Tent hospitals in Cuba were one thing. In New York, Camp Wikoff was something else. Now that the newspapers had discovered the primitive conditions here, the scandal would have politicians scrambling to improve everything from the dirt floors to the food.

The door at the far end of the tent opened, giving a brief glimpse outdoors. The ground was churned to no more than mud flats, but farther on Trey glimpsed the deep greens of late summer in New York. A sliver of homesickness stirred inside him.

Kansas wouldn't be green this time of year. The native grass dulled and yellowed early there. On the ranch, his father's hands would be looking forward to the fall roundup. Farmers would be harvesting fields of wheat and oats shimmering gold in the sun.

Let me walk again, and I'll go home and make what I can of it. I won't crawl back, but if I can walk, I'll go.

Aah, who was he fooling. He'd like to see his mother and Alice again, but the last eight years had made no difference in his feelings about his father. In his wildest imaginings, Trey couldn't conceive of a path to a civil, much less friendly, relationship with his father.

However God felt about the mess that was the Van Cleve family, He certainly knew Trey would never offer any bargain that included an attempt at reconciliation with his father if there was any possibility of having to keep it.

Approaching footsteps sounded behind him. Trey turned to see Jamie Lenahan swoop up the twenty-five dollars from the bed and do a pretty good job of stomping off—for a skeleton.

THE ROOMS JAMIE rented in New York City were more Spartan than Trey would have settled for, with bare floors and plaster walls stained and yellowed with age. Jamie, on the other hand, considered a ground floor apartment with running water and a wash room an unconscionable luxury, one more proof of their very different backgrounds.

Without admitting he had never needed the few dollars from their original bet, Trey reassured Jamie about the cost. After all, bare wood floors made maneuvering the wheelchair easier. Trey and Jamie became experts at ways to get in and out over the front steps.

Jamie benefited from regular gifts of food from Mrs. Farrell on the second floor and Mrs. Long on the fourth. The pharmacist's concoction of quinine, methylene blue, and other ingredients that sounded more likely to kill than cure didn't stop the Irishman's recurring bouts of fever and chills, but the attacks came further and further apart and with less and less intensity. As late summer gave way to fall, he began to gain weight and fill out.

Trey did his best, but his appetite had disappeared with the use of his legs. He remained what Jamie derisively called a sack of bones, although ruthless exercise began to rebuild some strength in his right shoulder. Not enough that he could lift himself out of the bath yet, damn it.

"Need some help here," he yelled to Jamie for the second time.

"I'm coming. You don't want me burning Mrs. Long's good soup now, do you?" Jamie hurried into the room, helped Trey to the chair beside the tub, and handed him towels.

"I don't want you burning anything, but the water's getting cold and so are my feet." Trey heard his own words and went still. "It's a memory," he whispered. "I know the water's cooling, and it's a memory."

"Let's make sure," Jamie said, disappearing through the doorway and reappearing with a fork in his hand.

"If you think stabbing my feet with a fork will prove something, forget it."

"If I wanted to stab you, I'd have a knife now, wouldn't I?" Jamie sat on the edge of the tub, pulled one of Trey's feet to his lap, and ran the tines of the fork over the sole.

Trey stopped breathing. "I felt it. Not a memory, the real thing."

"Your toes moved."

"No, they didn't. I didn't see it. You're imagining it."

Jamie repeated the stroke with the fork. Trey watched his big toe and the one next to it twitch. Slightly, so slightly, but unmistakably.

That night, for the first time since Cuba, Trey buried his face in his pillow and wept.

"Spare me the virtues of your Joseph," Deborah said, beginning to lose her temper.

"All right, I will. You see Uncle Jason every day. He's a good man. You know all men aren't like our pa."

"You have no idea what he was like," Deborah said. "You were less than a month old when he was killed."

"I know he was strict and harsh. Judith told me what he was like. You just have to be careful and pick someone nice."

Strict and harsh. Deborah stifled an ugly laugh, but no matter how heated any argument with either of her sisters grew, she would never tell them the truth, never speak of it to the few in the family who did know.

Go ahead and marry in a cloud of silk and joy. No matter how angry you make me, I will never spoil that for you the way he spoiled it for me when he came in the night, put his hand over my mouth, and whispered of a daughter's duty. You will never learn from me about that kind of fear and pain and betrayal.

"You were only seven when he died," Miriam said, twisting to see the back of her dress. "You can't remember."

Deborah caught herself tugging at her skirt seam and hid her cold hands behind her back where no one could see them twisting against each other.

"Judith was five, and she's your authority, but nothing I say matters because I was only seven? I guess you're right. All that matters is that I want something different. I'm happy for you that you have Joseph, and I'm happy for Judith. Why can't you let me have what I want and be happy for me?"

"Because what you want isn't right. It isn't *natural.*"

"So I need to change because I embarrass you? Did your future mother-in-law say something about your old maid sister?"

"She just wondered why—like everyone, she wonders. You're beautiful."

"Oh, and aren't you just giving yourself a pat on the head."

Dark hair, dark eyes, skin that kept a pale gold hue no matter how carefully shaded from the sun, Deborah and her sisters looked so much alike if they styled their hair the same way, only close family could tell them apart at any distance.

Accusing Miriam of conceit didn't distract her. "You're beautiful, you're clever, and you're kind when you're not behaving as if you're the only one ever hurt, like now. You're not too old yet. All you'd have to do is smile at one of the eligible men Aunt Em is always rounding up for you. There's no reason...."

"Oh, so you and Judith chose husbands carefully and are ensured of everlasting happiness, but I'm supposed to marry one of the lazy old men or boys with spots all over their face that Aunt Em drags over every Sunday and twice on holidays. Why don't you marry one of them? They'd suit you so much better than Joseph the paragon." Her voice had risen and gone shrill, and she didn't care.

"Don't settle then. Make an effort and you can attract...."

"I'm not making an effort. I'm not going to marry, and you will just have to live with the humiliation of having a shriveled up, old...."

The bedroom door opened, and Deborah stopped the furious flow of words. Aunt Emma walked in, the wide-eyed innocence on her face marking her as a co-conspirator. No one right outside that door could have missed hearing the quarrel inside.

Pretending she had heard nothing meant Aunt Em knew full well Miriam intended to broach forbidden subjects. In fact Aunt Em, who had spent the last eighteen years determined to find a way to "cure" her oldest niece, had probably orchestrated the whole thing. Maybe Miriam had a point about the foolishness of anyone planning to live out her life quietly here on the farm.

Panic welled in Deborah's breast. Without a word, she darted out the door, down the stairs, and into the barn, where she hid in the hayloft until she mustered the composure to walk back in the house and begin helping with supper preparations as if nothing had happened.

JOSEPH'S FAMILY HAD rented the town hall for the wedding celebrations. Deborah helped with the decorations, shed a few tears in the church as she watched her sister become Mrs. Joseph Timmerman, smiled through endless toasts and congratulatory speeches, and made sure everyone saw her dance with each of her uncles when the dancing started that evening.

Duty done, she picked up her wrap from its hiding place under a ribbon-festooned table, and escaped into the darkness outside. Slipping away from gatherings like this was always easy. So long as she reappeared tonight in time to pretend to try to catch the bridal bouquet, no one would miss her. The little garden behind the hall with its facing benches provided a perfect haven she had used before.

Deborah sat carefully, not wanting to damage the skirt of her best dress on the wood bench, drew in a deep breath of the fresh spring air, and tilted her face up toward the stars.

The door to the hall opened again, and a large shadow lurched out. Another followed, steadier on his feet, but cursing as he stumbled over the slight step down to the walk.

Deborah jumped up, heart pounding. No one had ever come out that door while she had hidden here before.

The two men blocked the easiest way to return inside, but she could sneak around the outside of the hall to the front door.

So much for her plans to sit in the coolness of the night and enjoy a little solitude. The men were strangers to her and drunk. The one slurring as he argued with the other was very drunk.

"All I'm saying is a man ought to be able to get a decent drink when he wants it. What the hell kind of party is it with nothing to drink but that fruity piss. I shouldn't have to empty my own flask to get a decent drink."

"Be quiet, will you. If her family hears you going on like that, they'll pound you into the floor. Hell, if Joe hears, he'll stomp you himself. Come on, we can get a few drinks at the saloon and head on home."

"Mm not leaving. Drinking right here if I want to."

Deborah froze at the sound of a third voice, one near her, not by the door.

"There's a lady out here, gentlemen. Home or the saloon, you need to move on."

"Like hell. I'm not going...."

Steps crunched across the gravel, and a thump changed the spew of drunken words to gasps. A punch? The man who had spoken so courteously had punched the drunk?

Deborah sidled along the bench, intent on getting around it and away.

Her defender spoke again. "Here's his hat. Why don't you get him home and let him sleep it off?"

More gasping, grunts, subdued cursing. The halfway sober one urged the drunk along, and the sounds faded. Deborah hesitated. Should she thank the man who had intervened on her behalf before leaving?

"If you came out for a little fresh air, please don't leave because of them—or me."

His voice was strangely appealing, right in the middle ranges for a man, soft and smooth. Even drunk he'd never sound stupid or crude. And where had that thought come from, some silly female fairy tale?

"Thank you for making them leave," Deborah said, "but I only meant to sit for a minute and take in the quiet and a little fresh air. I'd best go back inside now."

"I'm sorry you heard any of that, but you must have meant to stay more than a minute. Please. Come back to your bench, and I'll go. I shouldn't even be here."

"You're a guest. Of course you should be here."

"I'm not a guest. I was out walking and heard the music, so I've been sitting here listening, stealing a moment."

His voice swirled around her like a soft, warm blanket in the cool night. She should say a few more polite words and let him go on his way.

As if drawn by an invisible hand, she moved back to the bench and sat, forgetting about the skirt of her best dress. "Please stay and enjoy the music. With you here I won't need to run into the dark if another drunk staggers through the door."

His laugh was as alluring as his spoken words. "Did you recognize him? From what they said it must be a wedding party. Were they really invited guests?"

Maybe Joseph the paragon had invited those ruffians. No one in her family had. "Yes, it is a wedding party. I don't know everyone invited, but they must have been guests."

She heard steps on the gravel again, saw the darker shadow as he sat across from her. The hedges surrounding this small enclave darkened the moonless night further. She couldn't discern a single feature, couldn't tell if he was short or tall, broad or slim.

Her breath caught then steadied. She'd been right to tell him to stay. A man who forced two drunks to leave because he knew a woman was present didn't pose a danger. If they shared the night in silence, he could enjoy the music that had brought him here, and she could pretend to be alone.

The music sounded distant and tinny. Pretending to be alone didn't make it so, and his voice.... If he spoke again now that the danger had passed, his voice would prove ordinary.

Fear and nerves could cause goose bumps on her arms and a flutter in her stomach. An unseen stranger's voice couldn't do that.

Long minutes passed. Her skirt rustled as she shifted on the bench, and the stones underfoot ground against one another. She fought the urge to cough, cleared her throat instead, and gave in to the urge to make him speak again.

"Do you walk this way every night?"

"No, I'm only visiting a friend here in town. Tonight was the first time I walked this way."

"Oh, then you don't live near here."

"My family lives almost a day's ride away, and I'm staying with them. I haven't lived here since I left for school in the East."

College! Back home from college. He must be young. She tried to think of a family in the area that would have sent a son to college in the last years and came up blank. "I envy you. I wish I could have attended college."

"Maybe you still can. A lot of women do these days, except.... I'm sorry. It's not that easy for everyone, is it, and a husband and children make it impossible for women."

He started to position the cane to use to lever himself upright, then swished it through the air like a sword instead. Until tonight the thing had been nothing but one more symbol of what he could no longer do.

Driving the cane right into the drunk's belly had knocked all the air out of him more effectively than a punch, and finding a way to shut up a lout like that felt good. More than good. Trey gave the cane another swish through the air. Just as well no moon shone tonight or he'd be howling at the sky.

He walked slowly back toward the street. He should be ashamed about lying to the woman about the music, but what kind of man admitted to a woman he couldn't walk a half mile without resting at the halfway mark? At least his pride still worked as well as ever.

Maybe he should have introduced himself, but then she hadn't given her name either, and not knowing had advantages. Let her stay a mystery, and he could imagine her any way he wanted, petite and blonde, tall and brunette, young, pretty, and of course, fascinated by a sack of bones who couldn't walk as well as most one-year-olds.

3

WATCHING COUSIN CALEB win Hubbell's annual Fourth of July shooting contest was a Sutton family tradition. As always, Deborah's family filled most of the front row of chairs set up for spectators, and as always, Deborah sat at one end, Miriam on her right and open space on her left.

Deborah fingered the fluffy bits of cotton in the pocket of her dress then withdrew her hand. When the shooting began, she'd stuff the cotton in her ears. Until then she wanted to know what was going on in the crowd behind her.

After the first two or three years, Deborah had expected to hear resentment over the way Caleb dominated the contest. To her surprise and amusement, and that of Caleb's wife, Norah, the town chose instead to take a fierce pride in its very own former gunman.

No one in Hubbell spoke of winning the annual shooting contest any longer but of "beating Sutton". Last year Mannie Ascher had gone so far as to purchase an old buffalo gun like Caleb's, and Ascher had practiced with it for months. Not that it did him any good, he'd missed his target in the fourth round.

Other towns had contests with elaborate rules and ways of scoring shots and determining the winner by the total score, but Hubbell kept things simple.

Paper targets hung on nails pounded in tree stumps. The first time a man missed his target, he was eliminated. Shooting started at a hundred yards, and the successful contestants moved back twenty yards after each round.

Deborah counted eight shooters on the field. Behind her, men placed bets on how many of the eight would make it to the second round. Mannie Ascher's father sat directly behind her, and Deborah could hear every word of his conversation with Mr. Lawson, who was behind Miriam.

"Last fall he bought one of those Mauser rifles the Spanish used in the war," Mr. Ascher said. "They're supposed to be the best, but I told him it's not the gun, it's the eyes. Sutton was just born seeing distances better than most men. It's a gift."

Deborah said nothing, but good eyesight alone wouldn't win this contest. Strength and steady hands entered into it.

And practice. Caleb didn't let his Sharps hang on the wall unused more than a few days at a time. He'd let Deborah hold that buffalo gun once. It was heavy, and in this contest a man had to heft his rifle. Contestants could shoot from any position, but they couldn't use a tripod or any other support.

"Yep, not one of them down there is going to beat Sutton," Lawson said. "They ought to just give him the trophy and cash now and save time, but I reckon when you let a man enter a contest, you have to give him a chance."

Deborah stopped listening as she scanned through the spectators. She had watched all morning, but she never saw anyone who could be her mysterious stranger.

She didn't know whether to feel relief or disappointment. Her stranger wouldn't be back in town, and if he was, did she really want to see some callow youth who wouldn't fit that voice?

She spotted an unfamiliar face, not in the audience but among the shooters. Her breath caught for a moment, but he couldn't be her stranger. The man on the field needed a cane to walk and had to lean on it heavily just standing there.

A man like that wouldn't stroll through town in the evening for pleasure. She doubted he could walk very far unaided. Not only that, he was her own age or even older, no college boy.

The men behind her started talking again. They recognized the stranger even if she didn't.

"Well, I'll be.... Look who's down there," Ascher said. "You got to give him credit for nerve. He looks like the recoil from a .22 would knock him over."

"He looks like a strong breeze would knock him over," Lawson said, "but I guess that's an improvement. I heard when he crawled home this spring he was on crutches. I don't see nothing but a fancy stick now."

How exactly could a man crawl on crutches? Deborah studied the man with the cane.

Most of the others, like Caleb, wore work clothes for the contest, but the man she watched had on gray flannel trousers and a white shirt. Tight around his skinny middle, his belt divided his body into two distinct halves. Someone should make him a gift of suspenders.

When he pulled his hat off and mopped his face with a handkerchief, she saw the bones of his face angling out sharply under pale skin. Only a thick, unruly thatch of medium brown hair showed any sign of vigor.

She tried to imagine him healthy. Handsome, she decided. Handsome in that elegant way some men had. A rifle hung from his right hand. He leaned on the cane in his left. The fancy stick.

"Webster Van Cleve is a right bastard, but even he doesn't deserve a son like that," Ascher said, "begging the pardon of any ladies who heard my lapse there."

Van Cleve! A quick glance to her right showed Miriam deep in conversation with Judith, oblivious to what the old men behind them had to say. No one sitting farther away showed any sign of having heard the name.

Deborah squinted at the man again. Even though the Van Cleves had been enemies of her family since she'd first come to live with Uncle Jason and Aunt Emma, she could only remember seeing any of them a few times, and the one she remembered was Mrs. Van Cleve, beautiful and haughty, her golden blonde hair perfectly styled, her shapely figure showcased in the latest fashion.

"I heard he don't even use his old man's name," Lawson said. "His name is the same as his father and grandfather before him, but he calls himself Trey. I guess plain American ain't good enough for him, so he picked out some foreign word for three, Spanish or something."

For goodness sake, hadn't either Lawson or Ascher ever played a game of cards? Didn't everyone learn the one, two, and three-spot cards as ace, deuce, and trey? Despising the Van Cleve family because they were arrogant, corrupt, and even criminal was one thing, making ignorant, ridiculous comments about a man's name was another.

"Maybe he's got reason not to use the old man's name," Ascher said. "You sure can't see any sign of Van Cleve in him. He must be more than half a foot taller."

Deborah's hand dove in her pocket and fisted over the bits of cotton. The two old gossips fell silent, as well they should.

Someone braver must have given them the evil eye and let them know they'd gone too far. No, Mr. Lawson started in again on the same ugly speculation.

"If you're right, maybe he didn't run off as soon as he was full growed. Maybe Van Cleve kicked him out."

Ascher wasn't done yet either. "Except for the darker hair he looks just like his mother, at least he did before he got that bullet in the back running the wrong way in Cuba. She's a real beauty, but it's not natural for a man to look that pretty."

That was it. From the fussing still going on in the open field where the contestants stood, the shooting wouldn't start for another five or ten minutes. Deborah shoved the pieces of cotton in her ears anyway.

Whatever Ascher and Lawson came up with next, she wasn't listening to one more malicious word about Webster Van Cleve, III. Even if he was as wicked as his father. Even if he outdid his father by a factor of ten. In fact she hoped the Third won this blasted contest. Well, maybe not, but she hoped he was first runner up behind Caleb.

TREY TOED THE shooting line and tried to estimate how many shots he could make before falling flat on his face in front of half the town, which would be doubly embarrassing because most of them would cheer. The Mayor droned on about the rules, prizes, and history of the country back to Columbus.

Sweat beaded on Trey's forehead and ran into his eyes. The morning was not yet half gone, and already every man's face shone with moisture as the temperature and humidity rose in tandem.

The Mayor's voice grew shrill as he reached the events of 1776. Resplendent in top hat and coat, meaty face slowly darkening from red to purple, he'd have to wind down soon. Trey lowered his rifle to the ground and centered the cane in front of him, curling both hands over the knob on top and leaning heavily.

At this rate he didn't have to worry how many contest rounds he could endure. He'd be an undignified heap on the ground before the first shot was fired, which would serve him right for wasting good money to enter this contest on a whim.

The whole thing was Jamie's fault. If Jamie hadn't gone off with his latest lady love, he'd have been around to play the voice of reason.

The other contestants stood gazing into space or staring at their feet. At least they'd known what they were getting into. They probably heard some version of this speech every year.

A flutter of white caught Trey's eye. The man at the other end of the line had his handkerchief out and was rubbing the barrel of his rifle with it. Every shooter straightened, smiles breaking out on sweaty faces as the Mayor stuttered to an abrupt halt and scurried out of the way.

The handkerchief man turned his head and looked down the line. Trey dropped the cane and jerked upright, heart hammering. Cal Sutton. At this distance he seemed unchanged from the monster who had haunted Trey's boyhood nightmares. Hard face. Lean body under broad shoulders.

Trey stared, hate, or something close to it, twisting in his belly. Memories flashed one after another—of Sutton breaking in on his family at breakfast and frightening them half to death, of dead bodies and fire in the night, of holding hands with his hysterical mother on one side and his weeping sister on the other as they boarded the train taking them away from

Hubbell, away from home and the bloody destruction Sutton wrought.

Sutton lifted his hat and ran his forearm over his face. Sun glinted off silver frosting his dark blond hair at the temples. At least time had affected the devil a little. He must be close to fifty now.

Taking a deep breath, Trey looked away, leaned down, and picked up his cane and his Winchester. He knew now what he hadn't back then—Sutton had fought his side of the land war with bloody ruthlessness, but Webster Alexander Van Cleve, Jr., had started the war and hired killers to fight it for him.

The emotions Trey had felt as a boy would only make a fool of him today. Still, to hell with collapsing. He'd collapse after he beat Sutton, and Jamie could decide whether to drag him to a doctor or the graveyard.

The field was clear. The Mayor shouted, "Fire at will!" Trey raised his rifle, snugged the stock tight against the scar on his shoulder, and sighted as if this were a life or death shot.

Only four men qualified for the sixth round. Only two for the eighth.

Trey hobbled to the new position on shaky legs, his jaw clenched. His shoulder radiated pain as if it had been beaten with a sledgehammer. If only he'd thought to fasten some kind of pad over the scar before signing up for this, his chances of getting through the next round would be better.

The Mayor hustled up to him, carrying a chair.

"Here. There's no rule that says you can't sit for a minute while the targets are checked."

The chair looked inviting. Sitting for a few minutes would make it possible to continue. Trey waited for Sutton to object, but Sutton just shrugged.

Sitting did help. Enough he hit his target, even if a little off center. Trey managed the ninth round by force of will but couldn't pry himself from the chair for the tenth, much less lift the rifle.

Losing was bad enough, but losing to Sutton? A bitter taste flooded his mouth as he shook his head at the Mayor, unwilling to concede defeat in words.

Leaving his position, Sutton sauntered over to join Trey and the Mayor. Trey's hands tightened on his rifle as he imagined jamming the barrel in the man's stomach and pulling the trigger at the first gloating word.

Sutton reached in his pocket, brought out a single gleaming two-and-a-half-inch brass cartridge, and held it in the palm of an outstretched hand.

"I got a little overconfident this year and only brought a dozen of these with me. Used two warming up. How about we each take a last shot and call it a draw? Next year when you have some meat back on your bones, we'll show them what real shooting's like."

Trey couldn't believe the offer, or the civil, straightforward way it was made, or the fact he didn't have the strength to accept it. "It'll be half an hour before I can get to my feet even with the cane," he admitted.

"The rules only say you have to shoot from the line. They don't say you have to be standing when you do it. I killed your father's men stretched out on my belly. I bet you can hit that target from yours."

Trey didn't have to go down on his stomach to make the last shot. Pure fury surged hot through every vein, lifted him to his feet, and gave him strength.

He fell back in the chair, sure he'd hit the target dead center. Sutton didn't have any doubts either.

"Give Mr. Van Cleve the trophy, and I'll take the cash prize," he told the Mayor. "Norah doesn't need another one of those things to dust, and Mr. Van Cleve doesn't need the money."

Sutton didn't wait for anyone to agree but strode away toward the viewing stand. More than a dozen of the spectators poured off the platform and met him halfway.

He lifted a dark-haired woman right off the ground, knocking her wide-brimmed hat askew as he spun her in a circle and kissed her on the mouth. Age and child-bearing had stolen any slimness of youth, but her face lit up as she hugged him around the neck and kissed him back, laughing up at him when he finally released her. That would be his wife, the one Trey's father to this day referred to as "the Hawkins woman" and blamed for involving Sutton in the land war.

The rest of the men and women crowded around, slapping Sutton's back, hugging. How could a cold-blooded killer provoke admiration, hugging, and celebrating from anyone, even family?

How would a man feel surrounded by a family like that? How would it feel to kiss a wife in public and have her laugh and kiss back? Better than sitting here alone in an exhausted heap that's how.

Except Trey wasn't alone. The Mayor, who had hustled off after the last shots, returned, carrying the trophy, a large wood carving of a rifleman with an engraved plaque at the base. After handing it over, he hovered, oozing concern.

He'd be on the Van Cleve payroll. The Mayor of Hubbell always was. He must be a minor crony, however, one who didn't know helping the son wouldn't earn favor with the father.

Then again, maybe he was a genuinely kind man, and cynicism was out of line.

"You sit right here, and I'll find someone who can bring a buggy for you. Are you staying at the new hotel?"

"I'm staying with a friend, and he'll come looking for me soon. You're due to lead off the parade, aren't you? You go on, and I'll just sit here until Jamie comes."

The Mayor dithered a few minutes, but in the end he left.

Trey slipped off the chair, stretched out on the grass, and closed his eyes. A trace of the scent of gunpowder lingered in the summer air. A reminder, not bad at all.

The sun beat down hot, red on the inside of his eyelids, but it felt good now that he wasn't fighting to stay on his feet. Jamie would show up sooner or later, and with luck he wouldn't have the giggling Miss Caroline Tindell with him.

Trey was half asleep when a shadow blocked the sun and a hand closed over his shoulder. Jamie. The horse he had with him must be borrowed or stolen, and Trey didn't care which.

"You said you were coming here to watch," Jamie said, frowning. "And I take it from that ugly wood thing, you went and got your rifle and wore yourself to a frazzle instead, didn't you? At least you won."

"Tie. He got the cash. I got the trophy."

"Better than losing."

"It is. Where's the lovely Miss Tindell?"

Jamie gave up the disapproving air and grinned. "She decided she'd toyed with me enough for now and went off with some of her lady friends."

"Is she toying with you?"

"Of course. You don't think that girl is serious about an Irish Papist who does the lowest kind of manual labor at the mill, do you?"

"You could stop being stubborn, come back to work for me for twice the money, and save your back."

Why did he even bother offering? Jamie had quit the day they'd reached Hubbell and found a job at the local flour mill. Except for driving Trey out there the first time, Jamie had never set foot on the V Bar C.

"And live with you at your da's big ranch with my stomach in a churn the way yours is all the time? Taking your money would be stealing when you don't need help."

"In case you haven't noticed, I need help right now, and here you are helping when you could be charming Miss Tindell into taking an Irish Papist seriously."

Trey grabbed Jamie's offered hand and used it to haul himself off the ground and back on the chair.

"Helping a friend now and then isn't a job," Jamie said, "and I don't want her to take me seriously."

"I thought Miss Tindell was your true love."

"The only lady I'll love will be a good Catholic girl, and even here in this heathen place there are a few. Caro is using me to get her family to let her go to Europe with some cousins, and they'll probably pack the clever girl off tomorrow. Her grandmother almost had an apoplexy in the street today when she saw the girl with her hand on my arm."

Trey searched his friend's face for signs of injured pride and couldn't find any. Even so.

"You shouldn't let her use you like that."

"Why not? I'm enjoying it and getting an education on the workings of the female mind." Jamie led the horse close. "Now can you get on this noble beast by yourself, or do I have to pick you up and throw you across the saddle?"

"Give me one chance to crawl up on my own, then throw me."

Jamie didn't exactly have to throw him, but Trey didn't make it on his own either.

THE DINING ROOM in Hubbell's new hotel was everything Deborah had heard rumored. Deep carpet underfoot. Pristine starched white linen on each table. Gleaming silverware and crystal at each place.

Every year Cousin Caleb spent his prize money on dinner for the whole family in a nice restaurant, at least for the adult Suttons. It was another family tradition, but nowhere they'd been in years past had come close to this.

Conversation from other tables provided a low, contented hum in the background, accented by the occasional chink of a fork or knife against china. The rich scent of roasted meat filled the air.

Deborah took a seat between Aunt Emma and Miriam in happy anticipation, smiling to herself at the sight of Uncle Eli and Aunt Lucy with their heads close together, consulting over a single menu. Plump, blonde Lucy had gentled Uncle Eli in ways no one had thought possible and everyone appreciated.

Years ago Deborah's uncles had looked as much alike as she, Judith, and Miriam did now. They were tall men with dark hair and eyes, olive skin, and strong features. Nowadays, no one would mistake Uncle Jason, with his deeply lined, careworn face and stooped shoulders, for his younger brother. Nothing would ever stop Uncle Jason from worrying about the entire Sutton family and trying to fix everyone's problems.

Too bad Uncle Jason wasn't sitting right beside Aunt Emma because Aunt Em looked a little too impressed with their surroundings. Downright intimidated even.

Aunt Em's once red hair had faded to gray years ago, but reading emotion in the color suffusing her pale redhead's complexion had always been easy. Right now two bright red spots flared on her cheeks.

A fierce wave of protective love washed through Deborah. Aunt Em could be infuriating in her attempts to reshape Deborah into the image of Judith or Miriam, but she was also the woman who had taken in her husband's three orphan nieces with open arms and done it less than a year after her marriage. No fancy restaurant should ever be allowed to intimidate Emma Sutton.

"Judith was right about how we should dress, wasn't she?" Deborah whispered to her aunt. "Look. Not one lady here is any more elegant than we are. Your blue silk is perfect."

Aunt Em stopped staring fixedly at the tablecloth and took in the room and people around them. Her rigid posture slowly relaxed.

"You're right, and you and your sisters are the most beautiful young women here, although it's time we made you something as stylish as what your sisters are wearing."

Just like that, Aunt Em's initial awe disappeared.

Content in the gold bengaline that had served as her best summer dress since she was Miriam's age, Deborah studied her menu.

The food listed matched the elegant scrolled printing. Oyster soup. Usual fare such as beef and pork, but also baked pickerel in wine sauce. What would that be like?

"How does roast *domestic* duck differ from not domestic duck?" Miriam asked.

"You can chew without worrying about breaking a tooth on a shotgun pellet," Deborah said.

Miriam switched her disapproval from the menu to Deborah. "Well, I'm having roast beef, and it better not come drowned in some silly sauce."

Unlike her sister, Deborah regarded the Fourth of July dinners as opportunities to experiment. She'd have the soup and the pickerel, and her mouth watered at the thought of chocolate pudding with sabayon sauce, whatever that proved to be.

Oyster soup was—interesting. She wouldn't order it again, but now she knew. She half-listened to the conversations swirling around the table until Miriam's husband Joseph caught her attention with a question to Caleb.

"Miriam says the Mayor always stops rambling when you bring out your handkerchief. How did you ever get such a windbag to agree to that?"

"I had a little accident with the rifle the first year," Caleb said. "I started rubbing a spot of dust on the barrel, and somehow I shot the heel off of one of the Mayor's boots."

Smiles broke out on Sutton faces around the table. Judith laughed out loud. Joseph's stunned look marked him as new to the family.

William Dalton, an easygoing blond bear of a man, had been married to Judith for almost five years. He merely looked resigned.

Those who married into the family got used to Cousin Caleb, but you had to be born a Sutton to really appreciate him—or love him the way Norah did.

"Speaking of the contest," Uncle Eli said. "Why give a tie to Van Cleve's son of all people? He'd already quit, or as good as."

"He earned a tie. I had to provoke him a little to get him out of the chair for the last shot, but he hit the target dead center."

"Well, I don't think you should have let his father have even a tie to brag about. Nobody ever went shot for shot with you at the end like that before. You should have let him quit."

"I don't figure to hold who his father is against him unless he makes me. In your shoes I wouldn't judge a man by his father either."

Anxiety knotted in Deborah's stomach. The family usually stayed away from the subject of her grandfather. Henry Sutton had been as bad as her own father in a different way and done terrible things to her mother, her uncles, and Caleb, who didn't even know who his father was.

Pushing Caleb on the subject of fathers was like poking a grizzly with a stick, and Eli knew better. Norah patted Caleb's arm, and Deborah relaxed. A touch like that from Norah always gentled Caleb.

"Why judge by his father when you can judge by his own actions?" William said. "I heard the reason he ran out of steam today is he took a bullet in the back in that little war in Cuba."

Judith ought to touch *her* husband. Better yet she ought to pinch him or throw water on him.

"Men who have been in wars would tell you they get knocked around and turned around, and the site of a wound means nothing," Deborah said, letting aggravation starch her voice.

Everyone at the table went still and stared at her. She hardly ever spoke up at family gatherings. Now that she had started, she might as well finish. "I heard all sorts of gossip about him from Mr. Lawson and Mr. Ascher before the contest started."

She ticked off the accusations on her fingers. "He's called Trey because he's Webster Van Cleve, III, and Trey sounds foreign, so it's a sign of putting on airs."

She paused and gave her Uncle Eli, no slouch with a deck of cards, a knowing look. "He's an ungrateful son who left home as soon as he could but came crawling home for help when he was hurt. Of course they didn't explain how walking on crutches is crawling. He's taller than his father and looks like his mother, so he can't be his father's son. In fact looking like his mother means he's so pretty he can't even be a man. Oh, and as William said, since he was shot in the back, he's a coward."

"Well, he's pretty enough to inspire a spirited defense from someone who won't look at ordinary men," Uncle Eli said with a grin.

Aunt Lucy didn't touch his arm but elbowed him in the ribs. He kept smiling, and so did everyone else around the table.

Deborah hoped the heat spreading across her cheeks and over the top of her ears wasn't visible as a blush and feared it was.

"A man doesn't have to be in a war to have gunfire turn him around. I turned a few around myself back in the day, and anyone who says he's a coward is a flannel-mouthed fool. He was going on guts alone by the time we started shooting." Caleb paused to swallow a spoonful of his soup then added, "I can't judge how pretty he is, but I can see his father in him. He has the old man's ears."

Sounds of disbelief came from around the table.

"I'm telling you, I had to grab hold of one of Van Cleve's ears once. They're uncommonly small and close to his head and so are the son's." Caleb fingered one of his own full-sized ears as he talked. "He's got the old man's chin too. His mother's is more pointy like."

"You certainly remember Mrs. Van Cleve's chin well after all these years," Norah said frostily.

This time Caleb patted her arm. It didn't work as well for him as it had for her.

Uncle Jason, ever the peacemaker, tried to help Caleb out. "Whatever else he is, he's an uncommonly good shot. If he gets his health back, he might just beat you next year."

"Not unless he gets a rifle with longer range. I won't get caught short on ammunition again, so if he can stay on his feet, and if he's as good as I think he is, we'll go past 500 yards next year."

Thank goodness Uncle Jason succeeded in moving everyone to speculation about next year. The waiter whisked away her empty soup bowl and replaced it with a plate of what must be pickerel in wine sauce.

Deborah took a tentative first bite. Not bad. Different.

Now if she could just find the courage to go ahead with her plans for tonight.

4

JAMIE'S RENTED ROOM was small, and the washroom was down the hall, but the walls were freshly painted a soothing blue, the place smelled like floor wax, and the few pieces of furniture were decent.

Trey particularly appreciated the soft bed Jamie dumped him on top of when they got back from the contest. Appreciated it so much he slept there like death until he heard Jamie returning and woke to a room dim in early evening light.

He yawned and watched Jamie change into a fresh shirt and fuss with the collar.

"If you're back among the living, get your arse out of my bed and come along and have some supper with Miss Tindell and me."

"You said she was through toying with you."

"She is. Now she's going to ease my broken heart with one last romantic evening before she leaves tomorrow."

"They're really sending her away that fast?"

"They are."

"Then why are they foolish enough to let her have one last romantic evening with you?"

"They aren't. She's spending the evening with her lady friends."

"Aah."

"Yes, aah. Now get up and come along."

"If I come along, you won't get your romantic reward. I'll get up and get something to eat, Granny. I promise."

Jamie gave him an assessing look. "And then what. Back here?"

"No, as a matter of fact, I have a quiet place all picked out, and I'm going to sit and watch the fireworks like the rest of the town."

"There's a lot of men celebrating with drink by now," Jamie said, working on his tie, "and most of them don't much like your family."

"Afraid I can't run fast enough to get away?"

"I'm afraid you haven't got enough sense to run. Come with us. It's going to get dark enough I can steal a kiss or two whether you're there or not, and the lady isn't more generous than that."

"Thanks anyway. I'm not going to try to defend my family's non-existent honor, or mine, such as it is. There's a bench behind the town hall where I can sit and see the fireworks, and I'll stop at the café down the street on the way there. Okay, Granny?"

Jamie didn't look happy, but he put his jacket on over the fresh shirt and left. Trey sat up and ran his fingers through his hair, still yawning.

If he was going out, he needed more than a fresh shirt and collar. Whether the grit on his scalp was dirt or gunpowder, it needed to go, and his mouth tasted as if he hadn't used a toothbrush since New York.

He needed to scrub from head to toe and get into the last of the clean clothes he'd brought to town with him.

Maybe he'd just get something to eat, come back here, and sleep some more. His mystery woman wouldn't be waiting on a bench behind the town hall. She wouldn't join him if he waited there. She'd said her family lived so far from town they only came in occasionally for supplies or special occasions.

Then again, what could be more special than the last Fourth of July of the Nineteenth Century? She must be in town with her family tonight, somewhere in the crowd gathering in the park to watch the fireworks. No one would come near the town hall.

Thinking about her, he shook his head ruefully at his own stubborn foolishness. The false image he'd conjured up that night of a pretty young woman with intelligence obvious in her face hadn't faded over the months but settled in his mind as truth. He shouldn't want to meet her again, maybe see her and shatter the illusion, but he did.

Damn it. You could expect a sick man to obsess over an unsuitable woman, but a recovering man should have more sense, and he *was* recovering. His appetite was back. He'd actually gained a few pounds in the last weeks.

Still berating himself as seven kinds of a fool, Trey rose and headed down the hall.

SHE WAS LIKE the boy who cried, "Wolf!" After years of pleading headaches, fatigue, and other obscure ailments to escape any gathering larger than a family dinner, Deborah couldn't make a single person believe she didn't feel well enough to walk a few blocks to the park.

She massaged her temples, not just for show. If they didn't stop fussing at her, the headache would soon be real.

"Deborah, honey, please do come with us," Aunt Emma begged. "You know what happened last year will never happen again."

"I know, but I can see everything from the yard here, and the sounds won't be so loud. If bursts of light make the headache worse, I can lie down and rest. Please, Aunt Em, go on. I'll be fine."

Deborah avoided looking at either of her sisters. The others might argue, but they only suspected Deborah of being Deborah. Given half a chance, Judith or Miriam might guess what she was up to, or something close to it.

They all left, finally. Parts of the family were staying with Judith and William or with Miriam and Joseph. Caleb, Norah, and their three children were at the hotel, and they'd all soon meet at the park on the south edge of town, chatting and laughing, ready to ooh and aah over bursts of colored fire lighting up the sky.

Inventing aches and pains to get out of large social events, or at least remain at the edges, had never bothered Deborah before, but she couldn't pretend this was a small fib. She had just lied to people who loved her in order to do something she wasn't sure she should do or had the courage to do. Worse, the desire to do it was plain silly.

If only her stranger were the age of Van Cleve the Third, she wouldn't feel so foolish. Not that she was *interested* in him. She couldn't be. She couldn't be interested in any man, but her stranger was interesting, which was different. And he was sympathetic. No, empathetic. And his voice....

She was being silly, female, and foolish. She would stay right here the way she had promised she would. She could remember the conversation with him here the same as she had at home a hundred times.

After all he wouldn't be there. He had returned from the East and college to spend time with a family that lived far from Hubbell. He had only been in town the night of Miriam's wedding to visit a friend.

Even if he was still staying with his family and even if he had come to town again for today's celebrations, he'd watch the fireworks in the park along with everyone else. The town hall sat dark and empty tonight. No one would be there.

Foolish or not, she left her best dress on and wished she had given in to Aunt Em's oft-stated desire to replace the aging gold dress with something more stylish, a more complimentary color. Which had to be the silliest wish she'd ever had. No one would see her. No one would be in the little garden behind the hall.

Still, she wanted to sit in the place where it had happened again, remember his voice, his words, the way talking to him made her feel.

If she let herself dwell on the memory of the drunk and his friend and thoughts of how many like them would be on the streets tonight, her nerve would fail. Deborah floated out of the house and down the front walk wrapped in a cloud of her own nerves, icy hands and feet unaffected by the hot summer night.

A laughing group of young people approached, stragglers on their way to the park. Deborah paused by Miriam's front gate until they passed, then followed as close as she dared. Let anyone watching think she was part of the group.

Her unwitting chaperons led the way right to the town hall. No moon lit the walk around the dark building. Clouds hid even the stars. Her footsteps on the gravel path crunched so loudly she half-expected her family to hear, come running, and drag her to the park, scolding all the way.

At last. Her outstretched hand touched the rough back of the same wood bench she had occupied the night of Miriam's wedding.

A trace of spicy, masculine scent drifted to her on the warm air. Could scent be nothing but a memory?

She scanned the shadows under the trees, afraid to believe what her eyes told her was the blacker shadow of a man on the opposite bench, even more afraid the shadow was the wrong man until he spoke.

"I hoped we'd meet again, but I didn't dare hope it would be tonight."

A wave of pure joy washed away nerves and fear. "Oh! I didn't expect you to be here either, but I...." How could she explain being here without embarrassing herself? "It will be one big crowd in the park, and it's quiet here."

His low laughter rippled over her like a caress. "And you don't like crowds. I'd forgotten about that, but I'm glad of it now, and I'm glad you're here. But tell me you didn't walk here by yourself tonight."

"I-I didn't. I was with a group of people right until I reached the hall."

"And they left you here by yourself?"

"Not exactly. I escaped again."

"You esc.... Is that how you think of it? As escaping from where you're expected to be? Doesn't your family miss you?"

"Oh, no. Most of the time they know where I am. Tonight, though, they do think I'm at my sister's house. They wouldn't approve of my being here any more than you do."

"But I do approve of you being here. I just don't like to think of you getting here without a safe escort."

"I really did come with a group."

"Mm hm."

The sound he made was full of disbelief, but at least he dropped the subject. Sort of. She moved around the bench and sat.

"Last time we talked, when you said you had escaped, I didn't think you were serious."

"I wasn't. Not really. Saying I escape makes it sound as if someone forces me to go places I don't want to, and that's not true." She paused then decided to tell the whole truth. "My aunt and my sisters lure me and bribe me and try to convince me I'll have a good time. By the time I was ten, I realized it's easier to go along with them and then slip away than to hold out for peace and quiet to start with."

"Clever lady."

"Have you ever been in the park for the fireworks?" Deborah asked. She didn't wait for him to admit he hadn't. "Every square foot of the park has a person sitting on it, and last year boys lit firecrackers and threw them right in the crowd." Uncle Eli's boys, but she wasn't mentioning that. "There was screaming and shouting, and some of them exploded right next to me and frightened me out of my wits."

"Were you hurt?" He sounded upset at the thought.

"No, but the sparks burned holes in my skirt and ruined my dress. Everyone fussed over it the rest of the night and most of the next day. It spoiled the evening and the whole trip to town."

"They fussed too much, and it embarrassed you."

How could a stranger understand what her family never did? "Yes, exactly. I wasn't hurt, but you'd think I had an arm blown right off. I really do love them dearly, but they're—overwhelming."

"Aah. Overwhelming. That's a good word for family some-times." His voice was as she remembered, wrapping the two of them in a private, intimate world.

For the past two months, in her imagination, *in her dreams*, he was a friend, a real friend who knew her secrets and didn't care. Before she could stop them, words spilled out as if that were true.

"They treat me as if I'm simple minded and delicate to boot. Any woman who would rather read a book than pore over fashion pictures in *Godey's* or *Harper's Bazaar* has something wrong with her. A woman's whole life is supposed to center on finding a husband, and since mine doesn't, it's lacking, and I need to be guarded or guided—I'm never sure which—but all they do is make me want them to leave me alone that much more."

Hearing the passion in her own voice and realizing what she had just revealed to a stranger, Deborah felt heat race across her cheeks and blessed the darkness of the night. "I'm sorry. I should never.... I can't believe I just...."

"Don't be sorry. I understand all about how family can make you want to run away and never come back. I even tried it once. At least your people have good intentions."

"The road to hell is paved with good intentions," Deborah said tartly.

"It often is."

A soft whistle sounded in the distance. Deborah forgot he wouldn't see her and pointed to the south as a fountain of golden fire shot across the sky.

"Oh, look. Isn't it beautiful!"

Before the last sparks faded, more rose.

"Do you ever wonder if men like Washington, Adams, and Jefferson expected that people would be celebrating what they did with the Twentieth Century right around the corner?" she said.

"I don't know if they expected it, but I know they hoped it. They knew how great an experiment they started, and they wanted it to last."

Deborah settled back against the bench, enjoying a discussion of the country's history with him more than the displays overhead. She spent as much time searching the shadows for any glimpse of his outline as watching the fireworks.

When the last sparks dissolved in the sky and quiet returned to the night, she said, "I know I should introduce myself, but...."

"But talking to a shadowy stranger has an allure that plain Mr. Smith would not."

"Yes." No one had ever understood any of her feelings before. He seemed to understand them all.

"I feel the same way, but I've wasted far too much time trying to decide if you're blonde, brunette, or even a redhead. Settle that much for me."

"Brunette."

"Are you? Me too."

He might have wondered about something so basic, but he couldn't have spent as much time thinking about her as she had about him.

"Will you go back East soon?" Why ask him that? Yes, he was going to leave. Tonight was an unexpected gift.

"I'm not sure. I'm not even sure where I'll go when I leave or what I'll do, drift around and see the parts of the country I've missed maybe. What about you? Have you thought of applying for a position that would let you escape your overwhelming family for more than an hour or two at a time?"

Applying for a position? Traveling? Her stomach flipped. "Oh, no, I'm content with my life. I don't want anything different."

"I see."

Did the soft way he said those two words indicate disappointment? Did he imagine her to be a stronger, braver woman than she was? If he questioned her more along those lines, he'd learn the truth. "I'm glad you were here. I enjoyed talking to you again, but I need to go."

His shadow rose from the opposite bench. "I enjoyed it too, but at the risk of spoiling our invisible acquaintance, I'm going to walk you home."

"Oh, no, you don't need to do that. It's only a short way, and I'll be fine."

"I do need to."

"No!" Deborah stumbled around the bench and took off running.

She didn't want to see him, didn't want to have proof positive he was no more than Miriam's age. She didn't want him to see her, at least half a dozen years older. And she didn't want the mystery ruined.

TREY ONLY TOOK a few steps after her before returning to the bench, cursing. Even if she was older than he thought and stout, there was no use pretending he could catch a healthy woman running from him, and if he could catch her, what would he do? Behave like the sort of ruffian he wanted to protect her from in order to force her to accept his escort?

At the thought of throwing a woman over his good shoulder and promptly collapsing to the ground, smothered in petticoats, skirts, ruffles, and bows, his temper changed to amusement.

He sat for a while, wondering. Not stout. Surely a stout woman couldn't run like that. Brunette. At what age did a woman say she'd never married as if it were no longer a possibility? How much did it matter?

Unable to come up with an answer he liked, he groped around for the cane, rose, and headed back to Jamie's.

5

TREY HAD BEEN back and forth to town so often he didn't need to so much as twitch the reins to direct his tired little buggy horse to turn from the ranch road toward the main barn. She stopped with her nose almost touching the big door she knew separated her from hay, grain, and rest.

Shaking his head in sympathy, Trey rotated stiff shoulders, arched his aching back, and gave each leg a shake before climbing down, refusing to think about the days he would have, could have, jumped. Leaving Hubbell at first light and traveling at a steady clip meant he'd arrived at the V Bar C with time for a bath and nap before dinner.

Now, with the ranch house in sight, he wished he'd left later and traveled slower. The best way to avoid quarreling with his father and sister was to avoid his father and sister, and their presence at the dinner table was a certainty.

He slid the heavy door open and led the mare out of the hot summer sun into the cooler gloom of the barn and began unhitching.

"Here now. Don't you bother with that. I'll do it."

Trey looked up to see Herman Gruner reaching to unfasten the trace on the other side of the buggy. The old man's jaw jutted mulishly with his determination to take over even such a small task. Not many stove-up cowhands were kept on to take care of odd jobs and livestock, and those who were that lucky needed to be seen earning their keep.

"Sure," Trey said as he pulled the trace on his side off the singletree. "Let's get her unhitched, and if you hobble around and take care of the horse, I'll hobble up to the house and take care of me."

The tension left Herman's face. "You can't make us out to be a matched pair. You've got a few more miles left on you. All's you need is to get something big enough and get back in the saddle. There's a good bay gelding out back. Not a mean bone in him."

Trey shook his head ruefully. "I've been back in the saddle, and it hurts like hell. This little lady gets me around just fine."

He gave the mare an affectionate slap and left the barn before Herman could say more. No one else needed to know that after half an hour in the saddle, numbness started to creep up his legs. Trey saw no reason to gamble with frightening reminders of last year's helplessness.

Grabbing his cane and valise from the buggy, he headed for the house. As a boy, Trey had ridden and hiked over every one of the thousands of acres of the ranch, and almost all those acres were treeless grasslands. A slight rise in one spot or old buffalo wallow in another was often the only landmark for miles.

Here at the heart of the V Bar C, though, the land changed from flat to rolling, just a little, just enough. Cottonwoods grew along the creek. The buildings nestled among hackberry and walnut trees far enough from the water no spring flood had ever come close.

Trey knew his father would have perched the ranch house on a majestic hill if one had been available. As he labored up the incline from the barn to the house, Trey thanked Heaven for the ranch's singular lack of majestic hills.

The walk wasn't the struggle it had been a month ago, but it still left him short of breath. He paused and dropped the valise. Just in case anyone was watching, he tried not to lean too obviously on the cane and pretended to study the house he'd been born in, lived in happily for sixteen years and miserably for another two.

Massive, stark white even in the softening light of late afternoon, the house had never fit the landscape. The wide veranda was a mere decorative addition. No one ever sat there. Individual balconies jutting out from second-story bedrooms were more indicative of the nature of the Van Cleve family, although no one used those either.

His breathing almost back to normal, Trey shrugged and continued up the path. Living in tents, bunkhouses, and the bare rooms in New York had been better than living here those last years—or now.

Like the barn, the house was dim inside, a quiet, cool refuge from the heat of the afternoon sun. As expected, he found his mother in the small green and white parlor she called her own.

He watched her a moment from the doorway. A magazine lay neglected in her lap. She stared out the window, lost in her own thoughts.

Lorena Van Cleve had changed less than anyone in the family in the years Trey had been away. Elegant in a pale yellow dress that clung to her slim figure, she sat as perfectly straight as ever, her back not touching her chair. The strands of silver in her hair only made the gold appear paler, softer. From this distance the fine lines at the corners of her eyes and mouth were invisible. Lines that should have appeared years before they did.

He cleared his throat. "I'm back."

She rose gracefully and met him in the middle of the room, the light scent of her floral perfume enveloping him as he hugged her.

"Oh, I'm so relieved. I worry about you traveling back and forth to town alone."

Did she? No sign of relief showed in her expression. Her smile was as serene as always. His mother sailed through life, rarely affected by the emotions of others or showing her own.

If he had inherited that coolness instead of a male version of her bone structure, her green eyes, and the height of the men in her family, he might be able to deal with his father as easily as she did.

Stepping back, she patted his shoulder. "Tell me you're going to change into something respectable and join us for dinner."

Trey considered his dark blue denim trousers and cotton shirt respectable, even if not up to V Bar C dinner standards, but he didn't argue.

"I am. Bath, nap, and dinner."

"Excellent. You go on upstairs, and I'll let Edna know there will be six of us this evening."

Fatigue dogged Trey up the stairs and to his room. He collapsed on the bed, knowing if he let himself fall asleep there would be no bath, just a knock on the door when dinner was ready. Still, he drifted—quiet room his mother had redecorated in blues and grays sometime in the years he'd been gone, soft bed, soft pillow.

The door flew open so violently it banged off the stop, jerking him awake. Trey sat up and scrubbed his face with his hands before meeting his sister's angry dark eyes.

"And good afternoon to you too, my dear," he said. "How are you feeling?"

"As if you care. How do you expect to butter Father up if you keep spending more time in town with your Irish friend than you do here? Don't you think you should at least pretend an interest in what you're trying to steal?"

Any answer he gave would provoke more temper. He studied her in silence.

As much as he favored their mother and her family, Alice was their father's daughter, short and round, dark of hair and eye. Even as a boy he had recognized she would never have their mother's beauty, but he'd thought her pretty once.

Now anger, envy, and spite distorted her features into pure ugliness. Since he'd returned to the ranch, Trey had never seen her any other way. Did she relax into her old self when he was in town, or did his very presence less than a day's ride away keep her like this?

"You can't be doing the baby any good working yourself up this way," he said finally.

"That should make you happy. You'd love it if I lost the baby, wouldn't you? Especially if I lost a son."

"Alice...."

"You're not coming back after all these years and taking everything. You're not. I'll kill you myself first!"

"I've told you before, and I'll tell you again. I don't want it. I'll be gone again before winter sets in. I've told you, and I've told him."

"And I don't believe you. *He* doesn't believe you. You come back just long enough to make sure he knows you're alive and able, take off again, gallivanting around the country free as a bird, and all you have to do is show up before he dies and say what he wants to hear."

"Get out." Trey rose from the bed and moved toward her, ready to push her out of the room and shut the door in her face if he had to.

"Don't tell me to get out. I'll leave when I'm ready, and I...."

"Arguing like this is a waste of time and bad for both of us. If you keep this up, he'll outlive you and you won't have to worry about who inherits what. If I let you drag me into it, he'll outlive me. Out you go."

"It should be mine. I want it, and I didn't disappear for nine years. Just because you're male...."

He shoved her out in the hall, shut the door, and leaned against it until he was sure she'd given up and stormed off. Falling asleep before bathing was no longer a problem. Calming down enough to sleep before midnight might be.

If it weren't so depressing, it would be funny. Webster Van Cleve had only two children—Trey, who wanted no part of the empire his father had cheated, stolen, and murdered to build, and Alice, who wanted it all. And Webster Van Cleve would never leave an acre, a cow, or a stock share to a woman.

Trey stripped off his clothes, wrapped up in a robe, and headed for the bathroom. The year he'd decided he should dedicate to this impossible effort at reconciliation would be over right before Christmas. When he left Kansas this time, he wasn't coming back.

Whether her baby was a girl or boy, sooner or later Alice would have a son. She could damn well be satisfied with being mother to the Van Cleve heir.

UNABLE TO SLEEP or even focus on a book, Trey made it to the dinner table ahead of the rest of the family. He watched the others as they entered.

His mother smiled and thanked his father as he helped her to her seat at the foot of the table, never meeting her husband's eyes. Alice had herself under some semblance of control, nodding curtly to her husband, Vernon Forbes, as he performed the same courtesy for her.

A vivid memory of Cal Sutton lifting his wife in the air, kissing her on the mouth, and spinning her in a circle as she laughed up at him flashed through Trey's mind. He reached for his water glass and took a large swallow as his father marched to the head of the table like a general, ready to inspect troops and find them wanting.

Just as Trey wondered if inheriting beauty would have made Alice a happier woman, he wondered if enough extra inches of height would have made his father a better man. Not that going through life having to look up at his wife, son, and pretty much everyone he dealt with was an excuse for arson, theft, and murder. Still, at times like this, seeing his father standing at the head of the table, neck and shoulders stretched as high as possible, the thought always came to mind.

Once everyone stopped fussing with their chairs and gave him proper attention, his father bowed his head and said a short prayer of grace. Trey bowed his own head and bit his tongue.

With luck, keeping quiet through this farce would be the worst of it. His father and Vernon Forbes would talk about nothing but business from now until they retired to the study for brandy, cigars, and more of the same.

Vernon's brother, Daniel, would join the conversation now and then, but for the most part, like Trey and the women, he'd limit himself to polite pleases and thank yous as the serving dishes passed around the table.

Trey accepted the potatoes from Daniel with a smile and nod, wishing he knew more about both the Forbes brothers. He knew Vernon had managed the Van Cleve lumber mill up north, then graduated to overseeing several mills and factories. Now Vernon served as Webster Van Cleve's assistant in managing the entire Van Cleve empire, and Daniel had taken over Vernon's old position.

Unlike Alice, Vernon and Daniel were friendly, even giving Trey an occasional eye roll or wink from behind his father's back when things got tense. Maybe Vernon had married Alice to further his ambitions, but he treated her with courtesy, and Trey had glimpsed moments of what looked liked genuine affection between them.

What made Trey keep his distance was knowing Vernon and Daniel had to be aware they worked for a man not only corrupt, but criminal. Vernon couldn't do his job without being complicit. The brothers' round, open faces, sandy-hair, and blue eyes gave them a guileless look that could all too easily make a man underestimate them. Trey vowed not to make that mistake.

How much did Alice know about the workings of the empire she coveted? And what did she think about it? If it were all hers, what would she do about it?

Alice looked away from her husband, caught Trey's eye, and her pleasant expression hardened to fury. Vernon touched her sleeve, and Daniel turned the subject away from the potential of gasoline engines.

"You haven't told us whether you enjoyed the Fourth in Hubbell, Trey. I've never spent the holiday in a small town. What was it like?"

"I did enjoy it," Trey said. "It was about the same as anywhere in the country, speeches, a parade, good food on every street corner, fireworks in the evening. Everything is just on a smaller scale than in a city."

"And contests," his father said in a voice that froze everyone at the table. "They have a long-range shooting contest every year, and you didn't have the good sense not to embarrass yourself and the rest of us by entering. You can't walk from the barn to the house without resting half way, but you entered a shooting contest."

So his father had watched from the house and not been fooled by the pretense of stopping to admire the view, and someone had hurried from town to the ranch and earned a dollar or two reporting what happened at the contest.

"I never considered who I was or wasn't embarrassing," Trey said. "I saw a flyer about the contest, and it sounded like fun. So I entered."

"Fun! You let Sutton beat you in front of the whole town."

"It was a draw," Trey said. "I left the trophy at Jamie's, but I'll haul it out here and show it to you if you want to see it."

His flippant tone was bound to provoke, but it was better than giving way to the anger spiking hot in his chest. After all his plate was still half-full and his stomach half-empty.

"He gave you a draw. Condescended and gave it, and you let him get away with it."

Trey balled his napkin and threw it on the table, wishing his appetite hadn't returned. "Since you weren't there, maybe you're imagining it had to be the same for me as it was for you. Did he condescend when he gave you a draw?"

His father exploded from his seat, red-faced and shouting. "He didn't give me a damn thing! I fought him to a draw. Those plowed up scraps of land like his weren't worth what he did to your mother."

Trey rose slowly, wishing he hadn't left the cane upstairs. "He didn't do anything to Mother. It was what he did to *you* that scared her, and if you hadn't tried to steal that land, he wouldn't have done a thing."

"I offered good money for that land, and you know it. He was nothing but a gun for hire until the Hawkins woman got her hooks in him and turned him into a sodbuster."

His father was still sputtering and shouting as Trey made his way steadily out of the dining room and shut the door behind him. Maybe next time he was in town he'd see if one of the town's preachers could give some guidance about how far a man had to go to uphold his end of a bargain with God. Hell, maybe Jamie's priest would let him off the hook if he converted to Catholicism.

AT THE SOUND of the bedroom door, Trey turned from staring out the window at nothing but darkness. If Alice had returned to plague him, he'd pack and head back to town tonight.

Not Alice. His mother. She held a coffee pot in one hand, a cup and saucer in the other, making him wonder how she'd opened the door. Edna followed right behind, carrying a tray with everything he could wish for on the plates. Meat and potatoes. Bread and butter. Apple pie.

He watched half in disbelief as his mother set the coffee on the bedside table, moved the few other items on the surface to the floor, and Edna transferred the contents of the tray to the table. That done, his mother sat on the bed. Edna gave a shy smile and left.

His mother, for once, was not smiling. "Since we've gone to this much trouble, you'd better eat," she said.

"Yes, ma'am." Trey pulled the only chair in the room over to the table, sat, and broke open a warm roll, almost sighing over the yeasty fragrance as he slathered on butter. "You've never done this before."

"You wouldn't have eaten anything before."

"Couldn't have, but I am hungry tonight. Thank you."

He eyed her between bites. As a boy he'd been willing to do anything to please her. The desire rose as strong as ever, but this time what she was going to ask was impossible.

Finishing the pie, he washed it down with a second cup of coffee and pushed the chair back from the table.

"I needed that, and it was terrific. Thank you."

"You're welcome. I want to see you healthy again as soon as possible."

"With meals like that, it won't be long."

"With meals like tonight's, the rest of the family will lose *their* appetites and waste away. Your sister does not need this aggravation."

"No, she doesn't. Are you asking me to leave?" That would get him off the hook, wouldn't it? Wouldn't it?

"Of course not. I am asking you to stop provoking your father."

"You don't think he provoked me tonight?"

She hesitated, then admitted. "Perhaps he did, but you are the son, and he's right about Sutton. You know the man is dangerous. You shouldn't have anything to do with him."

"I didn't even know he was there. I was standing on the shooting line when I first saw him. You can't think I should have turned tail and run at that point."

She was kind enough to pretend running was even a possibility. "You don't have to run, but you certainly can turn in the other direction any time you see him. Part of his agreement with your father was that he would turn away any time he saw us."

Trey smiled at that. "Not us. You. And I bet he's never had to do it in all the years since because you've never been within five miles of each other."

"Be that as it may, since you spend so much time in town, you may see him again. You need to avoid him, and you need to make an effort to get along with your father. I thought you came back because almost dying in that horrible place made you realize you needed to repair things between you. You aren't trying."

What could he try? Nothing had changed except he'd made an impossible bargain in a desperate moment.

"How do you do it?" he asked her. "You can't tell me you don't know what he's done, what he's still doing."

Rising from the bed, she began gathering the empty dishes on the tray. "Business and financial affairs hold no interest for me. You have twisted and exaggerated pieces of information you came across into something ridiculous, and you've never been willing to admit your mistake."

"I see." Maybe he even did. How else could she stay in her serene shell? But he couldn't be that willfully blind.

"You are his son. You will inherit everything he has worked so hard to build. You owe him respect."

She managed to balance the tray on one arm and wrench open the door before he could get to it to help. It closed quietly behind her, the click of the latch emphasizing her anger better than Alice's door slamming ever did.

Trey sat unmoving for a long time, head in hands. His father was impossible, but there had to be some hope with Alice. If he could just make her believe....

An idea slowly formed and took hold. What if he signed papers now refusing any inheritance from his father? What if he signed something giving it all to Alice? There had to be a lawyer in Hubbell who could tell him if he could do either or both and how.

He raised his head. If nothing else, seeing a lawyer would give him an excuse to get away and go back to town for a few days. Too bad there was no way to know when his mystery woman would be there again. Right now he'd give a lot for a friendly conversation with a woman who didn't want something impossible.

6

THE OLD BROWN hen pecked Deborah on the forearm so hard she cried out and dropped the egg she had just stolen from the nest. The egg cracked wide open against the edge of the pail at her feet, the sound distinct amid the flurry of feathers and loud squawks of the hen as she ran from the chicken coop.

Rubbing her stinging arm, Deborah looked down at the pail. The egg she dropped had broken at least two others.

An intact yolk sat on top of the mess, peering up at her like an accusing yellow eye. She knew better than to try robbing that nest with the hen still on it, but she'd been wool-gathering. Again.

No blood showed on her sleeve. Too bad the summer heat had led her to dress in her lightest gingham this morning. Being careless around a broody hen didn't hurt so much in heavier clothing.

Her arm would sport a small bruise for a few days, but it was nothing worth crying over. So why were tears running down her face? The pigs could have as much of the ruined eggs as she could scrape out of the pail. She'd wash the rest at the pump and be more careful tomorrow.

And all the other tomorrows. The shock of that unbidden, unwanted thought stopped her tears. What was wrong with her?

Everyone had an occasional blue day, but lately melancholy followed her like a shadow. Doing chores in the cool of a summer morning had always filled her with a quiet joy. She preferred the subtle pinks of sunrise to the garish oranges of sunset. Ordinary sounds had a different, delicate quality to them in early morning.

Today all she saw was the clear sky overhead that heralded another scorching July day. Some gnawing discontent had hold of her and wouldn't let go.

Aunt Emma and Uncle Jason had begun to notice. They couldn't hide the worry in their faces when they looked at her any more than she could hide the nameless feeling that had stolen her peace of mind.

In the distance, she could see her uncles bringing the horses into the barn for a feed of grain before a long day of work in the hay fields. They'd be at the house soon, Uncle Eli to take his share of the morning's milk and eggs back to his own place, Uncle Jason ready for the breakfast that needed three of the eggs in her pail.

Deborah hurried toward the water pump. Before washing the eggs, she would wash her face. Enough cold water should hide any lingering signs of tears.

By the time Deborah made it to the house, Aunt Em had coffee brewed, potatoes and ham frying, and a stack of hot cakes keeping warm in the oven. Even though Deborah didn't want a heavy breakfast, the combination of familiar scents comforted.

Aunt Em reached for the eggs the second Deborah set the pail on the counter. "Why are the eggs all wet?" she asked, not waiting for an answer before cracking one after another into a frying pan.

"I was careless and that old brown hen pecked me so hard I dropped her egg. It landed right in the pail, and it broke and cracked two others."

"That old girl is living on borrowed time. She's too tough to roast, but once the weather cools enough for stew, she'll be in the pot."

Uncle Jason walked into the kitchen, hair still slick and wet from washing up. "If she's in the pot, we'll be short an egg every day. Maybe it's time to let her raise that brood of chicks she's pining for. We could use a few more laying hens."

He took his place at the table, and Deborah took a minute to pour him a cup of coffee before setting the table. Uncle Jason was the same age as Caleb, but he looked ten years older, his face heavily lined, his shoulders stooped as if he carried an invisible burden. He never shirked from his share of the butchering, but he didn't like it and was quick to find a reason to give an animal a little longer if he could.

Once Aunt Em perched on her seat and Uncle Jason gave the blessing, Deborah helped herself to small portions of everything, hoping her aunt wouldn't notice how small. A futile hope.

"If you don't start eating better, you're going to waste away. You've been as broody as that hen lately. Are you coming down with something?"

"Of course not. I'm just not hungry this morning. It must be the heat." She turned to her uncle. "I don't envy you working in the fields on days like today."

"I'd rather fork hay than be up to my elbows in a tub of hot water scrubbing clothes," he said, studying her. "You have been looking peaked lately. Your eyes even look red. Have you been sleeping?"

"I'm sleeping fine. I am fine, really. You worry too much. Both of you worry too much."

They ate in silence for a few moments until Aunt Emma changed the subject. "So what do you think of your cousin's plans? It's hard to believe Cal and Norah are allowing it, but they say they are. I don't care what they say about it being free either. It's bound to end up costing them a pretty penny, but I suppose they can manage."

Deborah had no idea what her aunt was talking about. Caleb and Norah had two daughters and a son, and one of them must be up to something, something that could end up being expensive, but how was she supposed to know what it was?

Aunt Em interpreted Deborah's blank look correctly. "Taking you to church is all but a waste of time. You don't stay in the pew long enough to hear what the preacher says, and you don't show any interest in the family afterward either."

That stung. And it was true, of course. Until three years ago, attending church had been a rare event. The church in Hubbell was just too far away.

Although she knew better than to admit it, Deborah had preferred it that way. The new church beside the Grange Hall was close enough to attend every Sunday, but far enough most families packed lunch and picnicked outside in good weather or ate in the Grange Hall on cold or windy days.

The problem was even sitting at the end of a pew with open space to one side, Deborah could only stand looking at all the people packed in rows like that so long before escaping outside. Sometimes she slipped back in and stood at the back for a while, more often not. As for the picnics, chatter, and gossip....

"It's not that I'm not interested," she said carefully. "I don't do well in crowds. You know that."

"And the Sutton family is becoming a crowd all by itself," Uncle Jason said.

Deborah nodded, glad of the excuse, but Aunt Em disagreed, "Oh, bosh, Judith and Miriam attend church in town now, and Judith's babies have never seen the inside of the new church."

Finished forcing her tiny portions of food down her unwilling throat, Deborah washed away the salty taste of ham with a swallow of black coffee. "So what is the news I missed?"

"Beth is going to go to normal school," her aunt said with pride. "Can you believe that? She'll be living in Emporia and learning to be a teacher."

Deborah's vision blurred. Her throat closed and her head tried to float away. Uncle Jason's voice sounded as if from a distance. "Not by herself. She'll board with other girls, her classmates."

"H-how can she be a teacher when she's never been to school?" Deborah said, hating the waver in her voice.

"Well, it's not as if she's ignorant," Aunt Em said, indignant on Beth's behalf. "She's studied at home just like you."

Deborah managed a jerky nod and stiff smile. "I think you may be right that I'm coming down with something. I need.... I'm sorry, but I need to lie down for a while."

She fled from the kitchen to her bedroom and barely made it to the wash basin before losing what little she'd eaten. Leaving the mess in the bowl, she crawled into bed, taking off nothing except her shoes in spite of the gathering heat.

A soft knock sounded on the door, and Deborah rolled to face the wall. She really didn't want to talk to Aunt Em now, couldn't. Before she decided how to ask to be left alone, Uncle Jason's voice reached her.

"Can I come in?"

Deborah rolled back over to face the door. She couldn't remember her uncle ever entering her room. "Of course you can."

He sat on the edge of the bed and gave her an awkward pat on the shoulder, so gentle she barely felt it. "Surely you don't begrudge your cousin the chance to do this."

Meeting his eyes had never been so hard. "No, but I envy her. Isn't envy one of the seven deadly sins?"

He shrugged. "Those seven never sounded any deadlier than a lot of others to me. I don't know if the school has any more open places this year, but if you want to go, we'll find out all about it, and you'll go. You're every bit as smart as Cal and Norah's girl. Smarter."

Deborah had to smile at his loyalty. "You're biased, but thank you. And I really wouldn't want to be a teacher. Can you imagine me shut in a room all crowded with children? I'd run out and hide in minutes even if there wasn't a single one like Uncle Eli's boys."

"Well, there are other kinds of schools. If you want to go, we'll find a way for you to do it."

"Thank you. Thank you so much, but I don't have the courage," she whispered, hearing an echo of what she'd told her mysterious stranger. "I envy Beth not because she's going but because she has the courage to go. I feel safe here, and I don't want to go anywhere. I'm content."

"A young woman like you should want more than content. You need to think on what would make you happy and stop worrying about Em and me. If you're happy here and want to stay, this is your home and that's fine, but this place will go to Eli's boys sooner or later. They'll marry, have children, and if any of us ever need taking care of in our dotage, they can do it. No one's going to be alone out here starving because you didn't play nurse."

Deborah sat up, thought about hugging him, and didn't, knowing it would be as awkward as his pat on her shoulder. "I love you, you know."

"We love you too. Take a little nap now, why don't you, and when you come back down find something to do other than helping with the wash. Lucy and Em can do that. You take it easy."

She ought to do the entire wash by herself after causing this much trouble. "I won't do too much."

If he caught her fudge, he gave no sign. On the way out of the room, he picked up the soiled basin and took it with him.

Caleb often said Jason was one of the few men in the world born purely good, a natural saint, and Caleb was right. Tears welled in her eyes again.

Miriam was right too. Uncle Jason and Aunt Em deserved better than a niece who thought about hugging and couldn't bring herself to do it.

Deborah wiped her eyes and reached for her shoes. Enough of this malingering. Yearning for things she wasn't brave enough to reach for when offered was as foolish as setting out for church every Sunday knowing she couldn't stay in the pew more than five minutes.

If she ignored these strange new feelings long enough, they'd fade away. They would. They just had to.

7

As THE REMAINING months of summer drifted by, Deborah's discontent didn't fade but settled deep inside, stealing all the contentment she had so prized. While she couldn't even put a name to the unsettling yearning, her aunt and uncle made a diagnosis and proposed a cure.

"How would you like to spend next month in town with your sisters?" Aunt Em asked one night at supper. "I'm sure you'd enjoy seeing Judith and the children every day, and Miriam has plenty of room."

"I don't think so, thank you. Miriam hasn't been married long enough to want a house guest for so long."

In fact Deborah wondered what combination of threats and bribes the family had used to get Miriam to agree to such a thing. Aunt Em would never admit what it had taken, but Deborah would find out sooner or later. Judith would offer up the story with a laugh the first time the two of them were alone.

Convincing Aunt Em to give up on the idea took a while, but Deborah knew if missing a sister were the problem, this strange emptiness would have started when Judith left with her husband five years ago. Judith was a friend and confidante. Miriam was too spoiled and too much younger for that kind of closeness.

Deborah went back to her supper, surprised Aunt Em had given up so easily. Busy pushing boiled carrots around on her plate, she almost missed the look that passed between her aunt and uncle. Aha! The month-long visit was only a first sally. They had another cure on offer.

"I miss those girls myself," Uncle Jason said, head bent over his plate as he cut a piece of chicken already bite-sized even smaller. "A month is long for a visit, but I think this year we ought to go in on Friday and have all day Saturday and Sunday afternoon at the fair. Come home Monday. Eli and Lucy think it's a good idea too. Their boys will love it. We'll find someone to ride over and take care of our livestock for a few days."

The carrots turned to tasteless mush in Deborah's mouth. Planning a trip to town for supplies that weekend and spending an hour or two at the fair was one thing, an annual family outing, but two whole days in the crowds and hubbub of Hubbell's Harvest Fair?

Aunt Em had her best wide-eyed innocent look in place. "Oh, that's a better idea, and we'll have an excuse to dress up Saturday night for the dance."

"Dance?" Deborah straightened in her chair, her breath catching in her throat.

"Oh, yes, the Harvest Dance is a big deal. Judith says the committee gets real musicians to play, and they decorate the town hall to a fare thee well. It will be fun. Promise me you'll dance with Hiram Johnson and a few other eligible men before you run off for the evening. You don't need to dance with your uncles."

Deborah nodded without considering what she was agreeing to. The light in the kitchen seemed brighter, the scents of fresh bread, fried chicken, and coffee more appetizing. Her carrots tasted of honey.

Her mysterious stranger wouldn't be there. He'd be back East again by now, attending college classes. Except what if he *had* graduated? He'd mentioned not returning East, so maybe he had. She should have asked when she had the chance. There must be positions in Hubbell these days for a college graduate, even if she didn't know of any. Surely he'd rather stay near his family than go off to some big city.

Busy calculating dizzying possibilities, Deborah smiled widely at her aunt and uncle without really seeing them. "That's a lovely idea. I'm sure we'll all have a grand time."

What harm could it do to have something to look forward to? No matter how slim the chance of meeting him again, for the first time in months, she felt like her old self. What harm could it do to slip away from the dance and steal some time? Maybe she would merely sit alone and remember. Maybe he'd be there, and his voice would reach out from the night and wrap around her like a soft blanket. Maybe....

Deborah grabbed hold of the idea of the Harvest Dance the way a drowning woman would a rope.

TREY LOOKED UP at the sound of a double tap on his bedroom door. At least he'd almost finished packing for a few days in town and could be gone in minutes.

"Come in," he said, his lack of enthusiasm for any visitor in this house in his voice.

The door opened just enough for a sandy-haired head to poke through. "Is it safe?" Daniel Forbes inquired with humor. "You don't sound welcoming."

"I suppose I'm not," Trey admitted. "I apologize. You weren't on my list of expected visitors."

"My brother has lured his wife into a walk while there's still a trace of coolness in the air. We missed you at breakfast."

"Did you?"

"Oh, yes, there was a marked conviviality in the group it lacks in your presence." Daniel crossed to Trey's unmade bed, sat, and ran his hand over the sheet as if checking the quality of the cloth.

Daniel's open face was full of humor. Trey regretted his own cautious reserve. Maybe the man could be a friend, an ally in winning Alice over. Even so, trusting anyone who held a high position in his father's empire meant trusting someone who at the very least looked the other way when criminal acts were committed under his nose.

Trey folded another shirt and piled it on top of the others in his valise.

"Do you really enjoy these jaunts to the thriving metropolis of Hubbell?" Daniel asked. "Or do you just hide out and lick your wounds for a few days?"

Trey had to laugh at the man's bluntness. "Licking wounds is an exaggeration. Hubbell may not be a metropolis, but it is thriving these days, and yes, I do enjoy it. There's a fair this weekend, a dance. You ought to come with me."

"And stay with Mr. Lenahan?"

"He hasn't got room. I suppose a place to stay might be a problem. The hotels will be full."

"Another time," Daniel said vaguely. "I'm sorry about Alice. She isn't usually so emotional, and Vernon thinks once the baby comes, she'll be better natured again."

"I'm hoping that myself, and once I'm gone for good she can forget all about it for another ten or twenty years."

"I think she's too smart for that and so are you. If something happens to your father, the lawyers will hire Pinkertons if they have to, but they'll track you down, and I bet Alice is right. Once it's yours, you'll change your tune."

Trey shrugged. "If I can't talk him out of it, I may anger him enough to change his mind. And who knows what may happen in the next twenty or thirty years? Maybe Alice and Vernon will have a son who makes a better heir. Father may outlive me, Alice, all of us. If Mother outlives him, I think she gets half by law. She can leave that to Alice."

"Really? Are you sure?"

"Pretty sure. I tried to talk to Alice about it once, but she just got hysterical. I suppose I ought to find out the details and make sure she understands. Maybe that would calm her down."

"Not much. No one wants to see this divided up." Daniel made a circling motion with one arm to indicate the entirety of the ranch. "No one but you."

"It's a waste, and you know it. This land could support thousands of families. There's enough land that's not much good for farming but can support cattle west of here."

"Good Lord, everything Alice says about you is true," Daniel said in mock dismay. "You really are a self-righteous rabble-rouser. Have they made you an honorary member of the local grange yet?"

Trey couldn't help but laugh at that. "Not yet, but I'm sure it won't be long." He finished packing, closed the valise, and gestured to the door. "Are you sure you don't want to take a chance and come with me?"

"Not this time. I'm not much of a gambler, and I like a soft, clean bed at night," Daniel said, giving Trey's bed a last appreciative pat.

Whistling every step of the way, Trey carried his valise, rifle, and a smaller case down to the barn and loaded everything in the buggy. Licking his wounds might be an exaggeration, but he'd be the first to admit finding an excuse to get away from the ranch and spend a few days in the relatively friendly atmosphere of town lightened his spirit.

Herman heard him and went to fetch his horse before Trey could do it himself. The sight of the bedraggled little mare Herman brought to the barn stopped Trey's whistle mid-note.

"What the hell."

An ugly bite mark marred chestnut hair dull with dirt. The little mare was covered with nicks and scrapes and several more larger wounds in the shape of horse shoes.

"I thought you agreed to put her in the south corral by herself," Trey said through his teeth.

"I did, and that's where I put her," Herman said defensively. "Somebody moved her in with the saddle string."

The wonder of it was that Irene wasn't hurt worse. How long had she been stuck in a corral with a dozen or more horses half again her size, every one determined to teach a newcomer her place? He'd have to abandon the trip to town or at least give her a day to recover.

"You can use one of the wagon team," Herman said. "A better horse will get you there quicker anyhow."

The insult to his willing little mare made Trey madder. She could have suffered a broken leg from those kicks instead of minor wounds. If she ate and relaxed for a hour or so while he groomed and doctored.... Trey led her into a stall.

"You fork some hay down for her, and I'll start cleaning her up."

"I'll do it. You go back to the house, and I'll let you know when she's ready."

"I'm not going anywhere. Help if you want to."

The two of them worked in silence, both grim with anger.

Herman finally spoke as he dabbed blue gall remedy on the wounds. "Some of the boys don't think much of giving a horse like this special treatment."

"I don't give a damn what they think," Trey said. "If anything like this happens again, some of them are going to be looking for other work. If I can't figure out who did it, I bet I can talk my father into hiring a whole new crew around here."

"Am I part of the crew?"

"I don't know. You decide."

Rather than insult Herman further, Trey stood aside and let the older man harness Irene, only stepping forward to make sure nothing rubbed on a wound. Holding the mare's head as Herman ran the buggy shafts up, Trey's anger faded enough for memories of lessons learned during years of surviving in wild and lonely places to surface. He ran his fingers over every bridle strap, moved on to the reins....

Each rein had a neat slice almost all the way through, hidden near the stitching that secured the rein buckle.

"Herman?"

When Herman looked around, Trey didn't say a word, just twisted the leather to show the cut.

"You ain't accusing me of doing that, are you?"

Trey stared at the old man a moment. He'd known Herman since he was a boy. "No, I'm not, but you must have an idea who did do it. How about those hands who don't like my horse?"

"Nah, there's a big difference between putting that mare in a crowded corral with bigger horses and cutting reins. Maybe you wouldn't get hurt too bad, but maybe you'd get killed, and a man who can't walk far would be in more trouble than most if he got tossed out of a runaway buggy."

Herman's anger switched from Trey to the unknown perpe-
trator. They went over the harness and buggy from end to
end. Nothing else was amiss on the harness, but one of the
buggy wheels was loose.

"Wheels work loose over time," Herman said.

Trey didn't bother unclenching his jaws to answer. No one
could calculate for sure, but this loose wheel would have
come off somewhere between the ranch and Hubbell, spook-
ing his horse, which he'd be unable to control when the reins
broke. Of course gentle little Irene might not have spooked,
or not enough. She might even listen to his voice.

They fixed the wheel, replaced the reins, and Trey did his
best to ignore the echoes of Alice shouting at him reverber-
ating in his head. *I'll kill you myself.*

HOVERING AT THE edges of the Harvest Fair for an hour or two
had never let Deborah appreciate the scope of the event.
Drummers, farm wives, and local craftsmen had set up tables
in any open space they could find and hawked everything
from patent medicines to fruit preserves. Jugglers, clowns,
and musicians performed on every street corner.

Deborah thought she spotted what had to be a gypsy
fortune teller in front of a garish tent painted with a moon
and stars, but her sisters dragged her in another direction
before she could be certain. In truth, ricocheting from one
sight to another with her sisters made Deborah realize her
aunts and uncles were right—she did miss Judith and
Miriam, even if missing them wasn't the cause of her recent
misery.

"Oh, let's get an ice cream." Miriam grabbed Deborah by
the arm and headed for the wrought iron tables and chairs
outside the ice cream parlor.

"There's no room," Deborah protested, but of course by the time they crossed the street, a table magically became available. Things like that happened for her sisters.

"I want one of those," Miriam declared, pointing to a chocolate sundae topped with a cherry redder than anything that grew in nature.

"Me too," said Judith, looking at Deborah expectantly.

The watch pinned to Deborah's dress showed noon was still an hour away, and on top of a perfectly satisfactory breakfast they had already had frankfurters, popcorn, and cider. Still, the day was warm for late September, and ice cream....

"Peach ice cream for me," Deborah said.

"That's what you always get."

"Because I like it." As she listened to her sisters chatting, Deborah scanned the groups of people passing by. So many strangers. The fair attracted people from neighboring towns and even neighboring counties. She could look right at him and never know. He'd asked about her hair color. Tonight she would ask him....

Stop it. He won't be there. Just stop it. She forced herself to pay attention to her sisters' conversation again.

"It goes to show you. The devil is probably handsome too," Judith said, gesturing with her spoon toward two men standing on the walk, waiting for a table. "William says he's a good worker. Too bad he's a Papist."

Deborah recognized one of the men. He had on a dark gray suit today, tanned skin golden against the white of his shirt. Under the brim of a slouch hat, his face no longer looked bony, and he no longer leaned on his cane as if he'd fall without it. His eyes met hers for long seconds, and all the chatter from her sisters and others around them faded to a slight hum.

"Don't stare." Judith's hand on her sleeve brought Deborah to her senses. She shifted and angled in her chair so she couldn't look again without turning. He was still staring. She could feel his eyes on her and feel heat spreading across her cheeks in response.

"See?" Judith said smugly. "You've never stared at a man like that before in your life. Admit it, he's a beauty."

Oh, yes, he was handsome as the devil, and probably was one, every bit as bad as his father. His slim elegance made every other man she knew seem coarse and ordinary in contrast, but a beauty? What an odd thing to say about a man. Not only that... "He can't be a Papist," Deborah said.

"Of course he can. He is. It's a rare Irishman who isn't."

What? "Webster Van Cleve isn't Irish. I don't think his mother is either."

"Not Van Cleve," Judith said impatiently. "The Irishman standing right there beside him. It's a good thing I love my husband because Mr. Lenahan is almost enough to make me wish I were still single and Catholic."

Deborah shifted the other way on her chair and glanced quickly over her shoulder. Her imagination had not played her false. Van Cleve the Third was still looking at her. If he was going to do that, she wished she could see his eyes better, see what color.... Appalled at the direction of her thoughts, she jerked back around, forgetting to look at the other man.

"Yes, I see what you mean. He's very handsome," she said, relieved her voice sounded normal in her own ears, and hoping her acquiescence would end Judith's interest. It didn't.

"I'm surprised they're still friends," Judith said. "He came out here with young Mr. Van Cleve, helping him when he first came home from wherever. He needed help. He could barely walk on crutches. And as soon as Van Cleve, Jr., made it out to his daddy's ranch, he let the Irishman go. How's that for following in his father's footsteps?"

"He's a third," Deborah said, then wished she hadn't.

"What?"

Her stupid remark had both her sisters staring at her, and the speculative look on Judith's face made Deborah even more nervous. "This Mr. Van Cleve, the one right over there, is not a junior. He's a third. I know because Mr. Lawson and Mr. Ascher sat behind me at the shooting contest in July, and I had to listen to them gossiping like old hens about him."

"That's right. You defended him that night at dinner," Judith said.

"Caleb defended him," Deborah said—defensively.

Two older women left their table, and the men moved toward it. After a few words, Trey Van Cleve took a seat and his friend went inside the shop.

"The poor man hasn't learned," Miriam said. "He's still waiting on Mr. High and Mighty."

Deborah clamped her jaw tight. She wasn't going to say another word on behalf of the Third in her sisters' presence. "I'm finished," she said instead, pushing her dish of half-eaten ice cream away.

"Shall we go find the rest of the family and see how the aunts are getting along with all the children?"

That distracted Judith finally. She had fussed and fretted before leaving her four-year-old daughter and year-old son, even with Aunt Em, even for a little while.

Deborah regretted ending the time alone with her sisters, but sometimes Judith was all too good at reading Deborah's mind, and right now Deborah was thinking she wished her mysterious stranger was not a college boy but Trey Van Cleve's age. The Third had to be closing in on thirty, definitely man not boy.

She took a last peek at him from under the brim of her hat as she rose and followed Judith and Miriam to the sidewalk. Imagining her stranger looked like that wouldn't hurt either.

TREY WATCHED THE Suttons with mixed feelings. Having women that beautiful nearby always improved the scenery, and the one, the most beautiful of the three, was downright inspiring. Still, those three were related to Cal Sutton in some way, which made them dangerous.

He caught sight of a ring on the left hand of the spoon-waver in the blue dress. She was the only one whose voice carried well enough he'd heard a few words, and those words made it clear Jamie had another admirer. Which made Trey wonder what kind of married woman she was.

The three of them were almost like peas in a pod, but not quite. Blue Dress had rounder, softer features. Pink Dress wasn't much more than a girl, definitely the youngest, with features just a little sharper.

Green Dress. Aah, the best of the three beauties was trying to hide in her plain, moss green dress and a hat with a brim so wide and floppy it shadowed her face until she tipped her head just so. Keeping an eye on her until she did that grace-ful little tilt again had been worthwhile. Big, dark eyes, even features as lovely in profile as when facing him....

If Green Dress thought the oversized plain dress hid the gentle swells of breast and hip and tuck of waist that the stylish, fitted dresses on her sisters highlighted, someone ought to point out her mistake. A shapeless sack couldn't disguise that much pure femaleness when she moved.

He wanted to believe if that one was married she wouldn't be waving spoons at Jamie. He wanted to believe she wasn't married and was the kind of woman who would wrap her arms around a man's neck, kiss him in public, and laugh with him afterward. He wanted one like that as much as Jamie wanted a good Catholic girl.

Trey grinned, earning a startled look from a matron at the next table. Sensations he'd worked at controlling as a boy shot through him unchecked, welcome. Green Dress had just provoked reactions in his body he'd been afraid had died in Cuba, leaving him sitting here feeling on top of the world.

He ought to track her down and thank her, but getting close enough to one of the Sutton girls for a hat tip and "good afternoon" could be fatal if Cal Sutton caught him at it.

Trey's mood turned dark at the thought. At least he'd have to do something to incur Sutton's wrath. Merely drawing breath had provoked yesterday's sabotage. And Sutton would do a quick, professional job. He wouldn't make a sloppy try at murder disguised as accident.

Confronting Alice with questions would only work her into a seething rage, dangerous for her and for the child she carried. And how could she loosen the wheel? Would her husband do it for her? Would Daniel, or one of the hands?

Trey didn't want to think it. She was his sister. They'd grown up together, two children alone among adults on the vast ranch. They had been best friends, played together, kept each other's secrets, conspired to drive tutors to distraction. How could he believe she'd really try to kill him? Yet who else would do such a thing?

The sight of Jamie, weaving through the other tables with an extra large bowl in each hand, pulled Trey away from his unhappy speculation.

"Is there really ice cream under all that?" he said as Jamie thumped the dishes down and dropped into the opposite chair. Heaps of whipped cream, fruit, nuts, and syrup hid any ice cream lurking in the bowls, which meant Jamie still clung to the belief Trey needed fattening like a bacon pig.

"There is, and you'd better eat every spoonful, or there'll be no supper for you."

"A starving lumberjack couldn't eat all that."

"But you will."

Trey explored until he found the vanilla ice cream under it all, made sure a little chocolate sauce was also on the spoon, and tasted. Cold and creamy. Sweet and good.

He dug in and didn't slow down until the dish was half empty. Jamie didn't do as well. In fact all he seemed to be doing was stirring things into slop.

"You seem preoccupied today," Trey said.

"I need to talk to you about something." Jamie made a face and threw down his spoon. "It's presumptuous. I don't want to do it, but my sister and her husband twisted a promise out of me. I wrote them they'd do better here than in New York, and so they came."

"Aah. This is the sister you wouldn't let me meet for fear she'd take pity on a crippled heathen and marry me?"

"The very one. Since she's safely married now, you can meet her."

"Oh, thank you. I suppose her husband's a jealous fiend."

Jamie shook his head. "He's working with me at the mill now, and he's too tired to be fiendish except for a few hours of a Sunday night. And there's an affection between them."

"That's nice to hear. So am I invited to dinner tomorrow night?"

"If you like." Jamie looked around. Close to noon now, the tables around had emptied, but he hunched forward and lowered his voice. "Am I right that you're rich, rich as Rockefeller as they say?"

Trey sat back and folded his arms over his chest. "That's a strange question after all this time. No. I'm not taking a penny from my father, and even he isn't in Rockefeller's class. I told you about the vein of gold I found in Arizona, but I'm not.... If you're in trouble I'll give you what you need, and I won't starve for lack of it. Is that what you're asking? How much?"

"No, no. I'm doing this all wrong. But it feels like asking, begging, and I'm having trouble finding words."

"Damn it, Jamie. If you need my good arm, it's yours. I owe you, and we're friends. If you need help, tell me what you need."

"There's no need to it. It's a dream, and it's not even mine. Maura's husband is fresh from Ireland. His family were mechanics. The trouble is they were also Republicans."

"So he's not a fiend. He's a Fenian."

They both laughed, and at least the embarrassment was gone from Jamie's face when he sobered. "These days he's just another poor Mick like the rest of us, and since he's a lot smaller than you or me, hefting hundredweights of flour is going to break his back sooner than mine."

Jamie stirred the slop in his bowl some more. "Mind you, I missed two days at the mill again last month with the fever. Mr. Dalton seems a fair sort, but I don't know how much of that he'll stand for, and Nolan, he's mad for these horseless carriages. He's sure if we could find a way to buy one or two at the factory, we could sell them here at a profit. He wants me to talk you into being a partner in an automobile business."

"I see." Trey thought a moment, then said. "No."

Jamie looked down at the melting mess in his dish. "That's wise of you, I suppose. I promised to ask, and I asked."

"I don't want to be a partner in an automobile business. Even if they work well back East, I can't see why anyone would want one out here, but if you're serious and willing to do it right, I'll loan you what you need as an investment. I'm not talking about bringing one of the things out here and selling it for a few dollars more than you paid. The two of you need to put together a plan."

"A plan?" Jamie said blankly.

"Yes, a plan. What will you buy, for how much, how many, where will you keep them, can you do it all yourselves or do you need extra labor? Add in living expenses for the two of you until you can make a profit, three years, five years, budget it out. Who do you think is going to buy these things and how many men like that are in Hubbell? In the county? In the state? Forget the dream and come up with a detailed plan, and if it looks good, I'll finance it."

Jamie's mouth had gone slack with astonishment. "And if he's only dreaming and not serious enough to come up with such a thing, you'll save your money."

"I'll save my money, and you'll save yourself. You don't want to be partners with a man who isn't serious."

"There's not many ways out of the mill for a man like me."

"Sure there are. You could open a hospital. After all, you have experience with invalids. I'll give you a glowing recommendation."

Jamie laughed out loud again. "You'll put me in a hospital with lectures like that. I'll talk to Nolan. We'll both find out what he's made of."

They left the table with its dishes of melting ice cream and started down the street. "So have you found your good Catholic girl?" Trey asked.

"Maybe. We're a long way from the priest yet."

"Do I have to wait until you're before the priest to meet her?"

"No, if she falls for a heathen like you, it will only prove she's not the right one for me."

"You're a romantic, you are."

Hearing his own words, Trey thought of his plans for the evening. He was going to sit on a bench behind the town hall waiting for a spinster he hoped was younger than she made herself sound to join him because she was the most interesting woman he had ever talked to. Did that make him a romantic fool? Or just a fool?

8

DEBORAH'S DISCOMFORT THREATENED to erupt into panic at any moment. How could she have agreed to dance with eligible men tonight? Men. Not just the ubiquitous Hiram Johnson, twice her age and always smelling as if he hadn't washed this week, but men, plural.

She couldn't remember doing anything so stupid, but Aunt Em would never make up such an unlikely story. The price of daydreaming instead of paying attention had been high before, but oh, how had she let this happen tonight?

If he was there.... He wouldn't be there. But if he was, how long would he wait? He'd come inside when he gave up on her. This wasn't a private affair like a wedding. Everyone in town and half the people in the rest of the county crowded the hall, making the dance area even smaller than usual.

Deborah craned her neck to see over Billy Potts' shoulder. No one had gone toward the back door, or come in that way that she'd seen, but she couldn't keep an eye on the door constantly and dance. And there was Aunt Em, smiling at Hiram Johnson and putting an arm on his to keep him nearby. Hiram had already had his dance!

Deborah stumbled. Billy caught her and, bless him, eased her off the crowded dance floor, and not near where her family gathered either.

"Are you all right?"

"Fine. I'm fine."

"No, you're not. If I was a lady, I wouldn't want to dance with Hiram either. Come on, I'll take you out for some air."

"Please don't." She backed away from him a step, flinched and moved forward again when she bumped into someone behind her. "Please just...."

"You don't want company, do you?"

She shook her head, wishing all the men Aunt Em rounded up were as nice as Billy. Of course he was a still a boy with a rash of red spots on his chin. He had to be even younger than....

Banishing that thought, she said, "Help me escape, and I'll be in your debt, and you can dance with Miss Carbury."

Billy blushed at the mention of Miss Carbury, but nodded, undoubtedly happy both to help and to be free to pursue that young lady. He pushed through the crowd and led the way outside through the front door.

"Thank you. I'll be fine now."

Other couples had come out for air. Deborah watched Billy assess the company and decide she'd be safe here.

As soon as he disappeared back through the front door, she began working her way around the building, passing first a couple lost in each other's arms, then two men embroiled in a heated discussion about the best variety of wheat. She made it to the back door and the path to the garden, out of breath from hurrying and from the fear it was all for naught. She'd never know if he had left before she got away or if he had never....

"I was about to give up." His voice floated to her out of the blackness of the night.

"Oh." Relief washed through her, leaving her weak in the knees. "I was afraid you would. If you were here that is. I had to dance with every eligible man my aunt could rope into it. She says I promised. I don't remember, but if she says so, I did." She felt her way to her bench and dropped down, heedless of her skirt or anything else. "I'm sorry. I'm babbling. I thought I'd never get away."

"I'm glad you did. Somehow I expected you this time, and I was starting to feel disappointed."

"Me too. I mean disappointed that I couldn't get away. You'd give up and go inside and I'd never know and never recognize you, and, well, I'm glad it didn't happen."

"Maybe it's time we give up the mystery and tell names."

Deborah hesitated, but she still didn't want to know—or to tell. "No, let's not, but—is your hair dark?"

"Plain old brown, the middling kind of brown. How about you? I took brunette to mean dark. Is it?"

"Yes. Almost black, but not quite." She settled back, ready to bring up the last book she'd read or ask him if he'd ever seen an electric car like the one the newspaper said won a fifty-mile race in two hours. Fifty miles in two hours!

"When we talked before, you sounded firmly established in the unmarried state, yet you admit you're dancing with eligible men. Have you changed your mind?"

"No. The problem is my aunt is stubborn as stone," Deborah said, more sharply than she intended. "The fact I'm not—enthusiastic just means she drags over any unmarried man with a pulse, the more desperate the better. When I got away, she had hold of this old, smelly...."

"You're angry."

"No, I'm not." She closed her eyes and took a deep breath. She didn't want to talk about Aunt Em or anyone else in the family, and how could she divert him to the kind of thing she did want to talk about? "Maybe I am a little. I've told her often enough that I don't want to marry, and she just keeps hoping and arranging and, and fussing."

"She cares about you and wants you to have a better life."

"Married isn't better, not for a woman."

"Aah. So your reading has included authors such as Mary Wollstonecraft and Susan B. Anthony, and you're an acolyte. If I try to debate their theories, you'll be angry with me."

As a matter of fact Deborah had never heard of Mary Wollstonecraft. Susan B. Anthony had been mentioned in the newspaper once—unfavorably. Deborah decided she needed to see what she could get her hands on written by those two ladies.

"I wouldn't be angry with you, but no one with an ordinary family would ever understand about mine."

"What's ordinary? My father believes the only real crime is getting caught, my sister makes Lady MacBeth sound sane, and my mother walks around with a smile on her face pretending she doesn't notice."

"My grandfather was so mean his own children wished him dead. Someone else killed him before anyone in the family could, but it was a close run thing. When I was seven years old, my cousin killed my father. I saw him do it—the same cousin who gives me books, the same cousin who couldn't bring himself to put his old dog out of its misery last week and had to ask a neighbor to do it."

He laughed. "You win. For a spur of the moment effort that was excellent."

"I thought so." She closed her eyes, relief giving way to sorrow. She should never have let resentment over his choice of subject provoke her into revealing secrets. How fortunate that her secrets were so outrageous he didn't believe them.

"You left out your aunt roaming the moors at the full moon with a lantern held high."

"She doesn't have to do anything that ordinary. In addition to trying to get me to the altar when I don't want to go, she spends her time poking and prodding trying to find out about my life before I came to live with her and my uncle when it's none of her business."

The laughter was gone from his voice. "You really are angry with her."

"I love her, and sometimes I hate her. Yes, she really upset me tonight. Would you like to trade her for your mother who always smiles?"

"I guess not. I don't suppose you'd take my sister instead?"

"She's really consumed with guilt over something she did?"

"No, she's like Lady MacBeth before the murder. She raves about wanting to kill someone. Me in fact."

"But she doesn't mean it."

"I hope not. She's expecting her second child, and she lost her first. I tell myself that's why she acts the way she does, and once the baby's born she'll be the way she used to."

Her small flare of resentment died, and the sadness intensified. "Family isn't always what you want it to be," she whispered.

"No one knows that better than I do. I walked away when I was eighteen, swearing I'd never come back, but then something happened, and here I am. You'd think nine years would change things, and in some ways it has, but not the things that made me leave to start with."

The sum of eighteen and nine stunned her so much she almost missed what he said next.

"I escape from the ranch every chance I get the same way you escape from crowds."

Her heart stopped then leapt to her throat as she jumped to her feet. "Ranch! You're not.... College.... The Third.... You liar!"

Unable to form a coherent thought, much less sentence, Deborah turned and ran. Yanking open the back door of the hall, she wove, darted, and pushed her way through couples waiting for the next dance to begin until she reached the place on the other side of the hall where Uncle Jason and Caleb stood talking.

By the time she got there, Caleb was already staring through the dancers, looking for what had upset her. Uncle Jason leaned in close as a lilting polka began. "What's wrong? What happened?"

Now that she'd stopped running, Deborah began thinking. If she told Uncle Jason and Caleb what had happened, they'd be disappointed in her and furious at the Third. Now that she was calming down, she realized the Third wasn't to blame. If he knew.... He still wouldn't know unless.... She stared through the dancers toward the door, unable to see any sign of the Third.

Having alarmed them, she had to tell her uncle and Caleb something. "Two drunks stumbled out the back door. One of them was very—rude, but another man who heard him came along and made the two of them go away. It's all right. I'm all right. I panicked, but I'm fine now."

Caleb had abandoned his search for danger in the crowd and returned in time to hear her. She ignored the pinch of guilt. She wasn't lying. Not really. It had happened exactly as she said, just back in the spring, not tonight. Setting Caleb loose on a man who needed a cane would be much worse than twisting the truth a little.

"Come on," Caleb said, taking her by the arm and ignoring her slight flinch. "Your sisters are out there somewhere dancing, but Norah and your aunt are over by the refreshment table. You'll feel better after you tell them about it."

Deborah nodded and watched a path open up in front of them. Being fussed over now wouldn't be so bad, and Uncle Jason would be quick to take her back to Miriam's if she hinted at wanting to go. Her heart still pounded wildly. The Third. Why couldn't he have been the college boy of her imagination?

TREY WENT AFTER her this time. Not quickly enough to catch her, of course. He might even have been unable to pick her out of the crowd inside the hall if she hadn't darted and dodged the way she did. Slim, hair so dark it looked black in this light, average height, agile as a doe.

Unwilling to push through the crowd, Trey moved along the wall beside the door, keeping her in sight. If she never turned, and he never saw her face, he'd have to find her later by her dress. Dark yellow? Brownish yellow? He saw nothing to distinguish it. The music started. Dancers whirled in a polka, letting him catch sight of her again as she stopped by two men.

A blow to the head could not have stunned him more. He'd thought her reaction to the slip that had given him away extreme, but as Jamie often pointed out, the Van Cleve family was not popular in some quarters of Hubbell.

Oh, hell. This was worse than a lack of popularity. That was Cal Sutton staring hard-eyed through the dancers, and Jason Sutton leaning in toward—toward Green Dress Sutton.

His mystery woman was the most beautiful of the Sutton girls, and if she told her uncle about three meetings alone in the dark with Trey Van Cleve, especially about the Fourth of July....

He watched Cal Sutton turn back. She talked. The Suttons listened. Cal took her by the arm and led her toward the women near the punch bowl, and he didn't have to weave through the crowd. They parted for him the way the Red Sea had parted for Moses.

Trey sank back against the wall. She couldn't have told them the truth, or he'd be explaining himself to Suttons right now. Except why exactly should he have to explain anything? It was a mistake, that's all, as much her mistake as his. Calling him a liar was a bit of female hysteria worthy of Alice.

He pushed off the wall and headed back outside, not giving way to laughter until the door closed behind him. Poor middle-aged spinster. Green Dress Sutton. The more he thought about it, the harder he laughed.

9

JAMIE SAW THE humor in the whole thing when Trey told him about it the next morning, but Trey didn't much like Jamie's advice.

"So she's the niece of your father's best enemy. Just forget it ever happened. You can bet she will. You made her feel foolish. So first she'll convince herself you did it on purpose, and then she'll do her best to forget all about it. If she sees you on the street, she'll stick her nose in the air and pretend she can't see you."

"You're cynical from letting too many women toy with you."

"I'm wise from studying many women who thought they were toying with me while I toyed with them."

"Nobody was toying. We met by accident and liked each other. At least she liked me until she realized who I am. She's probably been raised from the cradle to hate any Van Cleve. Well, not quite from the cradle. She and Alice were probably about the same age back then. You can't blame her for being upset. I feel like I owe her an apology."

"Upset is one thing. Calling you a liar is something else, and apologizing is the same as saying she's right—you knew and did it on purpose. You're thinking of excuses to see her again. Think about the uncle who kills men the way you and I swat flies and stay far away from her and her whole family."

"Cousin. He's her cousin. These are different times. He's been a farmer raising a family and minding his own business ever since he and my father made peace."

"Men like that don't change. The world is full of pretty women who don't hate you."

"She's more than pretty. She's extraordinary. I knew that from the beginning. Now—she's also beautiful. What more could a man want?"

Jamie gave an exaggerated sigh. "How about a woman who doesn't sneak and lie and then call you the liar when she finds out who you are? I'm not wasting more breath on you. You're going to go and make trouble for yourself. I can tell. When they find your body, I'll tell the police who did it, but that won't dry your mother's tears, will it?"

"My mother doesn't cry," Trey said. Not only that, but if Cal Sutton decided to kill a man, he wouldn't do anything so subtle as cut reins. Sutton would use a gun.

Finding out about the Suttons wasn't hard. Trey spent the next few days in one Hubbell saloon or another, hanging around the stables, the general store, and the gunsmith's. He sought out Hubbell old timers and drifted into casual conversation. When they inevitably wanted to talk about the Fourth of July shooting contest, instead of changing the subject as had been his wont, he encouraged them to talk, about Cal Sutton, about all the Suttons.

Trey already knew that Jason and his brother Eli farmed a full section of land bordering the V Bar C to the north. He knew Cal Sutton's land bordered the ranch farther south.

Now he learned that his mystery woman, Green Dress, was Deborah Sutton, the oldest of the three girls who had come to live with Jason and Emma Sutton years ago. The childless couple treated the girls like daughters.

The spoon-waver, Judith, and Pink Dress, Miriam, had married townsmen. In fact Judith's husband, William Dalton, was the manager of the flour mill Jamie referred to as a fair man. Talking about Judith always brought a smile to the speaker's face. As far as Trey could see, the whole town liked Judith, and Trey finally conceded his initial impression of her had to be wrong. After all, most women eyed Jamie as if they'd like to do more than wave spoons at him.

Trey put together the bits and pieces he learned. The wedding celebration Deborah had talked about escaping from the night they first met was her youngest sister's. Odd that she'd disappear from something like that for hours. Of course that was the problem with the little he learned about Deborah.

"Different," said Lawson at the general store. "If she had a penny for candy, she'd give it to her sister and take half what it bought rather than come up to the counter and buy for herself. At first I thought she was shy, but after a while— different. It happens sometimes."

"Strange," a farmer he met at the café said. "Emma Sutton took them little girls in and treated them like her own, but that girl is a strange one. My wife had ladies over for a quilting bee one time, and I saw that girl shove Emma away and say, 'Leave me alone. Don't touch me. I told you, don't touch me.' All Emma did was reach out to brush a speck of dirt off her dress."

"Odd." Trey flinched at the sound of his own word coming from the mouth of a faro dealer in one of Hubbell's saloons.

"Judith's a sweetheart. They spoiled Miriam to where she thinks too much of herself, but now she's married, maybe she'll get over it. Something just went wrong with Deborah, I guess. If any of the Suttons heard me say it, they'd beat me to a pulp, but they know it's true. They all know it, and they protect her as best they can."

Not very well, they didn't. After all, she was out in the night meeting strangers, and she had walked alone through town on the Fourth of July, but then she'd all but admitted to sneaking away on the Fourth.

Learning that Miriam's husband was Hubbell's newest lawyer reminded Trey of his earlier hope that a lawyer could help him with Alice and her fears. A visit with Joseph Timmerman proved a disappointment on all fronts.

Trey arrived at the lawyer's office mid-morning, expecting to schedule an appointment. A rosy-cheeked clerk who didn't look old enough to be out of Hubbell's grammar school, much less working in an office, greeted Trey cheerily, disappeared through a door behind his desk for a moment, and returned to escort Trey straight in to see Timmerman.

Papers piled high on the desk and on the seat of one of the red leather chairs in front of it hinted at a growing practice, or a sloppy filing system, although file cabinets along one wall proved intent.

Nothing about Timmerman himself looked sloppy. His pin-striped suit had been tailored to fit those square shoulders by someone better than the local man. Every dark hair was pomaded into place, and the reserve in his expression hinted at a cautious nature.

The only sign of recognition of the Van Cleve name Trey discerned was a momentary flicker in sharp blue eyes. Other than that, Timmerman treated Trey as a valuable new client, had no interest in discussing anything except Trey's problem, and no satisfactory solutions.

"You can't assign property you don't own to someone else. You can promise to do so in the future after you inherit, but a court would probably let you squirm out of such a promise if enough time passes."

"That won't do then," Trey admitted. Alice was bound to check anything he did with her own lawyer, and an opinion like Timmerman's would simply seal her belief that her brother was a conniving rat.

"You have the same problem if you disclaim it now," Timmerman said. "In theory it would work, but in practice, if the inheritance comes in ten or twenty years, you could go to court and claim you didn't understand what you were signing or temporary alienation from your father that was resolved, and I'd give good odds even if you didn't get everything, you'd probably get at least half."

Trey slumped in his chair. "So if my father is stubborn about leaving it all to me, the only way to stop him is to die before he does?"

"That's the surest way," Timmerman said, a smile lighting his narrow face. "Of course, once it's yours, you can do what you want with it. You can give it to anyone you please or, for that matter, to a charity."

Standing on the walk outside the office, Trey stared at the shops across the street without seeing them. Once Alice had her child, she'd stop this insane feud, and Jamie was right. No matter how beautiful, no matter that she was the first woman to quicken his interest or his body for more than a year, Deborah Sutton was trouble.

Why continue a futile search to find out more about her? Did he expect to stumble across some explanation for her behavior? She was not a woman who would throw her arms around him and kiss him, happy for his success. She had run from him twice; she was odd; she was trouble.

His energy needed to go toward finding out who had sabotaged his buggy and making sure it never happened again. His own arguments were so convincing, by the time he reached the V Bar C the next afternoon, Trey had conceived of a plan. A plan to see Deborah Sutton again.

DEBORAH SLIPPED OUT of the pew and the church and took a seat at one of the rough hewn tables in the field between the church and the Grange Hall. The October sun shone warm from a sky so blue staring at it evoked an ache in her throat. Then again, pretty much everything made some part of her ache these days.

A friendship hidden in the dark had never had a chance of surviving light. She had always known that, but if she hadn't reacted so terribly, so unforgivably, she and the Third could have said a few regretful words about their families' enduring enmity and parted friends. She would at least have the memories without what she'd done at the end spoiling it all.

A covered buggy pulled by a chestnut horse came into sight on the road. No one would come to the service this late, but where could the man be going? The road only continued for another mile and ended at the Hazlett place, and the Hazletts were inside the church, not at home. The driver didn't try to find a hitching place among the wagons, buggies, and saddle horses tied all along the road in front of the church. He turned his rig around in the church driveway, left his horse standing there, and walked toward her.

Even at the distance she knew him. Without the cane, she would know him. Deborah sprang to her feet and looked around, ready to run, but where? Into the church where all those faces would turn and stare? Across the fields until she ran out of breath?

He stopped at a respectful distance. Even so he was closer than ever before, and he looked more handsome than at the ice cream parlor, slim and elegant in a way the men she had grown up with never could be, not quite so tall as the over-six-foot Sutton men, but close. She had been unable to see the color of his eyes before. Green. His eyes were gray-green, framed by lashes several shades darker than his hair. His face showed nothing but pleasure at the sight of her, as if she had never called him names and disappeared.

Too late to run. She'd have to hear him out, apologize, and see him on his way before the service ended.

"Good morning," he said. "I hoped this was your church and that I'd find you outside. I'd like to talk to you."

His voice was more real in daylight somehow, but familiar, giving the same illusion of safety and comfort it always had. She wanted to talk to him. She wanted.... "How did you know it was me?" she said, hearing the belligerence in her own voice.

"I followed you. I saw you go to your uncle and cousin."

"And now that you know, you don't have enough sense to stay away? Everyone will be outside soon. They'll see you and want to know why you're here. Go away."

"Your preacher must be a quick one. I heard the services start at ten." He made a show of pulling a gold watch from his pocket and checking the time. "It's only quarter after ten right now."

"I'm not the only one who ever comes outside. Someone will come out and see you." What was the matter with her? She didn't want to argue. She wanted to apologize for what she'd said to him, but those words stuck in her throat, and the ones tumbling out were all wrong.

"If you're worried about your uncle and cousin thumping me with my own cane, let's ride down the road a little way. We can talk without worrying about who will see me, and if I leave Irene standing by herself much longer, she may get it in her head to go back to the ranch without me."

In spite of herself, Deborah reacted to his nonsense and his gesture toward the buggy. "No one would beat you. They'd just make you go away," she said as she started walking. "And what kind of name is Irene for a horse. No one names a horse Irene."

"Really? I think she looks like an Irene. She's stuck with it now."

As Deborah was stuck with him. He didn't take her hand to help her into the buggy, but held out his and waited. Through her glove and his she felt the warmth, the strength, but then she was on the seat. She sat tight against the side, eyes locked on the road ahead.

"I need to apologize," he said once they'd left the long lines of tied horses behind.

Her tongue came unstuck. Maybe it was the everyday sound of hooves clopping down the road. Maybe it was the fact he sat as far on his side of the seat as she did on hers. "No, you don't. You have nothing to apologize for."

"Maybe for slipping and giving it away and spoiling everything."

She hadn't thought of it that way. After all she'd always known there would be a bad ending. "I'm the one who needs to apologize. For what I called you. I don't know why I said it. I'm the one who lied."

"To me?"

She didn't even have to think about that before answering. "No, never to you, but to everyone else. That night I even lied again and told my family I was upset about a drunk that came along, that a stranger had to punch him to make him leave. I told myself it wasn't much of a lie because it did happen."

He laughed. "Is that what you thought? I couldn't have punched a pillow hard enough to dent it back then, so I hit him with the cane. The result was so salutary I decided to keep the thing whether I needed it or not, and I don't really need it any more unless I'm tired. I shouldn't admit such low behavior to you."

"Oh." Against her will, the corners of her mouth turned up. "I don't see what was low about it. He deserved it, but that means I didn't even get my lie right, did I?" She risked a glance at him, his eyes met hers, and he smiled too.

The misery that had been her constant companion since the dance eased. She wouldn't see him again after today. They'd never talk again, but they could part friends.

"From what you said, I had the idea you were still in college, or only graduated this spring. When I thought it over, I realized you never said that exactly, but I took it that way."

"I thought you were a middle-aged spinster, probably longer in the tooth than Irene. You didn't exactly say that either."

"Oh, but I did say.... I can see why you thought that. My sisters call me an old maid."

"Your sisters are wrong. What are you twenty-three, twenty-four?"

"Twenty-five."

"Aah. I take it back. That is old."

"You need to turn around now," she said. "We need to be back in time so no one sees you."

He didn't argue but reined to a halt and maneuvered the mare around in the road. Once they were headed back, he said, "Would it be so terrible if they saw me?"

She stopped taking short sideways peeks at him and turned to face him. "Of course it would. Your father...."

"My father got it into his head he wanted all the land to the creek and killed people trying to get it. Your people. I know that. You and I were children back then. I don't see why we can't be friends now."

"He had my grandfather killed," Deborah said, surprised he would admit what his father had done, "and my cousin Norah's first husband and half a dozen other people who had settled along the creek."

"Sins of the fathers?" he said, giving the horse an unnecessary slap with the reins. "Didn't you say your grandfather was a monster? Was that another little lie?"

"No, it wasn't. He was a very cruel man, but that doesn't mean he deserved to be murdered."

Trey—she couldn't think of him as the Third after this—sucked in a breath and blew it out noisily. "No, it doesn't. I'm sorry, but I don't see why old feuds that were over when we were children should keep us from being friends."

"But it's not over. The fighting is, but not the feelings. You have no idea how much people still hate your father, your family."

"Maybe I do. There are people in town who let me know they don't see much difference between me and my father, and I know how he reacts to the Sutton name. I just don't care what he thinks."

"I do care what my family thinks."

"Even though you've spent most of your life running and hiding from them?"

She glared at him. "Leave me at the church, go away, and don't come back."

He gave a curt nod and neither of them spoke again until he turned and pulled up in the place where she'd first seen him. He helped her down and kept hold of her hand. "I'm sorry. I never should have said such a thing. I could talk to...."

She jerked her hand free. "No! You can't. Please. Let's just say goodbye as friends and not make trouble. You said you were leaving Hubbell soon anyway."

"I am, but until then...."

"No. I can't do that to them. I don't want to."

He tipped his hat, rueful acceptance in his face. "All right, Deborah Sutton. And when the Fourth of July rolls around again, think of me. I'm going to remember you."

Deborah watched him go. If anything was sure in life, it was that she'd never stop thinking of him, remembering four all too brief encounters.

At last she turned away. She could stand at the back of the church for the rest of the service, join in the final hymn. A dark form moved on the church stoop, and Deborah froze, her mind racing. Hiram Johnson. How long had he been standing there?

If she could reach him in time, find out what he'd seen, and beg him to keep quiet.... She lifted her skirt to run, but he disappeared inside. Even knowing it was futile, Deborah hurried after him, into the dim interior of the church.

She stopped just inside the door and watched Hiram march to where the rest of the Johnsons sat and slide into place. He began whispering to his brother before his rear hit the pew.

As the final hymn began, Deborah tiptoed back outside and walked slowly to the picnic tables. Concocting a story to explain what Hiram had seen was beyond her. She was going to have to tell the truth.

NO ONE ASKED a question. They all joined her at the table, beside her, around her.

At least Judith and Miriam weren't here to smirk or frown and neither was Beth, who had left for school more than a month ago. Eli's boys, too young to care about what concerned adults, took off across the fields with half a dozen other children, and Cousin Norah sent her youngest two away with a few words.

"It was an accident," Deborah said finally.

"Did he threaten you?" Aunt Em asked, concern all over her face.

"No, he came to apologize because I.... Because I...." It all came pouring out then, the first accidental meeting, what she'd done on the Fourth of July, and what had really happened at the dance. Aunt Em looked more and more horrified, Uncle Jason sadder and sadder, Uncle Eli and Caleb grim, Aunt Lucy and Norah merely interested.

"I'm sorry," she ended, close to tears. "I'm s-sorry, but I thought he was a boy, a boy from a family we don't know who went to college, and t-talking to him was interesting and, and it didn't seem so terrible at the time."

"I can't believe you were so foolish," Aunt Em said. "Out alone on the Fourth like that. You had to know what could have happened, what he could have done. Webster Van Cleve's son! He killed your own grandfather, paid someone to do it."

"I didn't know who he was!"

"But you rode away with him. Hiram saw you coming back down the road in the buggy with him."

"He wanted to talk to me, to apologize. He apologized, and we're never going to talk again." For some reason, after admitting to lies and sneaking, the last bit started her crying.

The only thing Deborah hated worse than crying was doing it in front of anyone. She stood up and took off running, away from the fields where the children whooped and shouted, behind the Grange Hall and into the shadows there. She sank down at the base of the wall, out of sight of everyone, not caring in the least how much dirt got on her Sunday dress.

The tears stopped, and after a while so did her raggedy breathing. She ought to go back now, before someone came to fetch her like a sullen child. Instead she drew her knees up, hugged them, and hid her face.

Footsteps sounded, and she looked up, ready to tell whoever it was to go away more rudely than she had told Trey Van Cleve the same.

Norah sank down beside her, and Deborah relaxed. There had been a time when she fell asleep each night wishing she was Norah's daughter. Then she had realized that would mean Caleb was her father and moved on to other wishes.

"Hungry?" Norah unwrapped the napkin in her hand to expose a thick slice of bread, glistening with a liberal coating of butter.

"Yes, thank you." To her surprise, she was hungry. Deborah devoured the bread, used the napkin, and waited for a lecture, advice, or recriminations. Norah just leaned back and closed her eyes, a slight smile on her face. The silence lengthened. Deborah rested against the wall and closed her eyes too.

"You're my favorite Sutton, you know," Deborah said.

Norah smiled without opening her eyes. "Right now."

"Most of the time. You're good at letting a person be."

"Mm. Maybe because there are times when that's all I want myself."

"Do you ever get it?"

"More now than when the children were small, but even then sometimes Caleb seemed to just know. He'd round them up and take them off for a while."

More silence.

"I'm going to have to go back and face them soon, aren't I?"

"Unless you want to walk home. It's a long way. They won't say anything more in front of the boys. It will be all right."

"It didn't seem so terrible at the time. I just.... I *liked* talking to him."

"You like him."

"I do, but I can't, can I?"

"Did I ever tell you how I once lost a position because of Caleb?"

"No. A position? You took a position, a paid position?"

"I did. After Joe was killed, it was work or starve. I starved for a while, and then I took a position as a housekeeper in town. When Mrs. Tindell found out I was seeing Caleb, she told me it reflected poorly on her and on me, and I had to stop seeing him if I wanted to work for her."

"*The* Mrs. Tindell? The one everybody calls the grande dame of Hubbell?"

"Caleb calls her an old bat, but that's the one."

"So she dismissed you because of Caleb," Deborah said knowingly.

"No, I quit because of Caleb." Norah opened her eyes, turned her head, and raised her eyebrows. "We got married the first time I saw him after that."

"It wasn't like that!" Deborah said. "We enjoyed talking to each other is all. I never thought of him like that."

"Of course not, you thought he was a boy, way too young for a spinster like you. And I just thought you would like to hear what I did once upon a time when someone told me I couldn't see someone I wanted to see. Of course I was much older and widowed."

"How old were you?"

"Twenty-eight."

"That's only three years...."

"That's right, much older." Norah gave her a wide smile. "And now I'm older yet, so you need to get up and give me a hand. My knees aren't what they used to be."

Deborah rose and pulled Norah, who seemed as limber as ever, to her feet. They walked side by side back to where the family waited without saying more.

10

TREY MADE IT back to the ranch in early afternoon. The Grange Hall and church were close enough if the Van Cleve family were so inclined, they could attend in all but the worst weather. As he turned his horse onto the ranch road, he abandoned conjuring up scenarios where the Van Cleve family joined the faithful in the farm community.

Fantasies of outrage and even righteous violence enabled him to keep thoughts of his visit with Deborah at bay. So would focusing on the all too real problem of who had cut harness, loosened a buggy wheel, and tried to put Irene out of commission for a few days at best or cripple her at worst, except he didn't want to face that reality any more than Deborah's rejection.

Herman met Trey in front of the barn and didn't give him a choice. "None of the hands has said a word or even looked sly when your name comes up."

"Does my name come up often?"

"Some."

The old man refused to give names, and Trey had no faith a contemptuous ranch hand had gone to such lengths to do harm. Trey accepted Herman's promise to guard Irene like a hawk and watch for anyone nosing around the harness or buggy as the best he could do.

In truth, he didn't want anyone to catch Alice with a knife in her hand. A few more months, and he'd be gone from Hubbell, and his sister's emotional vagaries would no longer matter.

The next few days passed in relative peace so far as Van Cleve family relations went. Trey stuck with polite banalities, and so did his father. Alice seemed too caught up in the prospect of the coming child to worry about her unworthy brother. Vernon and Daniel Forbes had left for the north on business and would be gone at least another week.

Trey spent hours walking over the ranch. He'd never run a race again and expected to deal with backaches when fatigued for the rest of his life, but the cane would soon be an affectation, one he planned to keep.

He shared stories with his mother about her mother, a tough-minded old woman Trey had lived with while in college.

The peace ended as Trey knew it would, this time with an early morning summons to his father's study. Knocking on the door took him back to a long ago time when he'd vibrated with excitement over permission to enter his father's private domain, been fascinated by the map on the wall, bookcases, and cabinets.

The big smile with which his father greeted him worried Trey more than a scowl would have. If he'd done anything to invoke this bonhomie, he didn't know it and hated to think what it might be.

"Sit down. Sit down and let's see if we can't get past all these petty differences."

Trey took both a chair and a cigar with suspicion. At least his father didn't seem inclined to start pouring whiskey this early in the day.

The map of the ranch and surrounding properties had disappeared when Webster Van Cleve came to terms with Cal Sutton. Other than that, the room looked much the same as it had twenty years ago. Different drapes and wallpaper, but still a dark, masculine room with the same big desk and chairs facing it.

His father had changed, though. He carried more weight on his short frame, gray predominated over black in his thinning hair. His black eyes hadn't changed. They remained as piercing as ever.

His voice was the same too, deep for such a small man, with an underlying smug tone, as if he always knew things no one else did. "I'm glad you've finally decided to stay home for a while. All this travel back and forth to town can't be good for you."

Especially in a buggy with cut reins and a loose wheel. "It's not a problem. I'm almost back to full strength now, and sitting in a buggy isn't hard work."

"Hard on the back."

Trey shrugged. "A little."

"How's your Irish friend doing?" his father didn't wait for an answer, but went on. "I hear he's working at the flour mill. I could find him easier work for two or three times the money. Just ask."

"He wouldn't take it." *And hell would freeze over before I'd ask.*

"That's too bad. They're a thick-headed people. In truth I'm glad you're seeing less of him and showing more family feeling. Revenge isn't always profitable, but sometimes it's good for the spirits."

Starting an argument over the thickness of Jamie's head would have to wait for an interpretation of the revenge remark. His father was all too pleased with him at the moment. Trey didn't like it.

"I've had a talk with your sister, and Vernon too. You're my son. You'll inherit, but they won't exactly starve. Vernon's making enough now he'll be wealthy on his own by the time I'm gone. It's not like I'm planning on dying soon."

"Of course not. Only the good die young."

"You're never going to let it go, are you? When it's yours you can run it as a charity for all I'll care. You'll lose half of it, but there will still be enough for my grandchildren. My legitimate grandchildren."

What the hell was he talking about, and more important, what was he up to?

"I'm afraid you lost me at revenge," Trey said, "and if you have some notion you have illegitimate grandchildren anywhere, you're wrong. I may have sewn a few wild oats, but I was careful none of them ever sprouted."

His father's expression matched the knowing tone of his voice as he leaned back and blew a smoke ring. "I hear you were out at the grangers' church last Sunday."

So that's what all this was about. "You really have spies everywhere, don't you?"

"People know being friendly never hurts and sometimes pays. So you had one of the Sutton girls down the road with you. Got those damn Suttons all lathered up and bothered, the girl running off in tears. I wish I could have seen it."

The smile and jolly attitude had disappeared now, and Trey could see pure malice shining from his father's dark eyes. "So they already know a Van Cleve had her. Now you make sure you leave her with a bastard to remember you by. Let Cal

Sutton chew on that. Maybe he ought to start worrying about his daughters with a handsome young buck like you around."

Trey threw the cigar down, ignoring where it landed on the carpet, and pushed to his feet. "She has more sense than to want anything to do with a son of yours. I wish I had the same choice." He yanked open the door to leave, then paused, "And if you leave me one bloody red dime, I'll give it away. I'll give it to every charity that helps the kind of people you've cheated, beggared, and murdered to line your own pockets."

"The hell you will. You say that now in a self-righteous fury, but when it's yours, you'll fight to keep it."

"If you're stupid enough to do it, I hope the preachers are right about heaven and hell and you can see me throw it away from where you're burning. That's the only way you'll see me again."

Alice and his mother stood wide-eyed in the hall, drawn by the shouting.

"You fool." Alice walked into the study and shut the door behind her.

His mother put her hands on his arms and looked into his face. "You're leaving again."

"I am."

"I wish...." She stepped back. "Be careful."

He nodded and turned away. He wouldn't make Hubbell until after dark, and the morning's gray sky warned of fall weather at last. A cooler temperature and stiff breeze would be welcome. With luck the cold and wind would clear the lingering scent of cigar smoke from his head and his father's filthy words from his mind.

IN NO MOOD to indulge Herman, Trey hauled everything he'd brought to the ranch to the barn, caught Irene up, groomed her, and harnessed her inside out of the wind. Rifle, valise, bedroll, a large leather bag, he loaded them all and was ready to put Irene to the buggy when Herman hustled into the barn.

"You should have come got me."

The old man didn't need to know why Trey was in such a hurry or such a temper. "Sorry. Help me hitch, why don't you?"

Trey started to untie Irene as a small black streak ran through the open door, under the buggy, and disappeared behind the grain bin along the wall. No sooner was the animal out of sight than Lenny, Trey's least favorite of the ranch hands, charged into the barn, cursing.

"Where'd it go?" he yelled at Herman.

Herman pointed wordlessly then turned to Trey. "Let's get you on the road."

Lenny grabbed a buggy whip and poked behind the bin with the butt. "I got the other two sacked up, but this one took off."

Lenny shoved the whip back and forth along the wall. The little animal he pursued slipped out from behind the bin and under the bench next to it. Trey recognized one of the puppies he'd seen playing around the yard.

"Come on, now," Herman said. "You need to get town before dark." He grabbed Irene's lead rope.

Hurry or not, Trey was still in enough of a temper to resent being pushed, and if he had to guess who had moved Irene into the corral with the other horses, Lenny, with his cocky attitude and thinly disguised contempt for the boss's son, would be first on his list.

What's more, there were better ways to catch a puppy.

"Hold up," Trey said. "Shouldn't you be herding cattle, not dogs?"

Lenny stopped poking behind the bin and raised the lid, ignoring Trey and his question. "How full is this thing? Maybe we can just pull it out."

"It ran under the bench," Herman said, pointing again.

Trey left Irene to Herman and blocked Lenny's path to the bench. "I asked you a question."

After rolling his eyes toward Herman, Lenny said, "If you spent more time around here, you'd know cattle don't need herding this time of year, but yeah, I got better things to do. I'm last hired, so I get the dirty jobs. Like taking care of dogs. We got too many dogs around here, and I got orders to get rid of them."

"We always locked bitches up in the old smokehouse during their time," Trey said. "If we don't need more dogs, and you're the one who takes care of dogs, why are there puppies running around?"

Lenny's leathery face hardened. "I let the old bitch out, that's why. I got tired of cleaning up dog shit, and I let her out, and I'd do it again. Drowning them or shooting them is easier, so why don't you get in that fancy buggy and drive that lady's pony to town and leave me to it?"

"Because I'm firing you first," Trey said. "Go get your possibles, saddle up, and beat me and the lady's pony to town, or I'll know why."

"The hell you say. You can't fire me."

"Sure I can. I just did."

"You and what other cripple!"

Shouting the last words, Lenny rushed straight at him. Trey pivoted away from the charge and smashed the man across the knees with his cane. Lenny fell head first, screaming. Irene lunged and danced in place. Trey shut Lenny up with a second blow to the mid-section that left him no breath for more than a moan. Shaking with the effort at control, Trey held back from what he wanted to do—put all his strength into a third blow to the head.

He went to Irene, soothed her with a few words and soft touches. "I saw some men hitching a wagon over by the south corral," he said to Herman. "Tell them to drive around here, load this trash up, and dump it in town."

"Your pa ain't going to like this."

"Think again. How would you like to be the one to tell my father he's been paying a hand who disobeyed orders because he's too lazy to do his job? Maybe I should tell him. My guess is the foreman will find himself in that wagon with Lenny."

"This ain't important enough to bother Mr. Van Cleve. So everybody likes Lenny. So we let him get away with it this time. You can't fire men over dogs."

"I can, and I did. It wouldn't be just this time, and you know it. Now it's not a problem."

"Yes, it is a problem. Them dogs need killing. Are you going to do it?"

The puppy had ventured out from under the bench while they argued. It stayed far away from where Lenny groaned, hunched over his knees. Gathering courage, it pounced on the lash of the whip and pranced back under the bench with its prize, head and tail high. Floppy ears, black with white paws and tail tip, it looked exactly like the ranch dogs Trey had grown up with.

"You take care of Lenny," Trey said. "I'll take care of the puppies."

By the time the wagon creaked away with Lenny in the bed, Trey had found the other puppies and a wood crate large enough to hold all three. He dumped the jumble of equipment out of the crate and tied it on the seat of the buggy.

"What the heck are you doing?" Herman said, coming up behind him.

"I'm taking them to town. Help me find a board to put on top and keep them in."

"You figure they ain't got enough dogs in town?"

"I figure you're going to help me find a way to keep them in here," Trey said, feeling the pressure of time. Not only would he get to town long after dark, he'd prefer not to debate his reasons for throwing his weight around with anyone who knew he was leaving the ranch for good.

At least three unhappy puppies would keep him from thinking of Deborah Sutton, his miserable family, or what he was going to do with the rest of his life for most of the long hours of the drive.

Ready at last, Trey held his eager horse to a walk for a short distance down the ranch road. Finally letting her move into a ground-covering trot, he waved once over his shoulder without looking back.

11

By the time he was halfway to Hubbell, Trey had reason to regret his previous thoughts about welcoming colder temperatures and wind. His teeth chattered for miles even before the rain started. First thing tomorrow he'd buy a heavier winter coat—and oilskins.

Irene slogged the last miles to town through mud that made any gait faster than a walk dangerous and pulled up in front of the town stable long after it closed for the night. Her head hung. Water dripped from her nose, tail, and everything between.

Unwilling to argue about his horse or the puppies, Trey didn't roust anyone to help him. Irene finished a quart of oats and munched on hay as he rubbed her down, her attitude improving by the minute. After exploring the barn, the puppies settled in a pile of straw, growling over the rabbit Trey had shot for them before the rain started.

He left his undersized horse and canine waifs in accommodations reserved for their betters, grabbed his valise and rifle from the buggy, and set out for the First Street Hotel.

Waking a working man like Jamie this time of night would be cruel, and in truth Trey wanted a hot bath, not a walk down the hall to cold water, and a soft bed, not an old cot.

At times like this, he still needed the cane. Fatigue crawled up his spine and sat heavily on his shoulders. Mud and muck in the street gleamed under the streetlights as he tapped his way along the walk. The catty-cornered crossing from the south side of Main to the east side of First proved every bit as treacherous as he feared.

Slowed by the heavy going, valise in one hand, rifle and cane in the other, Trey stopped in surprise at the sound of a man's deep shout.

"Heeyaah!"

The shout came again and again, punctuated with whip cracks. Hooves splashed and sucked in the mud as a four-horse team tore toward him, wagon rumbling and creaking with the strain. No way to run.

Trey froze for almost fatal seconds then dove for the walk, rolling as he hit the street. A hoof glanced off his shoulder, another smacked his thigh, and then the wagon was gone, careening into the night, the madman in the driver's seat still shouting.

Trey crawled up on the sidewalk and sat there, scraping muck from his face with shaking hands. A man splashed across Main to where he sat. "Are you all right, mister? You almost got squashed like a frog in the road. He has to be crazy. Only a crazy man would run a team like that even in good weather."

Crazy, drunk, or murderous. A blast of beery breath in his face as he took the proffered hand made Trey decide to leave drunkenness out of possible explanations. At least in present company.

The fellow wasn't really drunk, no more than halfway. He squelched back into the street, picked up Trey's battered valise from where it had landed, and looked around until he found both rifle and cane.

As soon as Trey took the cane, his helper's cheerful expression dimmed. "Ain't you the Van Cleve boy? What are you doing out and about in town on a night like this?"

"I'm running away from home," Trey said with as much dignity as he could muster while wiping mud from the back of his neck.

"Can't say as I blame you with that family. Where you headed?"

"First Street Hotel."

"Gimme that case, and I'll help you there."

Trey handed over the battered valise, spit mud, and smiled, "Thank you, friend."

TREY EXPECTED MORE sympathy from Jamie when the two met for supper the next night.

"They can't weigh more than ten pounds apiece," Trey said. "How could they have done twelve dollars worth of damage in a single night?"

"Are you sure they didn't really chew that saddle?"

"Who could tell? It's an old hulk so worn out no one could tell if the marks he showed me were made last night or during the Civil War, and your landlord's being totally unreasonable."

"He rents rooms for people, not dogs."

"Well, you think he'd take a bribe. They'll be gone in a day or two."

Jamie snorted. "Sure they will. You need to be worrying about who's trying to kill you, and taking more care to see they fail than you did last night."

"No one could have known where I'd be and when to set that up."

"What about that Lenny fellow. From what you said, he must be feeling murderous."

"He should be in town, but I can't believe he'd be up to driving a team last night. And he's not the only one of the ranch hands who resented the boss's son showing up after years away and acting like the boss's son, but how could anyone know where I'd be?"

"Follow you."

That was an ugly possibility Trey rejected every time the thought popped up. "No one followed me to town."

"You were sure to leave the horse at the stables. He could follow you from there."

Trey cut into his beefsteak with more vigor than required. "It could be an accident. Some crazy drunk risking his neck and his horses."

"How soon are you leaving town?"

"As soon as I work out the details of my investment in automobiles and find homes for three dogs."

"The sooner the better," Jamie muttered over his coffee cup.

"So you don't think a killer will stalk me wherever I go?" Trey said, smiling at the thought.

"I hope not," Jamie said, his expression serious. "Stealing away quietly in the middle of a dark night and using a different name for a year or two might be a good idea. Maybe I'm glad I was born poor."

"He's getting a lawyer out there right now to change his will, so if anyone's trying to cut off my branch of the family tree, they don't need to any longer."

"Are you sure?"

Trey sighed. "No. Maybe if Alice has a son. He's a stubborn old coot."

"Then you take after him in at least one way."

"Absolutely not. There are stubborn people in my mother's family. It's all from there."

"Sure. That must be it. Now do these dogs of yours need to go to snobby heathen homes, or shall I try to peddle them to some good Catholic families?"

Trey saluted with his coffee cup. "Those puppies look like Catholics to me. Find them homes, and I'll finance an extra automobile."

OVER THE NEXT few days, Jamie sweet talked families of men he worked with into taking the two male puppies. Neither sweet talk nor bribes got anyone to take the female.

"You can't blame people for not wanting the bother of locking her up for weeks every year or dealing with puppies," Jamie said philosophically. "You'll have to take her with you when you leave. Or shoot her."

Trey glared at Jamie through eyes more than a little gritty after another sleepless night. He should be making plans for where he'd go after he left here. Instead every exchange in every conversation he'd had with Deborah Sutton kept running through his mind.

So did the memory of the sight of her in the green dress and the look of pleasure on her face as she sucked ice cream off her spoon. Not to mention the way she looked in her plain gray Sunday best as she placed her smaller gloved hand in his.

By the time he got to where she sat beside him in the buggy, bringing a singing awareness to every nerve in his body, he gave up on sleep and worked on cleaning mud out of his rifle, polishing boots, or trying to drown himself in cold water.

Trey never doubted the report of his father's spy. Someone at the church had seen him with Deborah that Sunday, told her family, and she'd had to confess. Of course she could have explained his presence with something less than the whole truth, but her family knew she had spent time with him. Cal Sutton knew.

All of which was why a truly insane idea came to him. "Don't worry," he told Jamie. "I know someone who needs a dog."

The next morning, Trey put the last puppy back in the crate, tied it on the buggy seat again, and sent Irene trotting along the road toward Cal Sutton's place.

TREY STOPPED THE buggy in the road twice and actually turned back toward town once. By the time he reached the long drive from the road to the Sutton farm, he had rejected all thoughts of retreat as cowardly. Or maybe he was too tired to care.

He passed between a pair of old soddys and pulled up at a hitch rail at the front of a two-story house, the cream color glowing close to yellow in the late afternoon sun. Judging by the porch swing and chairs on this veranda, it was well used.

At least no new dog barked at him. Spending a day driving out here with a night drive back to town to come was bad enough. Finding out the slim chance he was taking was no chance would be too much. Behind the house acres of wheat and corn stubble stretched as far as the eye could see, harvested but not yet plowed under in preparation for next year's crop.

Nothing moved in the quiet yard. Trey eyed the big barn, painted traditional red, and turned toward the house. Mrs.

Sutton would be starting work on the family supper about now. Seeing her would be easier than facing Cal Sutton first.

The barn door slammed and two women emerged. At the sight of him, the shorter one raced back inside. Trey could hear her yelling, "Pa, Pa!"

Norah Sutton walked toward him, no sign of her daughter's excitement in her face. "Good afternoon, Mr. Van Cleve. I suppose you know you're a surprise, and I suppose you're here to talk to my husband."

Trey tipped his hat and returned the greeting, unsure where to start. "Actually I'm about to ask a favor of both of you."

"Well, then, let's wait until Caleb gets here. Would you like to come in and have a cup of coffee?"

A small howl rose from the box on the buggy seat as Trey shook his head. "Thank you, but I think the favor needs out of there."

Before he had the puppy on the ground, he heard the barn door again and looked over his shoulder to see Cal Sutton coming across the yard in long strides, his son and daughter following at a jog.

Trey put the puppy down with a muttered, "This is your chance. Be charming."

She ran in a few frantic circles and squatted in the grass near the porch steps.

"What are you doing here, and why come with your dog?" Cal Sutton said, stopping beside his wife.

"I'm...." Trey cleared his throat. "It's not my dog. It's no one's dog and needs a home. Deborah told me, that is Miss Sutton said something that made me think you might need, er, want a dog. You wouldn't be so surprised to see me if you had a dog to bark when someone drove up."

Sutton scowled down at the little animal, which was still ignoring Trey's order to be charming and now scratching an ear. "It looks like the ranch dogs I knew on the V Bar C years ago."

In for a penny. "We had an accidental litter."

"Somebody got careless?"

"Lazy."

Sutton frowned as if he knew the rest of the story. He scooped the puppy up and held her dangling out in front of him. "It's female."

"Yes, and that's why no one will take her. Mill workers took the males. I know it's extra trouble, locking her up during her time and all."

Sutton put the puppy down and looked at his wife. "There's no way to name a female."

Mrs. Sutton explained this strange statement with a smile. "All our animals are named after Confederate generals. It's a family tradition."

Trey stared at the puppy. She couldn't stay here because there were no female generals? "How about a spy?" he said at last. "Didn't Jefferson Davis think Rose Greenhow was as good as a general?"

Sutton exchanged a glance with his wife, and Trey saw the wink. "Rose it is then. Let's hope she's a better watch dog than her great, great grandparents."

The girl, who gave her name as Ginny, was already dragging one of the ropes Trey had used on the crate along the ground for the puppy to play with.

Mrs. Sutton renewed her previous invitation. "How about that cup of coffee now?"

Trey refused regretfully. He could use a cup of hot coffee before starting back. It might help him stay awake on the long drive ahead. "Thank you, but no, it's late already, and Hubbell's a long way."

"Hubbell? Aren't you going back to the ranch?"

"I'm not going back to the ranch." As the words came out of his mouth, Trey heard the bitterness in his voice and knew he'd given away more than he'd meant to.

"Driving all that way at night alone when you're tired is dangerous," Mrs. Sutton said, concern in her blue eyes. "Stay for supper with us and stay the night. We have room, and after all, the way you sneaked up on us proves we needed a new dog."

Astonished beyond words, Trey looked to Sutton, who gave a curt nod. He should refuse. Trey knew he should refuse, but the temptation to put off the long drive until morning won out. When he found his voice what came out was, "Thank you. Rose and I are both in your debt."

After taking care of Irene and helping the Suttons with a few evening chores, Trey trooped into the house behind Sutton and his son, introduced as Jason but called Jacey. And Trey fell in love. In love with the big kitchen painted in soft yellow and bright blue, with the scarred table in the middle of the room, with the soft light from oil lamps, and most of all with Cal Sutton's wife, who curved a hand over her husband's shoulder every time she leaned over him to place a dish on the table.

"I need to warn you," she said, setting a glass of milk at Trey's place. All we have here is goat's milk, and it has a slightly different flavor."

Trey didn't care if it tasted of boiled cabbage. He'd drink every drop. "I saw the goats in their pens," he said. "Don't tell me those goats are named for Confederate generals."

She laughed, and Sutton and the children grinned. "You caught us out. The nannies are exceptions, and Rose could have been too, but your suggestion was so inspired I'm glad we didn't miss it. The billy goat is Braxton, however."

"General Bragg may be whirling in his grave."

"He's a very handsome billy goat."

Grace here was not a travesty, and the meal was exceptional, well worth giving thanks for. As he ate, Trey added thanks for Rose's new home and his own easy acceptance by people his father had wronged.

Knowing farmers started their day before dawn, Trey half-expected to be shown to his bed before the dishes were done. No one showed the slightest inclination to turn in that early, though. Sutton picked up a book and eyeglasses from the sideboard, perched the glasses on his nose, and opened the book to a place marked by a ribbon.

"I'm sorry if this bores you," he said to Trey. "We're already at the halfway mark, so it won't make much sense to you."

Trey listened in wonder to a familiar section of *The Red Badge of Courage*. He pictured Deborah, reading the same book when Sutton was done and had passed it on. What would she think of a novel of war written so eloquently by a man who had never been a soldier? For that matter, what did Sutton, who had been in different kinds of wars, think of the story?

Mrs. Sutton and Ginny washed up and put dishes away as quietly as possible. Jacey listened as he punched holes in a length of leather that could be a new belt. Sutton cradled the book in scarred hands, head bent forward, reading out loud to his family. He didn't stop until after the last of the women's work was done.

Trey lay awake on the narrow bed in the blue and white room Mrs. Sutton showed him to and listened as Sutton came in from taking the puppy for a last walk. Murmurs sounded, a door closed. Quiet descended over the house. Trey tried not to think of Sutton, in bed with a woman who loved him so much it showed in every expression and gesture. He turned his thoughts instead to Deborah, as he had every night since the dance.

These people were her family. Cal Sutton was the cousin who gave her books, but he also had to be the one who had killed her father. How could a killer who had earned his living with a gun create a family like this?

Did Deborah's home with her aunt and uncle have this quiet warmth? If so, small wonder she didn't want to marry and leave.

Trey fell asleep without answers to his questions and slept as he hadn't for weeks.

SCENTS OF BACON and coffee woke Trey the next morning. He was the last one to the breakfast table and perhaps the most appreciative of the food.

After all, the others were used to Mrs. Sutton's cooking. Eggs with goat cheese mixed in? Chefs should take lessons from her.

His hand was on the door, his thanks and goodbyes said, when she handed him a packet of sandwiches. "I hope we see you again sometime," she said.

"I'll be looking for excuses. Thank you for everything."

Trey had Irene half-harnessed when Sutton materialized from inside the barn and helped him put her to the buggy. When they finished, Trey couldn't help but say, "I envy you."

"I'd expect an educated man like you to choose a different way of life. Farming's not the easiest."

Trey shook his head. "You're right. I'm no farmer. What I envy is your family. I'm going to leave Hubbell as soon as I take care of some unfinished business, but you give me a strong urge to marry and settle down."

"If you want what I have, choose your woman carefully. It all comes down to a woman who can—give." Sutton hesitated a moment looking off at the house, then went on. "I know there's something between you and Deborah. Norah and I have a strong affection for her and her sisters, but if you want what I have, she can't give it to you. She's...."

This time the pause lasted long enough for Trey to bet with himself on which word was coming—not *odd* or *strange* this time. Sutton would say *different.*

"...damaged."

Damn it. That was just too much. "She told me she saw you kill her father."

"Did she? So far as I know, she's never mentioned her father to anyone since that day."

"Well, she told me what you did. It would damage anyone. So why? Why did you do it?"

Unperturbed by Trey's anger, Sutton said, "If she wanted you to know, she'd have told you, wouldn't she?"

"I'm not sure she meant to tell me at all. I was moaning about my family, and she ran out of patience and decided to show me I didn't have it so bad. If it was a contest, she would have won."

Sutton laughed out loud. "Maybe I'm wrong and it's too bad you're leaving. Sneaking away to talk about books is one thing. Telling secrets is another." He stepped back away from the buggy. "You'd better get going, or you'll still be getting to town in the dark."

Trey looked back once as Irene trotted toward the town road. He saw Sutton striding toward the fields, the small shape of a puppy at his heels.

TREY DROVE TO town with hat pulled low and shoulders hunched as if thin white clouds streaking across blue sky presaged foul weather instead of an unseasonably warm fall day.

Shining yellow and brilliant orange flashed in his peripheral vision from cottonwoods and low-lying bushes along the creek. Trey never turned his head. Irene trotted along the flat brown ribbon of road without interference or guidance.

Yes, landlords and stablemen had proved resistant to both entreaties and bribes when it came to a puppy, but spending a day and night—that had turned into two days—on the road in hopes Cal Sutton and his wife would take her...? Without the hope of finding out where he stood with the Suttons, Trey never would have done it.

The invitation to stay the night had led him to believe this branch of the Sutton family had no problem with what had happened between him and Deborah. Yet Cal Sutton's last words had been a more effective warning off than threats and a gun barrel pressed between the eyes.

Damaged.

No matter how Trey fit together the few puzzle pieces he had, he came up with an ugly picture. Cal Sutton had killed Deborah's father in front of her when she was seven years old. She spoke of the killing in a flat voice with no emotion, prized the gift of books from Sutton, and accepted him as part of the family she couldn't bear to upset.

Trey could only think of one thing a man could do to a daughter that would justify killing and have her and her whole family acting like that. The thought brought waves of impotent rage and sickness. How had Sutton found out? Someone must have seen or heard something and told.

If only he could help her. If anyone knew about needing help, Trey did. From the search parties who had pulled him out of the jungle, to the nurses at Siboney, the doctors on the hospital ship and back in this country, Trey knew about needing help and getting it. Jamie claimed they had a mutual aid association going, but Jamie with his irreverent way of dishing it out, was the best help of all.

Shame sat heavy on Trey's heart. A better man would ignore Sutton's words. A better man could help a woman who so often fled into darkness find her way into the light.

Trey Van Cleve was going to leave Hubbell as soon as Jamie and his brother-in-law admitted their plan to sell automobiles was a pipe dream. Maybe he could talk Jamie into leaving with him.

They could winter in Arizona, head for Montana come spring, maybe even Alaska come summer.

12

"He did what!"

"He brought us a puppy," Ginny repeated. "He said you told him to, and he stayed overnight in Beth's room. I can see why you lied to everybody and sneaked away to see him. He is *so* handsome. His eyes are dark green. Not hard like a cat's, but deep, and just so, so beautiful. Even if he is a Van Cleve, Pa says you can't judge people by their fathers or where would he be? And after all, Trey left the ranch and isn't going back."

Trey? Unwilling to hear any more of her cousin's happy babble, Deborah interrupted. "He said that? He said he left the ranch for good?"

"Well, he didn't say it, but he *implied* it, and he said he's leaving Hubbell too as soon as he does some things, but maybe he won't. I don't want to go to normal school like Beth. I'm going to fall in love with a handsome man and marry him and live close to home. Do you think Trey is too old for me?"

Setting a bowl of hard cooked eggs on the table with a thump, Deborah gave her fifteen-year-old cousin a stern look.

"Yes, *Mr.* Van Cleve is too old for you, and if he said he's leaving, I'm sure he is. After all, he was gone for almost ten years before he came back last winter."

"Maybe he'd stay for the right woman," Ginny said dreamily. "He talked to me at supper and again at breakfast. Not like I was a little girl either."

Fond of her young cousin as she was, Deborah decided to get a breath of fresh air before she said something she'd regret. Oh, yes, Trey Van Cleve could charm a girl with talk, all right. Ninety-year-olds probably tittered and fell at his feet when they heard that voice. Seeing him and hearing him all at once would weaken the knees on females far older and wiser than Ginny.

Deborah shivered and folded her arms over her chest. Most of the families who'd attended church today had taken one look at the leaden sky and scampered for home. The Suttons and a few others were setting out lunch inside the Grange Hall, determined to enjoy family and friends for an hour or so in spite of the weather. No crowds today.

The cold bit through the fine wool of her burgundy dress, the one she saved for cold-weather trips to town when they stayed over. In the heavy gray wool she usually wore to church, she wouldn't be standing here freezing, even without a shawl, but she'd dressed for church these last weeks as if he might....

Might what? Come back and take her for another ride down the road? She'd told him to go, and he'd gone. Soon he'd be far from Hubbell and from Kansas, and that was fine. That was good. Unlike Ginny, Deborah wasn't dreaming of marriage. Some women weren't meant to marry, and she was one. She had a cooler nature than her sisters. At least she recognized her deficiencies and wasn't going to make some man miserable.

Before the occasional tear slipping down her face turned to more, she mopped up angrily and went back inside, where the old stove should finally be putting out enough heat to warm the building.

Finding a way to talk to Norah alone wasn't easy, but Deborah managed as everyone packed to go home. She scooped up an armload of empty dishes and followed her cousin to the family wagon.

Norah made no pretense of not knowing what Deborah had in mind. "He seems like a very nice young man. Caleb likes him too."

"He just drove up to your house and said, 'Here's a dog?'"

"Not exactly. He said he hoped we'd do him a favor and take her. They let some poor dog on the V Bar C have a litter and were going to kill the puppies. So Trey took them, and he and Mr. Lenahan found homes for the males, but no one would take the female. I'm glad you told him about our dogs. Caleb moped for months after Early died. He'd have done the same over Ashby, but now little Rosie has him charmed. He's quite taken with her."

Trey, but *Mr.* Lenahan. Rosie wasn't the only one who had them all charmed. "So he brought the dog, and he just stayed?"

"I invited him. He came from Hubbell to our place, so it was late afternoon when he arrived, and he was going to turn around and go back. Letting him do that would have been cruel when he looked so tired, and I'm glad he stayed. He was good company. He even drank a glass of goat's milk without wrinkling his nose too much."

"He's, he's an enemy. Everyone was upset with me for seeing him even when I didn't know who he was. I promised never to see him again." Deborah hated the shrill tone in her voice but couldn't stop it.

"Not everyone." Norah stopped packing things away and turned. "Sweetheart, you are a grown woman. If you want to see someone, say so and do it."

"I don't want to see him. I told you I thought he was someone else."

"Then say no the next time he comes to see you."

"He won't. I told him how I feel, and Ginny says he's leaving Hubbell again anyway."

"He told us that. Everything is going to work out perfectly for both of you then, isn't it?"

Before Deborah could answer, Jacey and Ginny arrived with the rest of the lunch leftovers, their father close behind. Deborah smiled brightly at them all and said her goodbyes. As soon as she was safely away, she stopped pretending.

How could her favorite cousin be so blind? Nothing was even bearable much less perfect. Having turned her quiet life upside down and made her miserable, charming Trey Van Cleve planned to disappear.

TREY STARED IN disbelief at the empty rack that usually contained the *Hubbell Herald*. "How early do I have to get here to get a newspaper?"

"Last week early. Old Richmond called it quits." As he spoke, Mr. Lawson continued twitching a feather duster over jars of brightly colored candy.

That explained why the racks for the *Herald* had been empty at the café where Trey ate breakfast, the barber shop he'd visited afterward, and now here at the general store.

"I didn't think Mr. Richmond would ever sell."

"He hasn't sold," Lawson said, changing his technique to broad swipes as he moved on to the shelves along the wall. "He's been trying to sell the whole shebang for a year. Last I heard he decided to sell his equipment piecemeal any way he can. Says if he can't sell the building, he'll rent it or burn it."

"What's he going to do?"

"He's got half a dozen grown children married and living all over the county. Every one of them wants him to come live there. I guess he's going to give in and pick one of them to bless."

Trey had worked for a newspaper for a few months when he was in college, just sweeping up, delivering bundles of papers to newsboys, and doing other menial chores. Memory of the smell of ink on warm paper filled his nostrils as if he still held one of those bundles.

Maybe he'd stroll over to the *Herald*'s office and see if Peter Richmond would show him the press. Anything that would pass a little time and take his mind off of Deborah Sutton sounded good these days.

He had made his decision, logical, best for both of them. If he could help her—but he couldn't. For all the hours he spent gazing into space trying, he was unable to devise a single plan that had any chance of convincing her to stop hiding in the midst of an overprotective family and venture out into the broader world. His world.

If only he had been able to leave Hubbell as planned. By now distance and new places would have begun to fade the memory of those secret meetings and the woman who was Deborah but not Deborah.

Leaving Hubbell would have to wait, however, for Jamie and Nolan had come up with a reasonable plan to visit half a dozen companies manufacturing automobiles, starting with the St. Louis Motor Company in Missouri, and ending with the Columbia Automobile Company in Hartford, Connecticut. They would then decide which company to deal with, order the motor vehicles, and spend time learning how to operate, maintain, and repair them.

So Trey would be staying in Hubbell long enough to help the new Hubbell Automobile Company begin business. Introductions to his father's old cronies would help. They were the men in Hubbell who might buy something as frivolous as an automobile for no reason except to flaunt wealth.

Jamie could talk birds out of the sky when he was trying. Even so, Trey worried that men who could afford a horseless carriage might refuse to deal with an Irishman they knew had been a laborer at the mill only months before, no matter how well spoken or well dressed.

Time would tell, but right now, Trey was royally fed up with the extra precautions he'd been taking to foil further murder attempts. Between that and the lovely, unsuitable female whose memory haunted him, he could use a distraction. An hour or two learning about the newspaper business sounded like just the ticket.

PETER RICHMOND REACTED to Trey's request to see the *Herald*'s press with hostility. Most of the citizens of Hubbell had become accustomed to seeing Trey here and there around town. More and more of them accepted him.

The open speculation as to why he lived at Jamie's rooming house and no longer traveled back and forth to the ranch probably helped. After all, from Jamie's reports, the speculation was extremely accurate.

Which meant Richmond must have a better reason for anger and suspicion than most townsmen. Instead of walking away without another word, Trey paused, intrigued by the way a smudge of dirt across one cheek and a hank of thinning gray hair standing straight up on the top of his head gave a man who must be in his sixties a boyish look. Admittedly a churlish boy.

Trey considered. How much did he really want a tour of this defunct small town paper? Enough to at least be polite. "I apologize for imposing, Mr. Richmond. It was inconsiderate of me."

"Your father has no reason to care what happens here any more, but if you came to nose around and report to him...."

"I think you know better than that. I have no plans to speak to my father about you or your business." Or anything else ever again, but Trey left that unsaid.

Richmond moved back out of the door. Trey accepted the unvoiced invitation and followed him inside.

"Why would you want to see what's left of one more broke country newspaper?" Richmond said.

"The lure of the forbidden perhaps. I worked for a newspaper in Tennessee for a few months, and they never let me touch the press. When Mr. Lawson told me you'd closed shop, I decided this was a chance to touch yours before you sell it. I even thought I might inveigle you to show me how it works."

The front room of the newspaper office they stood in was small, the upper two-thirds of the walls a brown that might be yellow under years of accumulated grime. Dark wainscoting on the lower third added to the gloom. A long counter divided the room in two. Behind it, a covered typewriter peeked out from heaps, piles, and towers of paper that covered every square inch of the surface of a large desk.

"Do many people come here to the office?" Trey asked.

"Used to." Richmond evidently decided to expand on his surly two words. "People come to place ads, take out subscriptions, give us details for the obituaries or tell us something they think we should print. Sometimes they find out they missed a paper that mentioned their family or someone they know, and they come to see if they can get the back edition."

An open door in the back wall led to a much larger room and the heart of the paper. Trey immediately understood Richmond's dirty face. There had to be a word beyond "mess" to describe the stacks of paper, empty cartons, cans, and kegs that littered the floor.

"My wife made me keep things in better order," Richmond said. "Since she's gone, things got away from me, but I figure no one will buy the building until I clear it out."

That had to be an understatement of the effect this sight would have on a prospective purchaser. Ignoring it all, Trey wove his way along the narrow trail of clear floor to the larger of the two presses and flattened a hand on the feed board. How many thousands of pages had this machine printed in its years of service?

"Is the smaller one in case this breaks down?" he asked.

"No, the Campbell prints the paper. The job press is for flyers and such. We print anything anyone's willing to pay for."

"And this?" Trey walked over to a tall monstrosity only a committee of drunks could design. "A linotype machine? Surely once the word gets out that you have machines like this for sale, there will be a line of newspapermen around the block."

"We'll see. I wrote to a few men I know, asked them to get the word out. Trouble is there's always used presses for sale. No one can make a living from a country weekly."

The Richmonds had made enough of a living to raise their family in Hubbell. Trey said nothing, but didn't control his expression carefully enough.

"This town was better off before your father got too good for us," Richmond said defensively. "He hurt a lot of people when he stopped supporting local businesses."

"And the police and the city council?"

"No, he still...." Richmond stopped. Then said defensively, "I never printed an untrue word."

"But you left out some true words?"

Richmond sighed. "Yes. I'm not proud of it, but it's the only way we could do it. Sadie called it dancing with the devil, but that's not all that's wrong here. With her gone.... She was a better newspaperman than I am, and I didn't realize it until she was gone. Circulation started sliding the day she died."

"I'm sorry."

They stood there eying each other warily for a moment until Trey said, "Show me how it works, and I'll help you clean up. I'm good with a broom."

Richmond gave in and laughed out loud. "That's inveigling all right. You have a deal."

Trey spent the next hours learning how the presses worked. By the end of the day, he was ready to approach the linotype machine. By the end of the week, he owned a newspaper.

PETER RICHMOND AGREED to stay as editor of the *Herald* for as long as necessary to teach Trey the intricacies of putting out a weekly paper. After his first experiences with the linotype machine, Trey vowed to do anything necessary to keep Richmond for at least ten years.

Timmerman's clerk jumped at the offer of a temporary job sorting paper and filing several evenings a week. Cleaners scrubbed every nook and cranny of the office, but the walls resisted soap and water. Trey brought in painters, and the yellowish brown disappeared under two coats of pale green.

While they all worked, Trey read, and learned, and filled pages with notes on the problems he believed had brought the *Herald* to its current sorry state and ideas about how to fix them.

One of those ideas gave him an excuse to see Deborah Sutton again.

13

DEBORAH DIDN'T EVEN look up from her ironing when the knock sounded. Aunt Em would answer, and if a neighbor wanted Uncle Jason or Eli, send them to the back field. If wives or daughters had come along, she'd have them here in the kitchen soon, recovering from the cold November wind over coffee and gossip.

"May I speak to Miss Sutton, please?"

His voice shivered through her. Her hands and heart stilled, and her mouth went dry. She'd thought him gone. A hundred times a day she imagined him climbing the steps into a railroad car, taking a seat, the train pulling away from Hubbell.

"No, you may not. She doesn't want to see you, so you need to get back in that buggy and go back where you came from."

Deborah shoved out from behind the ironing board and ran. She made it to the door in time to stop Aunt Em from shutting it, then stood wordless, staring at him. The bulk of his long gray wool coat made him an imposing stranger looking back at her with Trey Van Cleve's eyes.

She needed to hear his voice again. "Your nose is red from the cold."

"And dripping too, since we're being so honest," he said, opening one gloved hand to show a crumpled handkerchief. "You're a sight for sore eyes yourself."

Her blue wool dress had faded to nondescript a dozen washings ago, her apron had a streak of dirt down the front, and hair straggling loose from its pins had been tickling her neck for the last hour.

"What do you want to talk to me about?"

"A job."

"A what?"

"I wish to discuss an employment situation with you, and if I have to do it from here, I'll freeze before I finish, and so will you." As if for emphasis, he rocked on his feet in that way cold people had.

"Tell him to leave," Aunt Em whispered.

"I don't want a job," Deborah said, "but you'd better come in and warm up for the trip home." She had to yank a little, just a little, to get the door out of Aunt Em's grip and open it.

The back of Deborah's neck burned with awareness of him behind her for the few steps from the back room to the kitchen. She'd stayed too long in the cold of the open doorway, her breath came quick and shallow.

Aunt Em sat at the kitchen table, chair pushed back, arms crossed over her chest. "My husband and his brother will see your buggy and be here any minute."

Deborah said nothing. Her uncles were working on an irrigation ditch in the back field, almost a mile from the house. Since they didn't have a telescope or binoculars with them, they wouldn't see the buggy, or return home before dark.

Ignoring his hostesses' rude failure to take his coat and scarf, Trey unwrapped and unbuttoned and sat where Deborah indicated.

"I meant what I said, you know. You do look good. It's good to see you again."

Unable to speak for fear her voice would break, Deborah poured three cups of coffee, put a plate of cookies on the table, and sat. Hiding behind her cup, just in case, she said, "It's good to see you too. I thought you'd be gone, traveling the country again by now."

Good wasn't the word. Dizzy with relief, giddy with joy, light-headed with pleasure.

"Jamie, my friend Jamie Lenahan, is starting a business and needs some help, so I stayed. Then I heard Mr. Richmond had closed down and was looking for a buyer for the *Herald*. We reached an agreement, part of which is that he's staying on and teaching me the newspaper business."

Staying. He was staying, but he didn't look happy about it. Deborah watched him fiddle with his coffee cup, turning it in place on the saucer. Had Mr. Richmond cheated him? That seemed unlikely, but something was wrong. "Are you sorry you did it? Have you changed your mind?"

"No. What I did was read years of back issues of the paper. I thought, everyone I talked to thought, that after his wife died, Peter lost heart and so the paper declined. We've put out three weeklies since we started up again. Not only have I read the papers before and after Mrs. Richmond died, I no longer believe Peter wrote anything that appeared in the paper before his wife died. She did it all. The sad truth is if the Atlantic Ocean swallowed the entire country east of the Mississippi, Peter Richmond could make it sound so dull insomniacs would fall asleep by the third paragraph."

Aunt Em sniffed. "The Van Cleve talent for business must be wearing thin in your generation. You'd better cut your losses and get going to wherever you're going."

Trey smiled, teeth white in his tanned face, and Deborah took a swallow of coffee to hide her expression. Why couldn't he have turned out to be a spotty boy?

"I rewrote every article in the last edition, and I can keep doing that. He didn't even seem insulted, but relieved. So that's where we are now. He can teach me to run the presses and the linotype, and I can do the writing. I think I'm halfway decent, certainly better than he is, and I'll get better still."

He pulled two newspapers, folded small, out of his pocket and set them on the table. "What I can't do is this. Mrs. Richmond was good with standard news articles, but she had a special talent with this, and I think it was a major part of what attracted readers in the paper's heyday."

Deborah managed to look from his face to the two papers he set by her on the table, but how could she read anything with him sitting there looking at her?

"What should I see?"

"One is a page from a paper printed a year before she died. The other is a page from last week. You can see the problem right there."

He tapped the papers one after the other and took a swallow of coffee. When Deborah didn't pick up the papers, he explained further.

"Christenings, weddings, anniversaries. She didn't just give the bare facts of who the event was for and who attended. She mentions the ladies' hats and dresses, little personal touches. Look at this one where she describes the way the baby reacted when he felt the water at his christening. I'd say he cried. Peter wouldn't mention it at all. She describes the expression on that baby's face, the *way* he cried and the way he waved his arms and legs. The whole item is only two paragraphs, but you read them and an hour later you remember that christening as if you had been there. I want that back in the paper, and I can't do it."

What he was saying, rather than the miraculous sight of him right here in Aunt Em's kitchen, finally struck Deborah. She heard the rest of his words as if from far away.

"I need a lady reporter, someone who can stand at the edge of events like that, notice details, and report them. Someone with ties in town who would hear what's going on with Hubbell families. If the paper is going to regain circulation, I don't think long articles that come across the wire about what's going on in Europe, or in Washington for that matter, will do it. People who live in Hubbell read the Hubbell paper to find out what's going on in their town. I want to tell them, and I want them to find it interesting."

She didn't wait for him to ask. "No. No, I can't."

"I think you could. I'm not asking a favor. I'm offering a respectable position, and I'll pay what it's worth."

"I can't. I'm sorry, but I can't."

"You...." He didn't finish whatever he'd been about to say but got to his feet and buttoned his coat. "I thought a woman who likes books might like working for a paper. If you change your mind, let me know. I'm not going to find someone who can do what I need easily. Thanks for the coffee, and.... Take care of yourself."

Aunt Em all but herded him out, her expression one of grim satisfaction.

The sound of the door closing almost but not quite hard enough to be called a slam spurred Deborah into frantic action. She grabbed the two papers Trey had left sitting on the table and stuffed them in the pocket of her apron. By the time Aunt Em returned, Deborah had the coffee cups in the dishpan.

DEBORAH HID THE papers under the mattress of her bed. Every night she pulled them out and pored over them, studying not only the brief descriptions of social events Trey had mentioned, but every word. The differences between the older paper and the new glared from the page.

Could she do what Mrs. Richmond had done? She scribbled descriptions of Miriam's wedding and the christening of Judith's son in the margins of both papers until every bit of paper not covered with print was covered with tiny handwritten words. Thinking about it was ridiculous. She had no more talent than Mr. Richmond.

Shoving the papers back under the mattress, she picked up her current book, then sat staring blindly at the page until a tap on the door brought her out of her trance. She called out, expecting to see her uncle. Aunt Em would never knock on a door so gently.

Her aunt and uncle both walked into the room and sat on her bed. As if that weren't surprise enough, Uncle Jason took Aunt Em's hand in his and kept it.

"The two of us have had some long talks about you and Mr. Van Cleve," he said. "We want you to know that no matter what you do, you are a daughter of our hearts and always will be."

Deborah's eyes pricked. She tipped her head back to keep the tears inside.

"I don't know him enough to dislike him," Aunt Em said. "What I dislike is his name, and I know that's not fair. He may be as honest as his father is dishonest. And I know that you want to take his offer. I didn't miss how those papers disappeared from the table. In fact something is crackling under me right now as I sit here."

Heat rose in Deborah's cheeks, and she couldn't help but smile at her fierce aunt. "We never did get away with hiding much from you, did we?"

"Your sisters didn't."

"We just wanted you to know," Uncle Jason said, smoothing over that awkward truth, "that you can take the position he's offering without upsetting us. And if you don't like it, you can come home again, or you can try something else."

She loved them both, loved them enough to tell them the unvarnished truth for once. "No, I can't. When he came to the church I told him we couldn't be friends because it would upset you, but that's not the truth. I always knew you'd get over any upset. The truth is I don't have the courage. I didn't then, and I don't now. You are sitting on those papers, and part of me wants so much to try, but I'm afraid, and I can't."

Her aunt and uncle exchanged a long look, and Uncle Jason wrapped his large hand more tightly around Aunt Em's smaller one.

"Courage is a strange thing," he said slowly. "I think everyone has at least a little in them, but some of us have to dig deeper to find it than others. I know that because I wasn't brave enough to face down my father until years after I was full grown and could have done it. Should have. And those were the years when he did the most damage to all of us. He married your mother and our sisters off in those years."

"That was different," Deborah protested.

"In most ways. What's the same is that finding courage is easier than living with regret. If you don't want to live in town and try the newspaper job, put it out of your mind and don't look back. If you do want it?" He smiled and shrugged. "The worst that will happen is you won't like it, and you'll be right back here with us."

Deborah didn't move as her aunt and uncle left. Uncle Jason was wrong. Falling in love with Trey Van Cleve was the worst thing, and that regret already sat heavy on her heart.

DEBORAH JOINED HER aunt in the kitchen the next morning, tired after a sleepless night, but at peace with her decision. She waited until they were all seated at the table for breakfast before saying, "The next time you go to town, I'd like to come and bring some bags and boxes along."

Aunt Em got up and busied herself at the stove. Uncle Jason nodded. "If the weather holds, we'll go tomorrow. We have enough of a shopping list a trip to town won't hurt."

"I'm coming too," Aunt Em said. "I want to see this newspaper office. I remember there are rooms on the second floor. The Richmonds lived there after their children were all up and out."

Aunt Em made rooms above the office sound ominous. Deborah smiled at the thought then wondered where Trey lived. Nearby. Not in those rooms surely. Her nerves, which had settled, started up again.

The weather held, but Deborah traveled to town with only Uncle Jason. Two of Uncle Eli's boys had broken out with ugly red spots the night before. Chicken pox. Two sick and one still running around had Aunt Lucy worn to a frazzle.

"It's only decent to stay and help," said Aunt Em, checking everything Deborah had packed for the third time. "I gave Jason more than a list of supplies. He has a list of what to look for in that newspaper office and what to find out from Mr. Van Cleve. You be patient with Miriam now. You're not girls any more. None of that squabbling you did when she was here."

A few tearful goodbyes, and Deborah climbed to the wagon seat, half-wishing a sudden outbreak of red spots would save her from her decision. Her own miserable, itchy bout with chicken pox remained clear in her mind, however, and Aunt Em swore no one ever contracted the pox more than once.

The hours of the trip to town passed quickly. After the emotional talk of the day before, Deborah dared ask about things that had always seemed forbidden—about her mother.

"I never really knew her," Uncle Jason admitted. "Pa didn't believe boys and girls should mix, and we hardly ever did. I look at you and your sisters sometimes and wish it was like that for us, but it wasn't. All I remember is three sad-eyed, skinny little girls who were always frightened. We were all always frightened."

"He was truly terrible, wasn't he, my grandfather?"

"Yes. He had an anger and a meanness in him that made him frightening. Eli had the anger, but never the meanness, and Lucy gentled him a lot."

Deborah remembered the anger. She'd been afraid of Uncle Eli for a long time because of it. "Do you think they're all right, your sisters?"

"I want to believe they are. They write once in a while and say they are, but then your mother wrote letters like that until the end."

They passed the trip talking about family history. For the first time Deborah heard how her aunt and uncle had met, and how Uncle Jason had refused to marry while his father lived.

"But if he hadn't been killed, he could still be alive today. You could have waited forever."

"We weren't waiting, we were saving. It's hard to come up with cash money when you're farming and it all belongs to everyone, but I squirreled away every penny I got hold of and so did Em. I hated the thought of leaving Eli alone with Pa, but Eli would never leave. The land has a hold on him it didn't on any of the rest of us. I figured to homestead somewhere farther west. There's still land for the taking in places like North Dakota."

"Not good land with water like here."

"No, it would have been a harder life in some ways. Easier in others, but then Pa was killed, and we got married, probably quicker than some thought decent, and we're still here."

"Killed by Mr. Van Cleve."

"On his orders anyway. He didn't do any of the killing himself."

"Did you ever meet him?"

"Not to talk to. I've seen him in town now and then. So have you."

"I remember. Tr—his son doesn't look like him."

Uncle Jason gave her one of his rare grins. "If he did, we'd still be home today, wouldn't we?"

Deborah looked away and changed the subject.

MIRIAM'S FACE SET into hard lines as she listened to Deborah's plans. Deborah didn't waste breath asking to stay with her. Uncle Jason made that mistake and gave Miriam the chance to say no and make her feelings clear.

"Do you have any idea how humiliating it's going to be for me to admit I have a sister *working for a newspaper?* People will wonder whatever is the matter with our whole family. And Van Cleve? He spends all his time with the *Irish.* He lives in some roach-infested room near the *mill.* No, you can't stay here. The whole idea is ridiculous and embarrassing enough without having to admit you're living with me."

Deborah headed for the door the moment Miriam started her rant and heard the last of it from outside. Uncle Jason handed her back up to the wagon seat, and neither of them said anything until he had the wagon turned around and started toward Judith's.

"It's as much your fault as ours," he said finally. "We all spoiled her."

That was the truth. Miriam had been such a cute baby, and Mama had died just days after having her. "Maybe we should go to the hotel. I'll see about a room at the boarding house tomorrow. Having me will be harder for Judith with the children."

"You can help her with them."

"I won't be there that much." At least not if Trey hadn't found someone else. That worry niggled at her. The thought she'd forced herself to come this far, and it might all be for naught brought bile to the back of her throat.

"Family takes you in," Uncle Jason said loudly, as if that would make it true. Of course when the ones faced with taking three orphan nieces in had been Uncle Jason and Aunt Emma, they had done just that, and without a complaint or second thought.

Judith rewarded Uncle Jason's faith. "Of course you can stay here. We'd love to have you. So you're going to be working for the newspaper, for that ugly Mr. Van Cleve." She wiggled her eyebrows suggestively.

Deborah stared at the floor. "I need to go there and see if the offer is still open. Maybe he found someone else. Maybe he's changed his mind."

"And I need to go with her," Uncle Jason said. "I need to inspect the place for cleanliness and see who lives in the rooms upstairs and how many doors there are between where Deborah will be and those rooms."

"Well, Trey doesn't live in those rooms." Deborah said tartly. "I have it on good authority he lives with the *Irish* in some roach-infested place near the mill."

"Woo hoo," Judith said. "Trey, is it? This job of yours is going to be interesting."

Deborah ignored the teasing and walked out. She reached the sidewalk before remembering she didn't know where the *Herald*'s office was.

14

THE *HERALD*'S OFFICE was only four blocks from Judith's. As Deborah walked beside Uncle Jason, her breath came more and more quickly until she gasped for air. She stopped with a block still to go. Uncle Jason peered down at her, his face screwed up with concern.

"Here, sit." He pushed her down on a wide window ledge that dug into her bottom. "Catch your breath, and we'll go back to Judith's."

Shaking her head frantically, Deborah managed, "No. Just one minute."

She thought of the way Trey looked buttoning up his coat and leaving the kitchen, thought of his voice. Her breathing slowed and steadied. When the numbness in her bottom turned to pain, she rose and brushed the back of her skirt, tightened her shawl over her shoulders. "Tell me taking on Grandfather was harder than this."

"I don't know if worrying about it beforehand was any harder, but doing it was. We brawled all over the yard. He broke two of my ribs, and I thought my jaw. He had me down and a board in his hands at one point. I think he'd have killed me then if Eli hadn't knocked the board away."

A single deep breath, and she straightened her shoulders. "Thank you. That puts things in perspective."

A narrow building that needed a new coat of paint housed the newspaper office. Gold lettering on the front window said, *"Hubbell Herald,"* in large letters, with *"Peter Richmond, Editor,"* underneath in smaller script.

A bell tied to the door sounded when Uncle Jason pushed it open. Deborah concentrated on taking even breaths as she walked inside. Pale green and dark wood. Before she took in more than that first impression, Trey appeared through a door behind the counter, wiping black hands on a towel, and she forgot everything else.

"Just let me get enough of this ink off my hands to...."

His words stopped when he saw her. For a fleeting moment she thought she saw something in his face, something that matched the way her own spirits soared at the sound of his voice and sight of him. He was in shirt sleeves, rolled up shirt sleeves that showed muscled forearms streaked with more ink.

"Can you get that off well enough to touch anything without leaving marks?" she said.

"Oh." He looked at his hands as if surprised the ink was still there. "Yes, there are solvents. My fingernails will look like a boy's for a few days, one who doesn't waste much time washing. I'm learning to work the presses."

He dropped the towel on the counter and came around the end. "Tell me you're here because you changed your mind."

"I'm here because I changed my mind—if you haven't found someone else."

"There is no one else."

At the sound of Uncle Jason's cleared throat, Trey hastened to add, "No one else that I know of who could fill the position, that is. I can't imagine how I'd word an advertisement for the position in my own paper."

Another harrumping sound from her uncle prodded Deborah to make introductions. The two men said the correct polite words, but they eyed each other warily.

"What exactly is Deborah going to be doing here? Where will she be working?" Uncle Jason said finally.

Trey looked around as if he hadn't thought of that before. "Here some of the time." He pointed to the big desk behind the counter. "I've posted the hours the office will be open by the door, and I want anyone who comes in to subscribe or place an advertisement to be guaranteed someone will be here to serve them. No waiting. With Peter, Mr. Richmond, alone here, that hasn't always been the case. The bell only works if someone is here and if the presses aren't running and drowning out the sound."

Deborah's heart sank. In spite of his talk about a lady reporter, what he wanted was a clerk to sit behind a desk.

"We're all going to take turns," Trey continued. "We'll have to work out whether that means by the day or certain hours, but with three of us, no one will be tied to the desk all the time. Other than that, I hope De—Miss Sutton will set her own course. We have customers who request we cover events important to them, and we oblige, of course, but we need to cover more of what goes on in the town."

"But I can't just attend someone's wedding without an invitation."

"Not all, but some, and as time passes, you'll be welcome more and more places."

"I'm not good with crowds," Deborah said doubtfully.

"You don't have to be in the middle of crowds. You're an observer, not a participant. Can you imagine the story you could have written about the Fourth of July shooting contest?" Trey laughed. "Not that there's ever much suspense about the outcome." He motioned to the back room. "Would you like to see the presses? We have a linotype machine."

In the back room, Trey introduced them to Peter Richmond, who was doing something with the larger of the two presses that required a wrench. He had ink on his hands, but wasn't covered with it the way Trey was.

Deborah wasn't sure what a linotype machine was. After hearing Trey's enthusiastic description of how the machine made it possible to set type by the line instead of by the letter, she knew more than she wanted to.

Uncle Jason and Mr. Richmond were still talking by the large press. "Don't tell me Mrs. Richmond operated this behemoth better than anyone else too," Deborah whispered.

Trey lowered his voice to match hers. "No, everything in here was Mr. Richmond's bailiwick. He's teaching me, but he's also agreed to stay. For the foreseeable future, not just a few months. So I'll learn everything I can from him, but he'll keep doing the work of getting the paper printed. You and I are responsible for coming up with what he prints."

"Mr. Richmond tells me he's going to continue to live over the office," Uncle Jason said, joining them. "Do you live nearby?"

Trey's expression showed he understood full well the purpose behind the question. "Right now I'm staying in Jamie Lenahan's room on Walnut Street. He's going to be gone until at least after the first of the year, and all I need is a place to sleep. Once he returns, I'll have to find a place of my own."

They drifted back to the outer office.

"When can you start?" Trey said.

His fingernails weren't all that looked boyish. His hair fell over his forehead, and his attempts to brush it back had left ink smeared over one eye. Deborah, who avoided touching anyone except her sisters when she could, had a sudden urge to reach out and wipe the smudge away.

"Tomorrow?" Her voice squeaked a little. Uncle Jason had talked about regretting things not done. He should have mentioned regret over biting off too much to chew—and over impossible dreams.

JUDITH WANTED TO know every detail of what had happened, of course. Deborah wanted to share, but they had to wait until after supper, after the children were in bed, and after Uncle Jason and William retired to the parlor for drinks and cigars.

"So," Judith said, pouring them each a cup of tea before settling down at the kitchen table. "Tell me everything."

"I'm in trouble," Deborah said. "He wants me to just— wander around town and find things to write about." She waved an arm around to illustrate and looked into her cup gloomily.

"Does he? Well, that's silly. Let's make a list of what you should look at." Judith dug through a drawer and came up with a pad of paper and a pencil. "Let's see. This week Mrs. Tindell is sponsoring some Eastern writer reading his poems to enlighten us ignorant hayseeds." She looked up and made a face. "The trouble with that is you'd better say nice things because if you get on the wrong side of Mrs. Tindell, you won't get through half the doors in town ever again."

"I won't say I like it if I don't."

"Then go and see, and if you hate it, don't say anything."

"Did you know that Norah once worked for Mrs. Tindell?"

"Of course, and she quit when the old bag tried to tell her she couldn't walk out with Caleb."

"How did you know that when I never did?"

"Because I don't go off by myself when interesting things are being discussed at family dinners. You have to stop that now that it's your job to hear things like that."

"I'm not writing about our family."

"If you keep adding things you're not writing about, you won't have anything left. Let's see, the Methodists are having a rummage sale, setting up tomorrow and officially open Saturday. Used clothes." Judith wrinkled her nose. "There's a new play starting at the theater. Oh, I know. You should go watch the first night they have anything new at the theater and then say what you thought in the paper so people will know if it's any good or not."

Deborah stared at her sister in wonder. "He should have hired you."

"Yes, he should have," Judith said smugly, "but he doesn't want a married woman or two little children running around his office. He wants you, unmarried and full of possibilities."

Judith did that silly thing with her eyebrows again. Deborah pretended not to notice.

The list grew longer until it filled the page. Finally Judith tore the sheet off and handed it over. "There. That will do for this week. In between times, you need to just go shopping and keep your ears open. I'll go with you when I can. As soon as Miriam stops being ridiculous, she can too. Having Hubbell's first lady reporter in the family is fun, and you should have seen William's face when he heard how much Mr. Van Cleve is paying you."

As she read down the list, the anxiety that had been building in Deborah ever since the visit to the paper waned.

"You're wonderful," she said to her sister sincerely. "You give me hope I can really do this."

"Of course you can, and in honesty I couldn't. I could go and chat and have a wonderful time flitting all over town, but I couldn't write about it afterward. I have trouble with thank you notes."

"I'll write them for you. Thank you. Are you sure William doesn't mind my staying here?"

"Of course not. He's hoping you'll stay with the children every time he wants to go to a restaurant—or a poetry reading. Having you here will work out for all of us, just don't let us overdo." Judith pushed the pad and pencil across the table. "Here, take this too. You need something to take notes on, and this will do until you can get a proper notebook."

Deborah folded the list and pushed it deep in her pocket. If the children got to the pad of paper before she did in the morning.... Maybe she needed not just a notebook but a purse too. The pockets on her coat barely held a hanky, and dresses sometimes didn't have pockets at all.

Judith's bright chatter had already changed the rumble of male conversation in the parlor to laughter by the time Deborah joined the rest of the family. Over the years she had sometimes envied and sometimes resented her sister's unfailing optimism and exuberance. Tonight gratitude brought a lump to her throat.

Deborah touched the paper in her pocket. The list changed the thought of her new job from something frightening to something to look forward to—almost like sneaking off to meet a mysterious stranger in the night.

15

DEBORAH WALKED TO the newspaper office alone the next morning. William had offered to wait and leave later than usual for the mill and walk with her, but as she explained to him, her new job would have her roaming from one end of town to the other soon enough.

"You're as bad as your sister," he said, with a look at Judith that said he didn't find anything about her bad. "Here, let me draw you a little map so you know which parts of town to stay away from."

"Are these all bad parts of town?" Deborah asked her sister after William had left.

"Bad enough you don't want to go there alone. I'll talk William into taking us there one day so you can see. He'll get all red in the face, but he'll do it. A newspaper woman should know what those areas are like."

Maybe so, but Deborah hoped William would resist her sister for once. Adventures like that appealed to Judith, but Deborah wasn't so brave. She could write about weddings and christenings without setting foot in the areas William had marked off on his map.

Trey looked up from the desk and smiled when she walked into the office. "Good morning. Are you ready to start?"

"Yes, I am."

No shirt sleeves today. He had on a black suit, and his hair was in place. Her nerves began playing up. Nothing else could explain the way her stomach flipped. Wearing any one of her own dresses would be embarrassing when he looked so fine. Thank goodness Judith had talked her into borrowing a dark blue wool dress with jet trim and velvet hat to match.

Deborah hung her coat on one of the pegs along the wall, but after a moment's hesitation, left her hat on. After all she'd be going out again soon. At least she thought so. "That's not true. I'm not ready because I don't know where to start. You were vague yesterday about what I should do."

He made a face. "Aah. That's because I don't really know. Maybe Peter can give you some ideas about how his wife went about things. He'll be back from the barber shop in a little while."

Sucking in a deep breath, Deborah took the list from her pocket and laid it on the counter. "Judith helped me make a list."

Trey rose and stood across the counter from her as he read down the page. When he finished, he said, "I'm not paying you enough."

"You're paying me too much. If you keep throwing money around like that, the paper will fail for you faster than it did for Mr. Richmond." She couldn't meet his eyes. "At least that's what William says, William Dalton, Judith's husband."

"He should know, but I don't need to make a profit."

"You mean—your father?"

Trey's face hardened, and she drew back. "I'm sorry. That's none of my...."

"It is. If you're working for me, you have the right to know I'm not crazy. Those years after college when I drifted around the country, I worked at any job that came my way. I tried prospecting in Colorado without any luck and then tried it again in Arizona and stumbled on a vein of high grade ore. Looking for silver and found gold."

"You have a gold mine."

"No, I pulled out as much as I could by myself with a pick and shovel and then sold the claim to a company that thought there had to be more if they went deeper. I have a five percent royalty interest, and the mine is still producing. I don't need to make a profit from this paper, but I do need to break even. Not making money is one thing, losing it is another. So we'll give it a couple of years and see how we do."

"You keep saying we, but you own the paper now. Do you mean you and Mr. Richmond?"

"Me, Mr. Richmond, and you."

His eyes gleamed as if he understood the effect those words had on her stomach. Deborah picked up her list and went back to her coat. "How soon do we need these stories?"

"Monday afternoon for Thursday's paper."

Deborah nodded and headed for the Methodist church.

DEBORAH WHIRLED WHEN she heard Trey's voice behind her. Sure enough, there he was, talking to Mrs. Yates. Men who owned big papers back East would probably pay to look as good as Trey did in that long gray coat, with black hat, black cane, devastating smile. In fact, Mrs. Yates, mother of six and grandmother of more than Deborah wanted to know, was simpering. Simpering!

He was here to check on her, of course. Deborah dropped the dress in her hand back into the box it came in and brushed her hands together as he left Mrs. Yates and strolled over.

"Mrs. Yates says you've been a great help this morning," Trey said as he reached her.

"I'm sorry. I know I'm supposed to observe, but they were so happy to see me and have help, and I just—got dragged in somehow."

"When I said be an observer, I didn't mean you always had to do it that way. Whatever works. I came to see if you'd like to have lunch with me."

"Lunch?"

"Lunch. Not a big meal like on the farm, but a sandwich at the café?"

She swiped at the dust on the front of Judith's dark dress. His eyes followed her hand across the bodice. Deborah dropped her hand as if it had been burned. "I don't think...."

Trey looked around the big room, empty except for tables with piles of the used household items and clothes that had been sorted for sale, and boxes such as the one Deborah had been sorting through.

"They have Bible study, church dinners and the like here, don't they?" he said. "Surely there's a wash room somewhere. If not, we'll stop by the office first."

He reached out and rubbed a finger across her cheek. "Or maybe not. You'll look better than anyone else there just the way you are."

Deborah stopped breathing. The casual touch raced along every nerve ending. All her life she had flinched and jerked away from anyone except Judith and Miriam. Now she stood staring into his eyes as if turned to stone. Gray-green, a charcoal ring around the outer rim. Beautiful eyes. Questioning eyes. Questioning?

"Y-yes," she stammered. "I mean, yes, there's a washroom. I-I'll go and...." She fled before she could make a bigger fool of herself.

THE LITTLE CAFÉ Trey took her to sat a block inside the area William had designated "bad" on the hand drawn map of town he'd given her the night before. The walls and tables alike were bare wood, but Deborah was grateful for the steamy warmth of the place after working all morning in the chilly room at the church.

Her stomach reacted to the scent of frying meat with an appreciative growl she hoped no one heard over the clatter of dishes from the kitchen and buzz of happy chatter from every table.

"Jamie found this place," Trey said as he pulled out a chair for her. "The food is plain but good. I should have asked you if you wanted something fancier."

"Oh, no, I like this." She spotted two other women at the tables and relaxed. After all William had only meant she shouldn't come to this part of town alone.

"Have anything you like. Sandwiches aren't the only choice."

"So what did you find out this morning?" he asked once they'd ordered his sandwich and her soup.

She hesitated, tempted to tell him nothing. "The best of what is donated never makes it to the sale. Mrs. Yates and her friends see everything first, and they take anything that's particularly nice."

"Do they now." Trey didn't look particularly surprised. "And do they pay what these items would bring at the sale into the treasury, so to speak?"

She had never considered such a thing. "I don't know."

"But you're going back this afternoon to find out, aren't you?"

A young man with plates balanced up and down his arms paused by their table long enough to slap down a plate with a sandwich and a soup bowl.

If he had hesitated for a moment, Deborah would have thanked him for giving her time to think.

"We can't put that in the paper."

"Why not?"

"Everyone will hate me. Us. When the Baptists have a fund-raiser. They'll slam the door in my face."

"If they do, we'll report that and let people make of it what they will."

Deborah put her spoon down without tasting the soup. "It's only a church rummage sale. Organizing it is time-consuming and hard work for those ladies, and they do it for charity. Everyone in town probably knows what happens."

"Do you think women like your aunt and cousin who live a day's drive away know? How many of them time trips to town for supplies with the church's sale thinking they'll get something they can use at a bargain price, only they don't know they'll never have a chance at the best things?"

Aunt Em had done that when she and her sisters were little. Aunt Lucy did it last year and probably would again. And today Mrs. Yates had "put aside" a lovely yellow dress with no sign of wear on it for one of her granddaughters.

"All right," Deborah said, understanding the point, even if she still didn't completely agree. "I'll go back and find out."

"Really find out. You have to either see plain evidence yourself or hear the same thing from more than one person you believe. Don't just take the word of some lady who's upset because someone else got something she wanted."

Deborah nodded and picked up her spoon. Chunks of chicken and vegetables floated in rich broth. The soup tasted as good as it looked.

"Don't look so sad," Trey said. "We're not going to make accusations. The trick is to write it as a matter of fact report of the way the sale is organized. Leave deciding whether that's a good thing or a bad thing to the readers. Mrs. Yates and her friends feel the way you do—they work hard and it's only fair they get the pick of the lot. If they believe that, let them defend it. If not, maybe next year they'll do it differently. Maybe next year they'll get more volunteers."

When he put it that way.... "But it is only a church sale."

"Sure, but we have to decide how we're doing things too. Pretty soon it's only going to be the town's decision as to who gets the contract for paving Main Street. If the Mayor's brother gets the job and no one else is allowed to bid, do we just print an article about all the benefits of a paved street?"

He looked so earnest and serious.

"I think I understand why so many people don't believe you're really Webster Van Cleve's son," Deborah said without thinking, then slapped a hand over her mouth. "I'm sorry. I don't know where that came from. I never should have said that. I am so sorry."

Not only was he not angry, he laughed, laughed loud enough to attract glances from people at the other tables. "You have no idea how much I wish that were true."

"Caleb says you have his ears."

"Excuse me?"

"Caleb says he had to twist one of your father's ears once, and yours are just like his."

Trey's eyes widened for a moment before he started laughing all over again. Even though her cheeks still burned with embarrassment, Deborah couldn't help but join in. They finished their lunch, amid continuing bouts of amusement.

"Your cousin is an old curly wolf, isn't he?" Trey said.

Deborah nodded. "I think he likes you."

"I don't think I can use that as a character reference."

They had finished, and Trey was helping her with her coat, when an older man walked in, his eyes searching every table.

"Hey, Herman," Trey said. "If you showed up earlier, I'd have bought you lunch. The food is good here. I recommend a ham sandwich."

"I already et. Your Ma asked me to let you know your sister had her baby. Healthy little boy, I guess. They're calling him Webster too."

"He's welcome to the name. Is Alice all right?"

"Fine. They're both fine."

"Are you staying over in town? I'd like to send something back for them with you."

"Yeah. I'll be at the old hotel tonight, but there's no use asking me about that other business. Nobody's admitting cutting reins, and nobody but Lenny went to town the night you got run down."

Deborah stared at the old man wide-eyed. *Cut reins? Run down! What was he talking about?*

Trey introduced her to Herman Gruner, who looked past Deborah as if she didn't exist but didn't remark on the name.

"I'll see you tonight then," Gruner said gruffly and left as if he had important business elsewhere.

"What was he talking about? Cut reins and running you down?" Deborah asked.

Trey made a dismissive gesture. "Nothing. A couple of accidents, that's all."

"Cut reins doesn't sound like an accident."

"Some of the hands didn't like the boss's son turning up after so many years and giving orders, that's all. Nothing happened."

"And running you down?"

"Runaway wagon team."

She didn't believe him. He was being far too casual about potentially fatal accidents, but he obviously wasn't going to tell her more. "Is Mr. Gruner afraid to be seen in my vicinity? He certainly wasn't sociable."

"He's afraid of losing his job, and I suppose being friendly with a Sutton could do that. Come on, I'll walk you back to the church."

Deborah straightened her shoulders, still wondering about those "accidents," but surprised to find after their discussion, she almost looked forward to ferreting out the truth about favoritism at the Methodist rummage sale.

TREY MADE IT back to the church half an hour before dark, determined to see Deborah safely home. The door to the room where the sale would be held was locked, as were all the others.

Staring down the street toward William and Judith Dalton's home, Trey considered. Deborah had promised to be home before dark. There was no reason to believe otherwise. He still wanted to knock on the Daltons' door and ask whoever answered about her, be sure she was inside and safe for the night. More than that, he wanted to take her home with him where he could watch over her himself.

He turned away, annoyed at his foolishness. He'd put her in a position where she would be all over town every day. Hovering over her like a mother hen would have her sneaking away from him the way she did from her family. He was her employer, her boss, no more.

Hadn't he taken Cal Sutton's warning to heart? Despite the attraction, Deborah was not the woman for him. He would help her break out of the shell she'd hidden in most of her life if he could. That's all.

If only flashes of his mystery woman didn't keep cropping up through her wary reserve. The list. Even if her sociable sister created it, Deborah had been the one to present it, to march off to the Methodists on her own and discover the small blot on the ladies' charitable efforts. And the way she laughed with him over his ears....

Trey forced his footsteps in the direction of the old hotel. Instead of undermining Deborah's confidence by checking on her, he'd buy Herman a drink and give him the gifts for Alice and the baby.

At least he didn't have to skulk through town worrying about another attempt to kill him. He hadn't lured Deborah to town only to put her in danger.

Alice, Vernon, whether one or both of them had wanted him dead, they no longer had a reason. Webster Van Cleve wouldn't mind news that his son had bought a newspaper, but knowing Trey had ink-stained hands and delivered bundles of papers to the merchants of the town himself would prick his father's pride.

Finding out a woman, any woman, was working in an enterprise owned by a Van Cleve, would be more like a slash than a prick.

A Sutton? Any dealing with the Suttons not loaded with malice would have his father ranting and foaming at the mouth.

Couple that with a Van Cleve grandson who could be the new heir—lawyers had to be working on a new will about now. Trey gave his cane a twirl and started for the hotel.

16

DEBORAH'S FIRST WEEK at the *Herald* raced by in a blur of weddings, a christening, a funeral, the preparation for the Methodists' rummage sale and the actual sale.

Introducing herself and explaining she had come on behalf of the paper became easier, if not easy. Observing Trey's approach when she accompanied him to a town council meeting and a retirement dinner at the flour mill helped, although his approach was too—male.

Her first test as the paper's social reporter came at a luncheon given by Mrs. Gilbert Snopes, one of Miriam's new friends. Deborah had not received one of the coveted invitations, but Trey had.

"Here," he said. "Take this, go have a nice lunch, and listen to enough of the nonsense to write something about it."

The guest of honor at the luncheon was a high muckety-muck from the Women's Temperance Union. "You don't believe in temperance?"

"I don't believe in laws that can't be enforced. That's my opinion, not the paper's. The *Herald* is staying above the fray."

Deborah folded the invitation inside her new leather purse and walked the half mile to the Snopes mansion. As she approached the imposing three-storied house with its turrets, pillars, and lovely bargeboard, butterflies took wing in her stomach. Hunger, of course. At this time of day ordinary hunger was to be expected. Why then did the thought of food turn the butterflies into nausea?

A trio of chattering women approached from a cross street, nodded to Deborah, turned and continued on ahead of her. Two of those women were acquaintances who had always spoken a friendly greeting when they met anywhere in town.

Heart quickening, trying to work up saliva in her dry mouth, Deborah followed the three of them through the wrought iron gate, up the walk to the front door. Mrs. Snopes greeted the women ahead of Deborah with enthusiasm. A maid took coats.

The other ladies were still in the tiled entry hall when Mrs. Snopes approached Deborah with considerably more reserve. "Miss Sutton, how nice to see you. I don't remember sending you an invitation, but of course dear Miriam is here, and since Judith sent regrets, you are welcome to take her place."

Deborah fumbled in her purse. "I do have an invitation. I'm here for the *Herald*."

Mrs. Snopes regarded the invitation as if Deborah had extended a used handkerchief. "I sent an invitation to Mr. Van Cleve. If he cannot attend in person, then Mr. Richmond would be acceptable. I do not approve of young women gadding about town behaving in ways unbecoming to a lady and taking a position a man with a family should have. I suggest you return to Mr. Van Cleve and relay that message, and I further suggest you stop embarrassing your family and return home."

The woman was tall and wide. Her strong-featured face loomed above Deborah as she gave this lecture. Her lavender satin and lace-covered bosom quivered with outrage all too close to Deborah's chin. Resisting the urge to retreat at top speed, Deborah managed to say, "I understand, and I will convey your message to Mr. Van Cleve."

One of the watching trio tittered.

"You *convey* that if he wants subscribers to his paper, he'd better stop flaunting immoral big city ways in our town. We won't have it. *I* won't have it. Tell him I expect him in person before Mrs. Lambert begins to speak."

Deborah gave in to the urge and fled.

Trey was unimpressed. "I'm sorry you had to listen to the old harridan. Next time, don't. Turn around and leave as soon as anyone starts in. Garden parties aren't really news. We're doing people like her a favor mentioning her pet project."

"It's not a garden party, and she wants you to attend and listen to her speaker or send Mr. Richmond."

"I want circulation to double next week, and that's not going to happen either. To hell, er, heck with her. Come on, we'll have plainer and better food at the café, and then we'll find something actually interesting going on in town somewhere."

He really intended to ignore Mrs. Snopes. Deborah was sure that wasn't wise, but she accompanied him to the café in a warm haze of appreciation.

Mrs. Snopes sailed into the *Herald's* office before Deborah had hung up her coat the next morning. Trey's low curses at the linotype machine and Mr. Richmond's patient instruction sounded from the back room. The two of them would be setting type for this week's edition.

"I wish to speak to Mr. Van Cleve." Without so much as a glance at Deborah, Mrs. Snopes stepped to the counter, tapping a gloved finger on the surface.

After letting Trey know he was needed in the front office, Deborah sat at the desk and pretended to edit the pages in her notebook.

He would apologize to the woman, she decided. He'd apologize and promise to do better next time.

Trey walked up to the counter still in the printer's smock he wore over his shirt and trousers. Curiously, although he also now wore gloves for the messiest chores and setting type wouldn't take him anywhere near ink, he was wiping ink-stained hands on a rag the same way he had the first time she had come to the office with Uncle Jason.

Mrs. Snopes gave him a narrow-eyed, disapproving look. "Did Miss Sutton inform you that I expected you or Mr. Richmond at my luncheon yesterday?"

"She did," Trey said, nodding. "I'm sorry for the misunderstanding. I hired Miss Sutton specifically to report on social events such as yours. Since you turned her away...." He gave a little shrug that completely negated his apology.

"I made a few notes myself," Mrs. Snopes said, pulling several sheets of paper from her purse. "I'm sure you can manage something appropriate from these."

Deborah sat at enough of an angle to see Trey's smile, all teeth, no warmth. "Maybe next time, Mrs. Snopes. We have this week's edition laid out, and we're setting type now. We filled your space with a story about Mr. Gardner's buggy being stolen and abandoned outside town."

"His nephew does that several times a year, and everyone knows it. That's not a story."

Trey shrugged again and repeated, "Maybe next time."

Mrs. Snopes had turned pale except for two bright spots on her cheeks. "You are an embarrassment to your father."

"I am. He's mentioned how he wishes he drowned me the first time he laid eyes on me."

Mrs. Snopes stormed out without another word, the bell jangling wildly as the door slammed.

Deborah joined Trey at the counter. "If you did that to make me feel better, you succeeded, but you really are going to go bankrupt if you keep it up."

He smiled at her, the real kind, white teeth showing, but eyes warm and crinkling at the corners. "That's part of it, I suppose. I wish I could claim to be a knight in shining armor, but it's mostly the fact we can't let tyrants like that tell us what to print and how to print it, or it won't be much of a paper. If she wants to impress her friends with mentions of her garden parties in the newspaper, she has to play by our rules. We're not playing by hers."

"You really are hard headed."

"Famously."

"And you have more ink on you than I've seen in days."

"I was hoping for a chance to shake her hand."

Deborah went back to the desk, light hearted. Her new job definitely had peaks and valleys, but she suspected working for Trey Van Cleve the peaks were going to prove so high the valleys would all look like shallow ditches.

ALONE IN THE office the Monday after the difficulty with Mrs. Snopes, Deborah stopped typing and rose from the desk when the front door opened and the bell gave a polite jingle. Her breath caught in her throat at the sight of the small, fragile-looking woman on the other side of the counter.

Snowy white hair, lined skin, and a slight tremble in the hand on the counter. Deborah ignored the signs of age and concentrated on the shrewd gray eyes assessing her from underneath the brim of a stylish hat.

"Mrs. Tindell, how nice to see you. I'm the only one in the office at the moment. May I help you?"

The older woman nodded acknowledgment of the greeting. "I'd like to arrange for someone from the paper to attend the welcome home celebration I'm holding for my granddaughter Caroline. She's returning from a European tour next week."

Deborah took a deep breath, held it, let it out slowly. "We'd be happy to do that, Mrs. Tindell. You understand I will be the one attending and writing about the event for the paper?"

"I do." The knowing gaze held amusement. "Unlike others in this town, I have no objection to young ladies working in respectable situations if it suits them. I employed your cousin as my housekeeper some years ago, you know. She was Mrs. Norah Hawkins then."

"Of course. She told me about it herself."

"A strong-minded young woman. She left my employ rather than give up the man who became her husband, but I suppose time proved her right. She has tamed him, and so far as I know she's been happy."

Deborah strangled laughter inside but couldn't suppress a wide smile. "I don't believe she ever tried to tame him, Mrs. Tindell. I doubt if anyone could change Cousin Caleb. Maybe that's why he thinks the world of her."

"As you say."

Mrs. Tindell left, a faint wisp of expensive perfume hanging in the air after her.

"Can you believe it?" Deborah asked Trey when he arrived. "She came in person."

"Of course, I can," he said, hanging his coat by the door. "Enlisting the newspaper on the Tindell side in the Tindell–Snopes war for social preeminence is too important to leave to minions. Mrs. Snopes ought to surrender right now. She hasn't got a chance, and we have just been blessed by the grande dame of Hubbell."

He grabbed Deborah and waltzed her around the counter, leaving her breathless and flushed. If Aunt Em had ever corralled someone like Trey at dances....

Oh, yes, more peaks than valleys.

17

BY MID-DECEMBER, Trey no longer worried about the direction he had taken the *Herald*. Circulation had increased, so had advertisements, which were the financial life blood of the paper. Deborah's amusing, quirky way of describing town events appealed to even those her reports tweaked.

"Are you sure you wouldn't rather stay here and do your write-up on the Christmas Pageant?" he asked her for the third time. "It's bitter out there, and the streets are sloppy."

Deborah swung her scarf around, bundling up to her eyebrows, and gave him a muffled third refusal to trade desk duty and stay inside and warm. "No, Mrs. Tindell's annual descent on the deserving poor awaits."

Trey watched her leave, watched her through the front window until she disappeared before returning to his own story on the town's proposed celebrations of not only the new year, but the new century.

The bell on the door sounded.

"Jamie!" They met at the end of the counter, hugging and pounding each other on the shoulders. "So you made it home for Christmas. Where's Nolan?"

"He's home hugging Maura, who's a prettier armful than you are. She's expecting. I'm going to be an uncle."

"Congratulations. I already am. Webster Van Cleve Forbes. Maybe I'll even meet him some day."

Jamie just shook his head. "You look good, and you bounced out of that chair faster than I could. You can't be spending every day behind a desk."

"I'm still walking a couple of miles around town every day, at least when it's not cold enough to freeze me mid-stride, and until I hire someone else to throw bundles of paper around, I'll stay in shape. So where are these automobiles? Why don't I see one out in the street? Did you leave them all at the train depot?"

Jamie leaned on the counter, his face grave. "Well, now, that's a little problem. There are no automobiles."

"But you bought four. Your letter said two Runabouts and two Victorias."

"We don't have any."

"They were stolen? How could someone steal four of those things? Where did you...." Trey stopped as Jamie's face changed to a big grin.

"Sold. We sold them all before we crossed the Mississippi."

Trey's mouth had fallen open. He closed it with a snap. "Back East? You sold them rather than bring them out here after all?"

"We loaded them on the train and got as far as Pennsylvania. We had to wait a day there—a wreck on the track shut things down in all directions. So we got off and started talking to people in the town there, and when they heard we had motor vehicles, they wanted to see them. You know how Nolan is. He couldn't unload one to show off fast enough, and damned if some fellow who owned half the town didn't want to buy it."

"You're making that up."

"So we got the idea, Nolan and I, that maybe traveling straight through wasn't the smartest thing to do. After that we stopped for a day in every likely place, and we sold them all. I know you never believed we could sell a one, but the fact is we did it, and the profit is more than either of us could make in a year at the mill."

Trey said a word he didn't use too often.

"Exactly. We already wired an order for five more, and we're going back after Christmas. Trey, they let us help build those things. Five more and Nolan will be able to take one apart and put it back together himself. Me, I'd rather keep my hands clean and do the selling, but I know what goes where and can fix most things in a pinch. Speaking of clean hands...." He gave Trey's hands a hard look.

"Ink," Trey said vaguely. "You didn't take promissory notes for them, did you?"

"Were we born yesterday? We did not."

It finally sank in. "So I'm never going to see one of these things? You'll keep getting them back there and selling them before you make it home?"

"We're thinking next time we'll stop trying after three and bring two here. If no one in Hubbell wants them, at least we know what to do."

"I'm still having trouble believing it."

"You're a heathen in every way. Why would anyone want to keep a horse when a nice little horseless carriage can sit in the barn without eating its head off or needing its shit shoveled? Now let's get out of here. I'll buy you a drink, or dinner, or a drink and dinner."

Trey shook his head. "How about tonight? It's my very own policy that the office is open every weekday. I can't leave until Deborah gets back. Peter's visiting his youngest son."

Jamie straightened and folded his arms across his chest. "Deborah is it now? That would be Miss Deborah Sutton? Why would we be waiting for a lady you decided to forget about before I left? Was that in a letter that never made it all the way back East?"

Trey examined the black rims on his cuticles. "It's a long story."

"Is it now. A whiskey story, I suppose. Since you can't leave until Miss Deborah Sutton returns, tell me you have a bottle stashed somewhere around."

"I don't, but I know where Peter keeps his, and I can buy him another bottle. Drag a chair from the back room out here, and I'll find glasses."

Once they'd settled at the desk, drinks at hand, Trey explained about the Richmonds. "So I wanted someone who could write in a way that appeals to female readers the way Mrs. Richmond did."

"And sneaky Miss Sutton popped right into your mind."

"She's not sneaky," Trey said irritably. "I wanted to help her stop hiding out on that farm and pretending to be an old maid. She's twenty-five for Heaven's sake."

"You wanted to help her."

"Yes, and I was right. She'd good at the job, and she's...." *Intelligent, beautiful, clever, exquisite, thoughtful, desirable.*

"So she's turned from an odd stick into the kind of woman you want who will throw herself in your arms, kiss you in front of the whole town, and laugh."

"I wish I'd never told you about that," Trey said, tossing down the last of his drink and pouring more. "No. She's never going to be that woman."

"Then why are you toying with her? Walk on by and find one who will be."

"I can't. It's like she's a magnet, and my bones are all iron. How do you do it? How can you just make up your mind to spend time with a woman who gets your blood going, get to know her, and walk away because she's not Catholic or not—whatever."

"They all get my blood going. Women are made that way, God bless 'em. Marrying, children, it takes more than a romp in a bed."

"I know that, but I can't stop thinking about her, thinking maybe...."

"Seduce her then. Scratch that itch a few times and it will go away. You know damn well if you marry her, she'll make you miserable."

Trey slammed his glass down. "Don't ever talk about her like that again. I didn't take it from my father, and I'm not taking it from you."

Jamie nodded and got to his feet. "Sure then. We'll have that dinner another time."

"So WHAT TIME is he coming by for you tonight?" Judith asked, leaning over to taste the stew simmering on the stove.

"You make it sound as if we go somewhere together every night," Deborah said.

"Do I? I suppose it only seems that way when you're watching someone else courting."

"We're not courting!"

"Of course you are. Everyone in town knows it, so you may as well stop pretending it has anything to do with newspaper reporting."

"Stop doing that with your eyebrows! It's, it's unseemly. We're going to the theater to see *Shenandoah*, and you can read a report on what we see in next week's paper."

"Calm down. I'm not accusing you of skipping the play and spooning in some corner all night. I know you're going to see the play, and I know you'll write about it."

"We'll work together on the review in the paper. If he expected me to go to the theater alone at night, you'd bar the door."

"Of course we would," Judith said soothingly. "And since the two of you have to bear each other's company, you might as well eat caviar at the hotel instead of stew here."

"They don't serve caviar!"

"Deborah," Judith said in that irritating, patient voice she used on the children, "even if you don't know what's written all over your face every time you look at him, you can't be blind to what's all over his face every time he looks at you. The two of you might as well hold up signs. Stop being silly. You're courting."

"No! We can't be. He can't.... I can't...."

"Is everything all right here?" William stood in the doorway, concern on his blunt-featured face. The children ran by him to Judith, gave Deborah baleful glares, and buried their faces in their mother's skirt.

Judith waved her soup-tasting spoon. "Yes, we're all right. Deborah is just being Deborah."

Deborah drew breath to argue further, looked at the children, and let it go just as a knock sounded on the front door.

"I'll let him in," William said.

Not *I'll see who's there,* or *I wonder who that could be,* but *I'll let him in.*

Deborah ignored her sister and stalked off to get her coat.

DEBORAH'S HEART BEAT a little faster when she took Trey's arm and walked down the street beside him. The first time she'd done it, she felt strong, confident. Knowing the heavy wool of both their coats, her dress, his jacket, and a few more layers were between the strength and warmth of his arm and her own helped.

At least that's what she told herself the first time she realized she was leaning into him instead of gritting her teeth and enduring the touch the way she did when she had to dance with every clod Aunt Em could pressure into asking.

Tonight Judith's words echoed in her head, and the small pleasure of walking with him was gone. Courting. Judith was growing into as much of a matchmaker as Aunt Em, and she was nursing ridiculous notions, just like Aunt Em. He was kind, that's all. Generous.

She made small agreeing sounds to Trey's conversation about his friend's successful automobile sales, lost in her own thoughts

The First Street Hotel didn't offer caviar, which was just as well. Deborah would have been as unable to taste that as the beef she ordered.

Trey's expression *did* seem particularly intent. She couldn't be looking at him like that. Except she couldn't look away, and heat flushed through every part of her, frightening heat spreading to frightening places.

"Have I got ink on my face?"

"No, of course not. You look fine."

Impossibly handsome. Broad forehead, high cheekbones that no longer angled sharply under his skin now that he'd put on weight, straight nose, a little long maybe, with one side of the bridge just slightly higher than the other. Everyone said he looked like his mother, and Caleb had described Mrs. Van Cleve's chin as pointy, but Trey's wasn't pointy, just tapered, just right.

He forked a bite of his own roast beef and chewed. Deborah forced herself to stop staring at his mouth, his lips, which were—perfect. Not wide, not thin, distinctly outlined.

Her corset was too tight, her breathing quick. Trey Van Cleve was a man any woman would want. Except one who couldn't. Shouldn't.

His head tipped to one side, and he studied her as if he could read her thoughts, his eyes dark in the restaurant light. "We'd better hurry. Can't miss the first act."

Deborah nodded and stopped pushing her food around on the plate. He didn't need her to attend nighttime events. She would tell him they couldn't do this any more. After the play.

Shenandoah was the second play Deborah had attended at the new Hubbell Theater. Like the First Street Hotel, the theater had generated excitement all over town when it first opened.

Tonight the ornate, gold-trimmed moldings and thick carpet underfoot were lost on Deborah. So was the play.

She sat in the aisle seat Trey had reserved especially for her and stared at the stage, seeing only the blackness inside her mind. She applauded when others did, let Trey help her with her coat when it was over, nodded to people she knew as they left, and saw nothing around her until they arrived on Judith's doorstep.

"You haven't heard a word I said since we left the theater, have you?" Trey said.

"Of course I have." He was a shadow in the night the way he had been when they first met, his voice even more compelling. The same sliver of moonlight that reflected from remnants of last week's snow gleamed on the skin of his jaw. The clouds of their breath mingled in the few inches of icy air between them.

"No," she admitted. "I've been distracted by.... Before I left tonight, Judith said you're courting."

"Would that be so terrible?"

"Yes! I can't be what you want."

"Are you sure you know what I want?"

"You want what all men want, a woman like Judith, like Miriam. I'm not like them. I'm not like other women."

"Aah. And is what makes you different the same thing that made your cousin kill your father?"

She jerked back so sharply the back of her head hit the door frame. Panic brought bile to the back of her throat. She would have run blindly into the night, but he held her by the wrists.

"Who told you that? Who told you?"

"You did." Trey's grip loosened slightly, tightened again when she tried to yank away. "You told me your cousin killed your father in front of you when you were seven years old, and Sutton admitted to me he's that cousin. So I had to wonder—what would make him do it, and why wouldn't you hate him for it?"

"He did it because Papa tried to kill him with a shotgun, that's why. That's the only reason." She sagged in his grip, all the fight gone.

"Deborah."

"No. My father wasn't like yours. I loved him."

"I know you did. That makes it worse, doesn't it? Betrayal by someone you love. Someone who should love you too much to do it."

"Don't. Please, please, leave it alone. Leave me alone." Oh, curse him. How could he understand so well what no one else did? Aunt Em had worried at it for a long time, not because she understood, but because she didn't. Why couldn't he be like all the others, pretending they didn't know, eyes sliding away from her whenever she did something strange?

Trey wasn't through with her. "You're right, my father isn't like yours. His is a different kind of evil, but I loved him too, and in a deep down, twisted way I still do in spite of what I know now, in spite of not wanting anything more to do with him."

"Let go of me," she whispered. "Let go of me and go away. I don't ever want to see you again."

He let go of one wrist, reached around her and opened the door. He didn't let go completely until she was inside.

18

HE SHOULD NEVER have done it. Confronting her with it had to be the stupidest thing he'd ever done, and frustration over her stubborn refusal to consider a future was no excuse. He'd frightened her, hurt her, probably done damage. *Damaged.*

The day of his quarrel with Jamie, Trey had taken a room at the First Street Hotel. Cursing under his breath, he walked toward the hotel now, oblivious to everything except his own anger. The huge shadow coming out of an alley as he passed never caught his eye. The gleam of streetlight on metal did.

Ducking his head low and swiveling the cane high, Trey deflected the smashing blow aimed at his skull enough to save himself. The cane shattered, the short piece left in his hand slamming into his face.

"Rich bastard."

The big man rushed again, swinging wildly. Trey danced backward, pivoted as the blow came. As his assailant's momentum carried him past, Trey jabbed what was left of the cane into the back of the man's thick neck. He roared, smashed an elbow into Trey's side and knocked him down in the street.

Trey rolled, scrambled. The pipe hit the walk where he'd been with a deadly thud. Grabbing the pipe end Trey kicked at the thick arm and bearded face on the other end until the man's grip loosened. Lunging to his feet, backing away, Trey flung the pipe into the night.

Shouts sounded down the street. His attacker turned to run. Trey tackled his legs, got a good hold on one and hung on, pounding the sharp end of the broken cane into anything he could reach.

The grunts and curses turned to shrieks. A blow to the temple knocked Trey sideways, fighting to stay conscious. His attacker disappeared into the night, running with a lopsided, limping gait.

Trey pushed up to sit where he'd fallen, gasping, and cradled his head in one hand until his vision cleared.

"Are you drunk? What do you think you're doing, brawling in the street like that?"

In the dim light, Trey made out one of the young constables on Hubbell's police force. "Trying to stay alive."

The man's face floated in the air in a most interesting way. Trey closed his eyes again. Maybe his vision wasn't quite back to normal yet.

"Mr. Van Cleve?"

"The Third," Trey said, not sure why, but finding it funny. "There'd be a Fourth if Alice could find a legitimate way to reproduce without a husband."

"You are drunk. Here, let's get you up."

"Not drunk. Tired," said Trey, doing his best to collapse back into the street.

"Up you come. Here now. Put an arm around my shoulders. We'll get you to the station and have a talk."

Once the young constable had Trey on his feet and moving and got a good look at him under a streetlight, he changed their destination to the doctor's office. "Drunk and brawling in the street," he said to the doctor disapprovingly.

The doctor leaned in close and sniffed.

"Go away," Trey said. "Don't want to kiss you. Want to kiss Deborah."

"Not drunk," the doctor said. "He's hit his head."

"I didn't hit it. Man with a pipe hit it."

"Leave him here," the doctor said. "I'll clean him up and keep an eye on him tonight, and you can talk to him tomorrow. He'll probably be able to make sense by then."

"Good idea, keeping an eye," Trey muttered. "Should have kept an eye." With that he gave up and let the doctor do what he would.

DEBORAH FINALLY FELL asleep in the small hours of the night and woke nauseated and shaky.

Unless the weather turned nasty, the whole family was traveling to the farm for Christmas in a few days. Until then she'd stay right here in this room. Once she was home, she'd stay there, where she belonged.

The house came alive with morning sounds. The children, squealing and laughing. Judith's voice. William's. A knock sounded on the front door.

Deborah shoved the knuckles of her fist in her mouth. No one could force her to see him again. Not ever.

She'd tell Judith she was ill. She'd make her own way back to the farm today. A soft knock came on the door, and Judith peered in. "Aren't you up yet?"

"I don't feel well."

"Oh, I'll bring you some tea and toast after I get William off, but I thought you should know. Mr. Richmond just stopped by. He wanted you to know the office would be closed when you got there. Trey, Mr. Van Cleve, was hurt last night, and Mr. Richmond is going to get him from the doctor's...."

"What!" Deborah jumped from the bed, scrambling for her slippers and robe. "Hurt how? Is he all right?"

"A robber attacked him. He spent the night at the doctor's, but Mr. Richmond is going to take him to the hotel now. He's supposed to rest today, but he'll be fine. What are you doing? You said you didn't feel well."

"I lied. If William's in the bathroom, tell him to get out. I need to get to the doctor's." Deborah threw off her nightgown and began pulling on clothes, barely aware of her sister's astonished gaze.

"Yes, ma'am," Judith said as Deborah pulled on stockings. "I will have my husband out of your way and in the clear in moments."

Deborah ignored the tangled mess of her hair, threw a shawl over her head, and ran. Trey's buggy was parked in front of the doctor's house, Irene standing hipshot in the shafts.

Was he hurt so badly he couldn't walk the few blocks to the hotel? Deborah pounded on the door, a stitch stabbing her in the side with every gasping breath.

In her imagination she had seen Trey prostrate and at death's door. In reality, he was sitting at the doctor's dining room table, finishing a piece of toast. He looked as healthy as a man with two black eyes, a swollen cheek, and several stitches near his hairline could look. Healthier than he had any right to in fact.

Deborah paused in the doorway for a few deep breaths. "You," she said, advancing on him, one finger stabbing air. "You have to stop this."

Peter Richmond put down his coffee cup with a click. "I'll just wait in the other room."

Deborah ignored him and kept right on stalking toward Trey. "Do you hear me? This has to stop."

"I didn't do this to myself," he protested. "A robber jumped me."

"That was no robber, and you know it," she shouted. "I don't care if she's your sister. You have to make her stop."

"First of all," Trey said, with infuriating reasonableness, "there's no way to be sure it's Alice. It could be Vernon, her husband—or both of them—or someone else I haven't even thought of."

"You can't just keep hoping to live through another attack. You have to do something. Surely your father would rewrite his will if he knew this one was going to get you killed."

"Why don't you sit down and have some toast and coffee?" Trey said.

She glared.

"Fine. Stand there. You want me to go and ask my father to rewrite his will? Do you have any idea what he'd do then?"

She didn't, so she said nothing.

"He'd blackmail me to come home and learn his damned business by saying he'd have Alice jailed if I didn't. Or something else just as bad I can't even conceive of. I'm not asking my father for any favors."

"She deserves to be jailed."

"She's my sister, and she has a month-old baby."

"Leave town then. Go to—Alaska."

"Oh, that would suit you, wouldn't it? It would solve your problem with me."

"So will your funeral," she said coldly, "you stubborn, pig-headed *jackass*."

She stomped out of the doctor's house as angry as when she'd entered. Angrier than she'd ever been before in her life. He wasn't going to do anything but try to dodge the next attack. Well, she was going to do something, and she even had a glimmer of an idea what.

TREY CONSIDERED GOING after her, decided he wouldn't be able to catch her, and even if he could, he didn't want to restrain her against her will again. There must be a way back in her good graces, but that wasn't it.

When Peter Richmond reappeared, Trey stopped staring at the doorway and took a swallow of tea. Foul stuff, but the doctor said no coffee today.

He watched with envy as Peter refilled his cup with coffee.

"Doc had to go out," Peter said, "You're to go back to your room and rest. He'll stop by and take a look at you in the morning and say whether you can come to the office."

Trey nodded, then wished he hadn't. Some vicious little devil had been banging a hammer inside his head from the minute he woke up this morning. Deborah's outraged yelling hadn't helped.

"I guess you know she loves you," Peter said.

Trey stopped chewing toast and stared at the other man. "That's love?"

"They don't get that mad at a man unless they care about him. The madder they get, the more they care."

The devil in his head slowed down, just a little. "If that's love, it's no wonder men avoid it."

Maybe the two of them could move to Alaska. As soon as the devil went back where he came from, Trey would think about it.

19

DEBORAH RETURNED TO the house to wash and dress properly before setting out again. Judith poured coffee and set bacon and eggs she'd kept warm in the oven on the table.

"If you're going to rampage around like that, you need your strength. Something happened last night, didn't it? I mean something between the two of you, not the attack."

"It did."

"And you don't want to talk about it."

"I don't."

"You're not keeping any secret. I've always known."

Deborah's stomach lurched. Her single bite of eggs threatened to come up. "Known what?"

"That it would take someone like him. Even if the men Aunt Em keeps rounding up for you were every bit as good-looking, you'd sneak away as soon as you could because they bore you. Whatever else he is, your Mr. Van Cleve is not boring."

"He's not mine."

"Whose fault is that?"

"Do you think the weather will hold and we'll make it to the farm for Christmas?"

Judith laughed and threw a dish towel across the table. "All right, I'll mind my own business, at least for the rest of the day."

Deborah's course was set, but her knees shook at the prospect of actually doing it. She almost asked Judith for help but didn't. A sister wouldn't be much help. A male escort was needed, but every man Deborah could think of would kick up a fuss, try to stop her, and probably succeed.

In the end she stuck her chin in the air, squared her shoulders, and went alone. Two blocks into the area William had marked on his map for her to avoid, she saw the building. It looked like what it had been, a big barn. A fresh coat of white paint and bright red trim made it stand out from its run-down neighbors.

Knocking on the big front doors brought no response. From outside the small side door, she heard sounds of a hammer and saw, decided whoever was working inside couldn't hear her, and turned the knob. The door opened to empty space. All interior partitions had been removed. Only a line of posts down the center of the building remained.

A sign leaned against one wall, "Hubbell Automobile Company." Deborah stood on dirt still flecked with bits of straw and hay. A pile of lumber loomed next to the door. Wood flooring covered the back third of the building, and two men worked along the edge, fitting more boards, nailing them down.

She stood there, watching, no longer sure the idea that had brought her here was a good one—or smart—or safe. Too late. One of the men straightened and saw her. The two exchanged words, and one came toward her. She recognized Jamie

Lenahan as the man who had been with Trey at the ice cream parlor, but that day she'd had eyes only for Trey.

Lenahan had none of Trey's chiseled elegance. The Irishman was handsome all right, but more like the men in her own family, rawboned, all the subtlety of a bull. He eyed her the way the men she'd passed on her way here had, with the same consideration cats gave mice.

Deborah took a step back, then stopped. Had she come all this way only to run at the first contemptuous glance?

He stopped a few feet from her. "I'm guessing you're Miss Deborah Sutton."

"Yes, and you're Trey's friend, Mr. Lenahan. Have you heard what happened last night?"

"I have. A few whacks on his hard head, and he's fine."

"I thought you were his friend."

"We're reconsidering that at the moment."

Deborah looked around the big empty space, the pile of lumber, the new sign. "He's helping you start your business."

"He financed the whole thing."

She hadn't realized Trey was so deeply involved. "Then you owe him."

"There's owing, and there's owing. We'll repay the money debt."

"Don't you care that he was almost killed?"

"Do you? Why don't you have a talk with your killer cousin?"

"My... Oh, for goodness sake, Caleb would never try to kill someone with a pipe. He hasn't killed anyone for years, and when he did, he shot them. He *likes* Trey, although why anyone would like that pigheaded idiot is beyond me. His sister Alice is the problem, and he's not going to do anything about it because he doesn't want her in prison, even though she should be. She should be hung. I thought you were his friend, and you'd help me since he's too stubborn to do it himself, but since you're *reconsidering*, I apologize for wasting your time."

She turned away, already debating the wisdom of enlisting Caleb's help, when Lenahan said, "Wait a minute. He told you his sister is behind these attacks?"

"When we first met, when we were—friendly strangers—he told me his sister wished him dead, and he doesn't deny she's behind the attacks now, he just says he can't be certain."

Lenahan frowned. "When he talked to me, he said he thought some of the ranch hands had taken a dislike. Your family has reasons to hate his and so do others in this town. The only time he talked about his sister he said he hoped she had a son who could inherit the ranch."

"Well, he admitted to me his sister wants that ranch and everything else so much she threatened to kill him."

"Why would she have to kill him for it? He and his father can't stand the sight of each other. Trey's gone from there for good and ugly words between them."

"Ugly words aren't enough. Webster Van Cleve is as stubborn as Trey, and he believes in primogeniture as surely as any poxy old European king. Trey is still first in line to inherit the V Bar C and everything else, in spite of the fact they're estranged. Even if Alice accepts she can never have it outright herself, her son can have it."

The moment the words left her mouth she wished she could take them back. She was talking to an Irish laborer, not Trey or Peter Richmond.

"It's the law in Ireland," Lenahan said. "At least it's the law for Catholics. My da was a third son, so it was a choice of the priesthood, starving, or America. I always appreciated he chose America."

She was as much a snob as Miriam. She couldn't meet the bright blue eyes. "Well, that's who and that's why. If you'll excuse me, I need to get home."

"Trey would skin me if I let you walk home from here by yourself. Come on, now. I'll go with you at least part of the way."

"No, you won't. You're too busy spending Trey's money." She waved at the pile of lumber, taking satisfaction from the way Lenahan's nostrils flared and eyes narrowed.

Before she reached the first corner, Deborah heard his footsteps behind her. She whirled to face Lenahan. "I can't stop you from following me, but if you touch me, I'll scream."

"Sure you will, and dozens of fine fellows will rush to your rescue. Suppose you tell me what it is you want from me."

"I want help to hire a guard."

"A guard. For *Trey?*"

His incredulous tone annoyed her even more. "Not to stand over him with a gun. Someone to watch from a distance and, and help him when something happens again."

"You want to set a guard to watch over him without telling him? What do you think is going to happen when he finds out?"

"He'll be angry with me, and I don't care. He can't be any angrier than I am right now."

A slow smile spread across Lenahan's handsome face. "A man who wants a sneaky woman deserves what he gets, I say. Do you have money to pay this watchdog?"

"I do." She thought she did. Except for the cost of her purse and a few new dresses, she had almost all her over-generous salary from the day she had started at the paper.

"All right. I'll find you men. It will take more than one, or he'll figure it out that much quicker."

Deborah tried to hide her relief. She didn't want her family involved in this, and telling one Sutton was the same as telling all of them.

At the sound of a knock, Trey shuffled to the door in his robe and slippers. A hotel waiter carried in soup, toast, and tea as expected. Unexpected was the sight of Jamie Lenahan, giving the room a thorough examination as the waiter set the dishes on the small table by the window.

The door had no more than shut, leaving the two of them alone, than Jamie said, "This place looks like the kind that has 'No Irish or Dogs' signs back East, but the fellow downstairs was so impressed with my superior tailoring, he decided to let me in."

Trey sat down to eat and watched Jamie bounce on the bed a few times, testing.

"It's a step up from my room, that's for sure," Jamie said.

"The facilities are better, but the company isn't."

"I'm moving up too. Nolan and Maura have rented a nice little house with a room for me."

"Good. Good for all of you."

Neither of them said anything while Trey ate soup, buttered toast.

"I've come to apologize. I should never have said what I did, and now that I've met the lady, I'm twice as sorry. She's a fine lady. I wish you luck."

Trey choked on the last of his soup and coughed while Jamie pounded him on the back. When he could draw a breath, he gasped. "You saw her?"

"We were in the same part of town, stopped, and talked a while. A fine lady, beautiful, friendly."

He was up to something. If Trey knew anything, he knew from the innocent expression on Jamie's face that he was up to something.

"What did you talk about?" Trey asked suspiciously.

"You. She's a little upset with you, but that won't last once the bruises fade. You are a sight to frighten small children and old ladies, you know."

"I know. What else did she say?"

"Oh, how she likes working at the paper and living in town, things like that."

If Trey didn't know of Jamie's determination to marry only a Catholic girl, he'd be worried. The man was too good looking to be safe. "Didn't you tell me before you went back East that you'd finally found a girl of your own? When is the wedding? Am I invited?"

"The faithless girl couldn't do without a man for a few months and found someone else. I'm lucky I found out before any wedding."

"You don't look broken-hearted."

Jamie leaned forward, his elbows on his knees, serious now. "I'll make some woman a decent husband some day, but a heart has to be softer than mine to break. Now what are you planning to do to keep yourself in one piece for Miss Sutton?"

Trey shook his head. "Watch every shadow again, I suppose. Maybe it's all a coincidence. The cut reins could have been one of the ranch hands who didn't like the boss's prodigal son showing up and giving orders. The wagon could have been a drunk, and last night he called me a rich bastard. Maybe he figured to knock me out and rob me at his leisure."

"Miss Sutton is right. You are a stubborn idiot, and she has a notion your sister was behind the man with the pipe. Why would she think that?"

"I said something I shouldn't have once in a fanciful moment. It's probably that ranch hand I fired. Lenny Somebody."

"This hot-tempered young fellow would pay somebody else to go after you with a pipe?"

"Maybe not." Trey made a face and pushed the tea cup away, wishing for coffee and a steak. "I tried to keep hold of the man last night, but I couldn't. If he tries to see the doctor, we'll find out who he is."

"He's in as bad shape as you then?"

"Worse, but he can hide it better. He broke the cane, and I got him in the goolies at least twice with the broken handle."

"They'll be wise to you now. You're nothing but bully bait, you are."

Unsure if that was a compliment or insult, Trey shrugged and changed the subject. They talked about the automobiles and the type of men who had bought the first four. Jamie left when Trey's eyelids started drooping.

Trey sprawled out in the bed, any chance of sleep destroyed by a sudden vision of what could have happened if Deborah had been with him last night. Until he could catch one of these incompetent assassins and find out who was behind the attacks, it would be better to let her stay upset and angry.

Her whole family planned to gather at the Sutton farm for Christmas. Much as he hated the thought, if Deborah decided to go into hiding out there again, she'd at least be safe. Maybe absence would make her heart grow fonder. He grimaced at the ceiling.

And he'd better find out what Jamie was up to, probably something harmless, but better to know than wake up to dozens of automobiles in the street one morning.

DEBORAH SPENT THE rest of the day at the *Herald's* office. Unable to write a coherent sentence, she practiced on the typewriter, doing the mindless, repetitive exercises set out in a booklet she'd found in a desk drawer. Peter puttered in the back room, without any more purpose, and they both greeted four o'clock with relief.

As she stepped outside, damp air bit through her winter coat, sending a shiver up her spine. Dark clouds hastened the coming of the winter night. She hoped the storm would pass quickly, leaving only a few inches of snow. More than that, and the Christmas trip home to Aunt Em and Uncle Jason would be in jeopardy.

Three men leaning against the hardware store straightened as she approached. Her steps faltered until she recognized Jamie Lenahan's tall form. They all stopped on the walk, assessing one another.

The men with Lenahan were older, closer to fifty than thirty, as Irish as shamrocks, their thick bodies emphasized by heavy winter clothing. The men knew what she wanted and had already agreed to work for a sum so paltry she almost offered more.

Shanahan would watch for Trey to leave the hotel in the morning. Maguire would take over at noon, and they would trade off from then on, giving each other time to warm up, eat, and sleep. If they were careful, maybe Trey wouldn't notice the same men nearby every day. Deborah started to give them instructions, caught Lenahan's slight headshake, and held herself to a polite thank you.

The men tipped their caps and disappeared into the gathering gloom. Lenahan said, "It's getting dark. I'll walk you home."

The first flakes floated gently down around them as they walked. "Those men look too old and fat to run and help anyone," Deborah said.

"Oh, and you're a fine judge of a fighting man, are you? They both spent years earning a living with their fists, and either one could take a pipe away from a man and wrap it around his neck. Do you want me to tell them the lady's changed her mind, forget it?"

"No, I.... I didn't know you and Trey weren't friends any more when I went to see you. How can I be sure I can trust you?"

"I never said we weren't friends. I said we were reconsidering. I reconsidered some more after you and I talked this morning and went and saw him. We're fine."

"You didn't tell him...?"

"No, I didn't tell him, and no, I'm not selling you two pigs in pokes. Now what do you want to do?"

She wanted Trey safe. She wanted to erase the bruises and swelling and stitches. "I want them to watch him. I want.... Will it work? Will he notice?"

"He'll notice. The question is how soon."

"Did you hire those men because they'll do a good job or because they need work?"

"Both. If they didn't need work, you couldn't hire them now, could you?"

At least he was honest about that. How did such a strange, one-sided friendship start between two such different men?

"Did you and Trey meet in the Rough Riders?"

Lenahan made a sound of disdain and amusement. "Rough Riders. Of all the stupid names. We left the horses behind in Florida and never rode anything but Shank's mare in Cuba. No, we met after, in the hospital."

"So you were wounded too."

"I'd have been better off. No, Cuban fever got me. Still does now and then."

He left her at Judith's front gate, disappearing in seconds in snow now coming down thick and fast. How could anyone watch Trey carefully enough on a night like this? On any night unless he stayed on the main streets under the lights?"

Fretting and trying to think of a better solution, she went inside to family, warmth, and safety.

20

DEBORAH ENTERED THE *Herald*'s office the next morning so slowly the bell on the door only gave a muted jingle. Trey looked up from the desk.

"Good morning."

"Good morning." She couldn't look at him, stayed just inside the door, studying the scuffed wood along the bottom edge of the counter.

"Did you write up a review of *Shenandoah* yet? We need it today."

"I can't," she whispered.

"Excuse me?"

"I can't. I don't remember anything about it." She dared a quick glance to see how he took her confession, but his head was turned.

He rose without looking at her. "That's all right. I'll do it then." He paused in the doorway to the back room. "It's only three days until you're due to visit your family, and you must have shopping and packing to do. We can manage here without you. Take the time off."

Her fear had been a knowing look, an attempt to talk about the exposed secret lying ugly between them. She shouldn't have even worried. He had guessed before, suspected. Now that he knew, he didn't want anything to do with her. Hadn't he even said something at the doctor's about her problem?

She left as quietly as she'd come, eyes wet, throat tight.

THE STORM HADN'T left enough snow to change out buggy wheels for sleigh runners. Deborah squeezed into the back seat next to Miriam and Joseph with no more than a nod and polite greeting. Bundled in hats and scarves, coats and shawls, gloves and muffs, boots over layers of wool stockings, they all pulled buffalo robes across their laps and high under their arms for extra protection.

In the driver's seat, William waited until everyone had settled in before sending the horses forward. Bright sun sparkled on ice crystals in the snow, iron-shod hooves rang on frozen ground, and the leather hood overhead whooshed softly as the wind filled it.

Beside William, Judith held Billy in her lap. Emmy snuggled in between her mother and father. As the miles passed, Judith sang to the children, told them stories, and occasionally exchanged a long look with her husband that brought heat to Deborah's cheeks and made her stare sideways at the flat, snow covered land passing by.

No one sang in the back seat. Miriam and Joseph sat silent, their faces blank. Deborah had spoken only a few polite words to her youngest sister since coming to town to work at the paper, but she sensed emotions swirling around the young couple that had nothing to do with her. Burrowing deeper in the layers of protection against the cold, she turned to her own unhappy thoughts.

Where would Trey spend Christmas? With Jamie Lenahan? Lenahan had family in Hubbell. Would they invite an outsider, someone of a different religion, to spend a holy day with them? Would Lenahan's family be full of matchmakers like her own? They wouldn't invite some unmarried Irish girl to meet Trey when he wasn't Catholic, would they? Her cold hands turned colder at the thought.

He didn't want her at the paper any more, and she didn't want to be there, but she had to go back. She had an agreement with the men watching Trey, and even if he no longer wanted even friendship, how could she hide at the farm when Alice would hire more men to arrange accidents and make attacks?

No matter how he felt, she still…. Her mind shied away from the admission, then she faced it. Loved him. Fool that she was, she loved him.

The trip dragged on forever. The children fussed, cried, slept, woke, and did it all again. Deborah never wailed along with them, but it was a close run thing.

FEWER SUTTONS HAD crowded around the table for the Christmas dinners of Deborah's childhood, but the happy chatter, chink of forks on Aunt Em's best china, and scent of roasted goose was the same.

Deborah savored her food, listening to conversations at both ends of the table. Thoughts of Trey Van Cleve were not going to spoil this rare time with the whole family home. The subjects were familiar, births and deaths, marriages and children. Only the names changed as the years passed.

When Judith mentioned the return trip home, Deborah lost interest in the other talk and paid attention.

"We do need to be back in town before the New Year," Judith said. "After all, William's family likes to see the children too, and if predictions of the end of the world at midnight on the thirty-first are true, it will be their last chance."

"Oh, bosh," Aunt Em said as everyone laughed. "Someone probably predicted the end of the world every century since they started counting. I understand how the Daltons feel, but I almost hope we get a storm, and you have to stay with us longer."

No almost to it, Deborah thought. Aunt Em would keep them all forever if she could.

"I want to stay," four-year-old Emmy piped up. "I don't want to go in the buggy ever again."

Judith tugged on one of her daughter's braids. "It's the only way home, and you want to go home and see your Grandma Dalton, don't you?"

"It won't be many years before there are quicker ways," William said. "Motor cars are going to replace horses before Emmy's grown."

Sounds of disagreement and disbelief came from all around the table.

"William is right," Deborah said. "I read about an electric automobile that won a race by going fifty miles in two hours last year. Can you imagine? We're going to see them on the streets in town soon. Tr- Mr. Van Cleve's friend Mr. Lenahan is going to sell them."

"Oh, do tell us about your *employer's* friend, *Mr.* Lenahan, Deborah. I'm sure we'd all love to spend Christmas dinner hearing about the doings of some Eye-riish laborer who's gotten above himself."

A sneer distorted Miriam's usually lovely face. Deborah regarded her sister as much with sorrow as anger, aware of the hush that had fallen over the table. Setting her napkin beside her plate, she got to her feet.

"I know the fact that you have grown into a vain, selfish shrew is as much my fault as anyone at this table. We spoiled you. I spoiled you. But I am telling you right now, if you ever sneer at me like that again, if you ever say the word Irish like that again in my presence, I am going to haul off and slap you silly. I'm sure you think I'm going to run out of here now, but you're wrong. I'm walking."

Outside in the yard, Deborah drew in great breaths of clean, cold air, noting the way the sky had darkened and the wind picked up. An occasional fat snowflake drifted by. She crossed her arms over her chest and shivered.

"Here. Put this on."

Judith had brought a coat and scarf. Deborah thrust her arms in the coat sleeves and buttoned up gratefully.

"After your dignified departure, our little sister tried for sympathy, and when she didn't get it, ran upstairs, crying prettily every step of the way. Don't you dare apologize to her. Every one of us wanted to say what you did."

"I'm not going to apologize. Joseph will make her feel better."

"Joseph is still at the table eating. Red-faced and grinding more than chewing, but at the table."

"But he's her husband. He should go to her."

Judith made a sound of disagreement. "That's not how it works. Being pronounced man and wife doesn't mean pretending your beloved is always right. Too much of this behavior, and our sister may find in spite of all the poetry about love everlasting, love isn't forever if you don't nurture it. He shouldn't have married her. She was too young."

"You were younger when you married William."

Judith gave her a knowing look. "You and I were always older than our years. We felt sorry for Miriam because she never knew Mama and was orphaned so young, but you and I are the ones who lived through bad times, aren't we?"

Deborah pulled up her coat collar and wrapped the scarf tighter. "I never knew you felt like that. You were always so happy."

"I am happy, but I remember being afraid. I remember crying and hearing you cry. We're lucky we had Aunt Em and Uncle Jason, but that doesn't mean it was easy."

"No," Deborah whispered. "It wasn't easy."

"I don't know what you and Trey quarreled about, but you need to fix it. You've been happy these last months, and now you're like you used to be. Don't be as foolish as Miriam and throw it away, fix it."

"I can't."

"Yes, you can. Kiss him a few times, tell him you're sorry, and promise not to do it again."

"Judith!"

"I mean it. You do what I say, or I'll slap you silly."

Judith mimed a slap to Deborah's face. Deborah made a fist and swung at air. Giggling like girls over their own nonsense, they walked back to the house arm in arm.

WIND ROARING AROUND the eaves woke Deborah in the dark of early morning the third day after Christmas. Lying there listening, she picked out the sound of thousands of icy pellets bouncing off the glass of the bedroom window. She snuggled deeper under her covers. Judith would be disappointed they couldn't travel back to town today. Aunt Em wouldn't even try to hide her delight.

Deborah's own feelings were mixed. Hiding here at the farm for the rest of her life was no longer a possibility. She wanted—more. What that meant wasn't clear in her mind, but she knew she would have to face Trey and find out.

Dawn never came that morning or the next or the next. The world didn't end at midnight on the thirty-first, but the blizzard finally did.

"I don't suppose they had fireworks and a band in town at midnight," Aunt Em said, hanging more wet woolen clothes in front of the stove to dry. "It's too bad because I wanted to read how you'd describe it all in the paper."

"Mr. Van Cleve is a very good writer. He'll describe whatever celebrations they managed to have so well you'll think you were there."

"Ha," Judith said. "I wish we had that paper right now. We could use more newspaper to stuff around the window sills. The snow is leaking in around this one again already."

"Just be glad you're not out there struggling to feed horses like the men. I'd have frozen stiff in that drift out there this morning on the way to the hen house if Uncle Jason and William hadn't pulled me out, and trousers under my skirt didn't keep me warm. They just soaked through and weighed me down more."

"You're staying inside with the rest of us until the paths they shovel stay open. The wind will die down by the time night falls."

Maybe so, but Deborah knew it would be at least another day before her uncles could haul out the prow-shaped wood plow, hitch up the draft horses, and break through to the road. In the meantime all she could do was help weather the aftermath of the storm and daydream about what it would be like to follow Judith's orders and kiss Trey a few times.

21

DEBORAH DID NOT creep back to the *Herald*'s office this time, but walked in as if everything was as it used to be. Wishing did not make it so.

The desk sat empty, the typewriter covered. Trey appeared in the doorway from the back room. Even though the tan printer's smock emphasized the fading yellow bruises around both eyes, no man had ever looked so handsome—or so stern.

"Why are you here?" he said.

"To start work again, of course. I couldn't get back sooner, but here I am, and I have an idea...."

"You're not working here any more. You need to leave."

She had already removed her gloves. Her fingers trembled on the buttons of her coat, and she stopped unbuttoning. "You're dismissing me because I couldn't get back when I said I would?"

"No, that's not...."

"Because I didn't write a review of the play on time?"

"No, I don't want...."

"Because I shouted at you at the doctor's?"

"No, listen to me. You can't...."

"Because of what you know about me now?"

"No! Because I don't want you hurt the next time someone comes after me with a pipe."

That was it? All the terrible things she'd imagined, and that was it? "You let me believe.... The way you behaved before I left.... Do you have any idea how much that hurt?"

"I'm sorry, but keeping you out of danger is all that matters. Don't make me hurt you again. Don't let me hurt you. Go home and stay there."

Deborah undid the rest of the buttons, took off her coat, and hung it beside her heavy wool scarf. She walked around the counter and stood in front of him. "No one is trying to kill me. I will not go away. I will not stay away, and you had better promise me you won't ever do anything like that to me again."

He closed his eyes for a moment, opened them looking more determined than ever. "Do you want me to go talk to your family and ask them to keep you away?"

"If you do, I'll go talk to yours and ask them to...." The problem with her threat was she didn't have the foggiest idea what she could request of anyone in his family.

"Stay away from my family! My father could be dangerous."

"Stay away from mine. Caleb *is* dangerous."

She met his eyes steadily, not giving an inch.

"Isn't it time, you got upset and escaped?" he said finally.

"No."

"Just like that? 'No.'"

"No."

The corner of his lip curled up, just a little, but he didn't give in. "You're wasting your time trying to threaten me with

Caleb," he said. "I have a lady friend who hired two retired prizefighters to watch over me."

"That rotten traitor. Mr. Lenahan told you!"

"No one told me. I had a feeling someone was following me, so I set a trap, doubled back through the hotel one morning, and cornered Maguire. He confessed."

"And I suppose you made them stop."

"I did. I paid them a bonus and sent them off with best wishes. I'll reimburse you."

"I don't want reimbursement. I want you to, to...."

"Move to Alaska?"

"Yes."

His expression sobered. "I've thought about it. I could leave Hubbell again. But I can't leave you."

Silence stretched between them, and Deborah thought she could feel the image of his face as it looked at that moment etching into her memory forever.

"Marry me, and we'll leave here together," he said, his voice soft.

Her vision wavered, her knees threatened to buckle. Pressing both hands to her rib cage she made it to the desk and the chair without collapsing. So often she had been unable to meet his eyes. Now she could not look away. "You know I can't."

"I know that I love you. If not Alaska, Montana?"

He couldn't mean it, couldn't. What he felt was responsible and protective, and he was just trying to make her cooperate. Still, saying *that*. Maybe she would crumble after all, fall right off the chair in a graceless heap.

"Love doesn't—it doesn't fix things. I can't."

"We don't need to fix things. We just need to—hobble on."

"I'm sorry, but I can't. I just can't."

"I won't give up, you know."

She tore her eyes from his and lifted the cover from the typewriter. Concentrating on small objects on the desktop banished the light-headed sensation, although her stomach still seethed, and her clothing rasped her skin with every movement.

"So you won't marry me and move to Alaska, and you won't go home and stay there until I figure out what's going on?"

"No, I won't. I work here, and I'm going to do my job."

"What if I pick you up and carry you home?"

Her stomach did a complete flip. "I'll come back."

"Deborah."

He ran a hand through his hair, making a mess. She squelched an insane urge to smooth it back down by concentrating on taking a sheet of paper from the desk drawer and rolling it into the typewriter.

"I have an idea for a story," she said, staring at her fingers on the keys. "There are people in town now who have no idea what a blizzard is like for anyone who lives out on the Plains miles from a neighbor. Joseph and William had no idea. I'm going to describe it for our readers. And farmers like Aunt Em and Uncle Jason who go through it almost every winter will love reading a story that's about them and their lives."

"That does sound good, but.... All right, you win, but we're not going anywhere together, and we're not even staying here together. When you're on the desk, I'll go out. Right now I'll go visit the police and see what the town miscreants have been up to lately and then the Mayor's office. I can have a talk with real miscreants there."

Deborah nodded and started typing. After he left, she ripped out the page of gibberish, wadded it up, and started again.

FOR THE NEXT two weeks, Deborah only saw Trey in passing. He was good to his word—if she was in the office, he was not. She fretted and worried. *Marry me. I know that I love you.* He didn't mean it. Couldn't. He knew her secrets, knew she couldn't be any kind of wife.

His determination to protect her was just plain male silliness. He was the one in danger. She wished she could talk to Jamie Lenahan again, but he and his brother-in-law had returned East to help build the new automobiles they had ordered. It would serve them all right if she said yes, lured Trey away to safety, and.... And what? Her mind refused to contemplate what came after the yes.

She missed going to late afternoon and evening events with Trey, missed noon meals with him at the café. Judith's words often popped into Deborah's mind. *Whatever else he is, your Mr. Van Cleve is not boring.*

No, Trey wasn't boring, but life without him was. Boredom and sympathy left Deborah vulnerable to a plea from Miss Florence Miller, who approached the counter in the *Herald's* office with hesitation. Deborah didn't know Miss Miller, but she knew of her. The owlish little woman eked out a living teaching music in a small house on the edge of the part of town William considered unsuitable for ladies.

Her request was impossible. Trey had committed to attending another of Mrs. Tindell's cultural events, this time a recital by a Russian violinist with an impressive name everyone in town pronounced differently. As Trey had said before hurrying out the door past Deborah, an hour of aural misery would almost be worth it if it settled the pronunciation mystery.

"I never thought of asking you to put our little recital in the paper," Miss Miller said breathlessly, "but yesterday Mrs. Green urged me to do so. Her Ned is my best pupil. Seeing his name in the paper would make her so happy. So I promised, but I know you can't. Even with proper notice, I know you wouldn't want to spend time with us, and you'd have to, wouldn't you?"

Fulfilling her promise had Miss Miller flushing red with embarrassment. "I didn't know Mrs. Tindell would schedule the same day, or I never would have done it, but I sent notes home with all my students weeks ago, and families have to plan. It's pretentious to call what my students are doing a recital, I know. Even Ned—a Russian violinist—only students— just parents."

Miss Miller finally stopped her incoherent ramble, and stood waiting for excuses and rejection.

"Your students are giving a piano recital for their parents tonight?" Deborah summed up.

Miss Miller nodded.

Deborah glanced toward the back room. Mr. Richmond had spent the day on the linotype machine. By four o'clock the lines in his face would be crevices, and his walk would be close to a shuffle. Still, if she asked him, he would go, or go with her.

"The problem is that Mr. Van Cleve has accepted an invitation to Mrs. Tindell's recital," Deborah explained. "I'd love to come to yours, but I'd need an escort, and I'm not sure who I can ask. Give me a moment to consider." Judith and William were taking the children to visit his family this evening, so she couldn't ask William.

"Oh, you mean you would..." Miss Miller's face lit up. "The Greens would be delighted to bring you with them. I know they would." Her face fell. "Of course, then you would have to stay to the end."

"I'd be happy to stay to the end," Deborah said, writing Judith's address on a scrap of paper. "I'll look forward to it."

Judith and William had already left when Deborah returned home. She had time to wash and change her clothes before the Greens arrived—and leave a note, since Judith and William would be home before she was.

TREY CLOSED HIS eyes and leaned back. Mr. Rostovtzeff was proving a pleasant surprise. Deborah would have enjoyed this, and he would have enjoyed having her beside him.

Alaska. He didn't want to go to Alaska or anywhere else. He wanted to smoke out this would-be killer, get him stopped, marry Deborah, and make a life here. Now that he had Herman co-opted into providing information about the comings and goings at the V Bar C, figuring out who was behind the attacks should be possible. Him. Not Alice. Him.

His eyes flew open when a hand closed on his shoulder.

"I need to talk to you," William Dalton whispered.

Deborah. "What's wrong? Is she hurt?"

"She's fine. At least I think she's fine, but I need to talk to you."

Trey ignored the glares as he followed William out of the room and into the hallway.

"What do you mean you *think* she's fine."

"Judith and I were out tonight. When we got home, we found this in the middle of the kitchen table."

William handed Trey a note. "I am covering a recital tonight. Since you will be home before I am, I didn't want you to worry. Deborah."

"Of course we are worried. She's always been bad about slipping off by herself, but in town at night in the dead of winter? She mentioned at breakfast she wished she could come here, so we hoped.... I said I'd find her and bring her home, but now I don't know what to do. I hate to go back and tell Judith I couldn't find her. I can't think where else she could be."

Neither could Trey, although he was having trouble thinking at all. Where would she go? This was the only recital in town tonight, this week, this month. Why say a recital? To tweak him when she knew he'd be here without her? If he found her unharmed, he'd wring her neck.

"Your wife doesn't know of anything else going on in town tonight?" he asked William.

"Nothing like a recital. The Baptists have choir practice."

"If you check with the Baptists, I'll check with Peter and see if she left an address or anything at the office. If I don't find anything, I'll meet you back at your house. If I do, I'll get word to you somehow."

Trey came closer to running than he had in the past year and a half and arrived at the *Herald* out of breath. Nothing on top of the desk gave any hint where she might be. He yanked open one desk drawer after another, searching for any clue.

A faint click made him look up. Peter stood in the doorway in his drawers and vest, a large black pistol shaking in his hand.

"Do you mind pointing that somewhere else before it goes off?" Trey said.

"Oh. Yes, of course. I thought you were a burglar. There's nothing much to steal, but I thought I should come look."

Trey took the revolver from him and let the hammer down gently. "Next time you think there's a burglar, lock your door and stay upstairs. You'll be safer."

Peter nodded, yawning, "I expect so. What are you looking for?"

"Any indication of where Deborah went tonight."

"I expect to Miss Miller's piano recital. That's what she was planning."

"Piano recit.... That frumpy little woman who lives on Water Street?"

"That's the one. She was in here today, and Miss Sutton promised...."

Trey already had his hand on the door. "Do me a favor and find someone to go and tell the Daltons where she is. Tell them I'm going after her and I'll get her home."

Trey yelled the last so he would be heard because he was out the door and almost-running again.

22

THE YOUNGEST CHILDREN went first and played very short pieces. As the performers increased in age, their performances increased in length and skill required. Ned Green must be a prodigy indeed.

Deborah wrote another name in her notebook. The only way to report on this modest little recital and do it justice would be to include the name of every child. Miss Miller and the parents had every right to be proud. Trey would be fortunate if Mrs. Tindell's Russian entertained so well.

Banging sounded from the front door. Deborah looked around, frowning. No one should be arriving and interrupting this late. The girl playing missed a few notes and stumbled to a halt as Trey hurried into the room.

"Excuse me. Excuse me."

Trey pushed through the clusters of parents standing around the piano until he reached Deborah. She jerked away. "What are you doing here? You're upsetting everyone. That little girl...."

"The question is what are you doing here? You're supposed to be home. Judith is worried, and William is searching town for you. Say your goodbyes, and I'll take you home."

Around her, parents whispered and frowned. Miss Miller had resignation on her face and a comforting hand on the shoulder of the little girl at the piano.

"I apologize for causing this disruption. Perhaps you can explain to the children that sometimes gentlemen act impetuously. Mr. Van Cleve and I are going outside for a moment," Deborah said to Miss Miller. To the little girl at the piano she said, "I hope when I return, you will be kind enough to let me hear you perform from the beginning again."

Deborah wove her way through parents and children, smiling and nodding, until she reached the front door, which she yanked open without waiting for Trey. As soon as the door closed behind them, she said, "I left Judith a note. There is no earthly reason for her to be worried or you to be here disrupting everyone's evening."

"She didn't send me. William came to the Tindell recital, hoping to find you there or that I would know where you were. They're worried because they have enough sense to know it's dangerous for you to sneak around town at night. If they knew you were in this part of town, they'd be here with the police."

"I came here in the company of Mr. and Mrs. Green and their two children, and they plan to take me home. I am not sneaking, and I am not stupid. I don't know what's gotten into Judith and William—or you. I left a note, and they have no reason to worry or interfere or enlist you to interfere. Go home."

"You really came here with one of those families?"

"Of course I did. Are you saying you think I'm not only sneaky but a liar?"

"Well, you have been known to...." Evidently reconsidering the wisdom of finishing that thought, he put his hands in his coat pockets, rocked on his heels, and changed the subject. "You must be cold."

"Yes, that's why I'm returning inside, where all those proud parents and excited children are now trying to pretend they aren't disappointed that someone from the paper isn't going to listen to their recital after all."

"I really was worried about you."

"You treated my worry about you as a joke and sent the men away."

"I didn't think it was a joke, but I suppose I hoped it meant more than it did. That red dress is pretty, but it's not warm enough to stand out here, and you're shaking. Let's go back inside. Will the musicians and their families forgive me if two people from the paper listen to the rest of the concert? Will you walk home with me instead of the Greens?"

"We came in their carriage." She pointed at the line of vehicles waiting in the street.

"Aah, I suppose you'd rather ride than walk then."

She open her mouth to agree, but what came out was, "I'd rather walk with you, but it will be a while, and you'd better show proper appreciation. I expect Ned Green to deliver a rousing finale."

Trey opened the door and sketched a courtly bow. Deborah swept back inside.

They left almost two hours later, thanks and good wishes from Miss Miller, parents, and children ringing in their ears. The same damp cold that had chilled Deborah to the bone on the carriage ride to the recital and when standing outside without a coat arguing with Trey no longer affected her. His gloved hand covered hers where it rested on his arm and warmed her better than the stove in Miss Miller's house.

"It was all your sister's fault," he said as soon as they set out.

"You are entirely blameless."

"I am."

"You didn't burst into the house in a froth, ready to drag me out of there."

"I object to terms like froth and drag."

"And you aren't worried about having spent hours in my company and walking me home."

"I am. I'm being selfish and self-indulgent. Surely we can enjoy one evening without guilt."

"Sneak it in, you mean?"

"I'm sorry. I was upset."

She laughed and hugged his arm tighter, unable to pretend anger over his worry about her. "You were, and you missed Mr. Rostovtzeff."

"I heard enough to write something that will keep Mrs. Tindell happy. Maybe we'll get a chance to hear him together some day. He's very good."

"As good as Ned Green?"

"It's a close call, but I'd say yes."

A buggy passed in the street and then another. One family from the recital walked half a block ahead, and another could be heard laughing and talking behind. "This can't be that bad a neighborhood," Deborah said. "We aren't the only ones walking home."

"None of the others are beautiful young women walking alone, and you wouldn't want to meet that fellow across the street by yourself."

He had noticed her new red dress. He'd just called her young and beautiful. She wanted to skip like Judith with the pleasure of it, and she couldn't argue his point. The man across the street leaned against a light pole as if he needed it to hold him up and had a hand under his coat doing something that didn't look quite like scratching.

Another ragged fellow staggered down their side of the street. As he reached the family ahead, the father pushed his wife and children almost off the walk away from the street and made a human barrier of himself until the drunk passed by.

Trey disengaged Deborah's arm with a pat on her hand and pushed her the same way, swinging his cane on the street side. The drunk muttered and swayed, seeming oblivious to everything around him until he was on top of them and stepped in Trey's path.

Deborah saw the flash of metal, heard a grunt of surprise and pain from Trey, and screamed. The men grappled for the knife. Trey's cane rolled on the ground. Deborah picked it up and hit the man struggling with Trey across the back with all her strength.

Footsteps pounded toward them. Men yelled. Women and children screamed. Deborah raised the cane again, but the drunk broke free, crossed the street at a run and disappeared around the corner.

"Are you hurt?"

"Are you hurt?" The families that had been ahead and behind surrounded them now, their questions drowning out Deborah's.

Trey stood very straight, his right arm clamped to his side, his face white under the streetlight. "I'm fine. He was just a belligerent drunk, and he frightened Miss Sutton."

Deborah yanked his arm from his side. "You are not fine. He stabbed you. That's blood."

The crowd around them broke out in buzzing chatter.

"He didn't stab me," Trey said. "The knife glanced off a rib. I wouldn't be standing here if he stabbed me, would I?"

A carriage drew up beside them in the street. The Greens. Deborah almost sobbed with relief. In less than a minute she and Trey had squeezed inside with the family, and Mr. Green sent his horses flying toward the doctor's home.

Relief ended on the doctor's doorstep. A sleepy housekeeper informed them the doctor had been called to a farm two hours west of town to deliver an uncooperative baby.

"Let's get Miss Sutton home," Trey said to Mr. Green, "and if you'd be so kind as to drive me to the hotel, they'll have bandages and disinfectant there."

When the carriage pulled up in front of Judith's, Deborah refused to get out without Trey. "You're coming in with me. The hotel may have disinfectant and bandages, but no one there is going to treat you. Judith can do it."

The fact Trey didn't argue worried Deborah even more. Blood wasn't dripping, but the stain on his coat had spread. Mr. Green helped them down from the carriage, walked them to the door, and left.

"I bet he wishes his wife never thought of trying to get Ned his first newspaper clipping," Trey muttered.

Judith heard them and rushed to the kitchen. "Oh, my goodness, am I happy to see you in one piece. Mr. Richmond said you were at some children's recital?"

"Never mind that, Trey's been stabbed, and the doctor's out of town. We need.... I need...." Deborah couldn't catch her breath. She leaned on the table for support.

"I haven't been stabbed," Trey said. "The knife just sliced a little. Calm down. Take a deep breath."

Deborah did take a deep breath, and it did help.

"Another," he said. "There, that's better. A little bit of bandaging, and I'll be on my way."

"You're not going out on the street again tonight!"

"Stop shouting. Didn't you promise you wouldn't shout any more?"

"No, I didn't. You promised not to get killed."

"I don't remember promising that, and anyway, I'm not dead."

Judith flew around the kitchen, disappeared, and returned. She banged a basin, carbolic, and bandages down on the table. "Stop arguing and let's see this stab wound."

Trey removed his coat with a grimace. The blood stain on his jacket had spread, his vest and shirt were soaked. Deborah wanted to weep at the sight.

Once he was bare to the waist, Judith swiped blood and peered at his side. "You're right it's just a slice, but it's deep and should be stitched. The reason William and I came home early is Emmy has a stomach ache and a fever. If William has to deal with her alone much longer, he's going to leave me. Deborah, you'll have to stitch this."

Judith couldn't mean it. Deborah stared at the wound in horror. "I can't stitch a person."

"Pretend he's a calf. You've stitched cuts on calves."

Judith whirled away again and returned with needle and thread and a folded nightshirt. "Since your clothes are all either ruined or wet, wear this tonight, and we'll find you a shirt in the morning," she said to Trey. "Emmy is crying. I have to go."

Deborah tore her eyes from Trey. A man who looked so elegant in a suit should not look so—male—unclothed. A puckered starburst of scar tissue marred his right shoulder. The rest of his bare skin curved smoothly over muscle and bone.

She swallowed and swallowed again, wanting to stare, afraid to look. She filled the basin with hot water and prepared to clean the wound. "He wasn't drunk, and he tried to kill you."

"No, he wasn't, and yes, he did. He could be the same man who came at me with the pipe. He didn't seem as big hunched over and stumbling like that, so I can't be sure."

"Can you stand up?"

"In a minute." He sounded tired.

"Never mind." She knelt beside the chair and washed the blood away.

"Have you really stitched up calves?"

"And pigs. My uncles held them down."

"Pigs are reassuring, but you don't have anyone to hold me down."

She wanted to lean her forehead against his arm and cry. Instead she disinfected the wound and the needle and thread and started stitching. "I'll marry you if you'll go far away."

"Just me? You won't come along?"

"Yes, I mean we'll go far away."

"Thank you for the offer, but I don't want you to marry me so I'll run away. I like it here."

"But you asked me. You said you would go if I married you."

"You turned me down and gave me time to reconsider. I don't want you to marry me to get me to rabbit off to Alaska. I want you to marry me because you can't live without me."

He sucked in a breath and held it as she started the first stitch, let it out while she tied the knot. "I don't suppose there's any chance you can't live without me?"

She dropped the needle. It hung swinging from the thread running through his skin until she picked it up again. "No." *I can live without you. It will be more like dying than living, but I can do it.*

"I was afraid of that. Then there's the fact that if someone wants me dead in Kansas, they'll still want me dead in Alaska. And if they can pay men to try to kill me here, they can find men willing to kill anywhere. More in Alaska maybe. It's still as wild up there as Kansas was before you and I were born."

"They wouldn't find you."

"Notice how you say they wouldn't find me, not us. It's a good thing I said no, or I'd find myself in Alaska, hiding out with a new name, and missing my wife because she escaped and left me a note the first chance she got."

Deborah ignored the teasing and concentrated on bandaging over the stitches, enjoying the warmth of his skin, the firmness of muscle. Long ago she had learned to endure the touch of people other than her sisters when she had to, but she had never learned to like it.

What made him different? He had always been different, a man she sought out instead of avoided. She could enjoy this much, just these small touches of her hands over his ribs.

"You hit him, didn't you?" Trey said.

"Yes, with your cane, but it didn't seem to make any difference."

"It did. He almost had the knife until then. Ladies are supposed to stand back, scream, and faint, you know."

"I did scream."

"Aah. Well then that's the best of both worlds. Clever lady."

Finished with all she could do, Deborah rose to her feet and for the first time saw the scar that covered the entire back of his shoulder. Lower down, a smaller scar beside his spine disappeared under the waistband of his trousers.

"Your back." She pressed her palm over the large grayish white blotch, wanting to hide it from sight, wanting to touch him even more.

"It's a mess, isn't it? Since I never have to look at it, I forget sometimes. The shoulder looks worse, but it was that little hole in the back that crippled me."

"Crip.... I heard someone say you came home on crutches."

"I did. Considering I was never supposed to walk again, getting out of the wheelchair was a triumph, and Jamie was glad enough to stop lifting and pushing."

"I didn't know. Does anyone know?"

"Jamie, and now you. We met in the hospital and went through it together. He was dying of fever, and I was dead from the waist down." Trey reached back and covered her hand with his own. "It's not something to talk about, is it? There's something embarrassing about admitting I needed Jamie to lift me from the bed to the chair for months. My left arm was about the only thing that still worked."

"There's nothing embarrassing about being shot!"

"There shouldn't be, but there is. Being one of the wounded just isn't noble somehow, is it?"

He turned his head and looked up at her, his eyes full of knowledge. And understanding. Not pity or revulsion but understanding. Even so, she pulled her hand out from under his and carried the basin to the sink to wash.

Behind her, his chair scraped on the floor as he rose. She sensed rather than heard his footsteps. One hand on her shoulder, one on her waist. She turned in his arms, closed her eyes when his hand cupped her face, his fingertips stroking into her hair, his thumb caressing along her cheekbone.

"Look at me."

Her eyes obeyed. He leaned close, closer. His lips brushed hers, warm so warm. The sensation shivered right down to her toes.

"Breathe."

Her lungs obeyed. She pressed the side of her face to his palm, happy to have this one moment, wishing it could last, knowing it could not.

"Touch me."

Her hands obeyed, curving over his shoulders. This kiss was no quick brush of lips. His mouth moved against hers, his tongue along the inner surface of her lips.

The hand still at her waist slid to her back, urged her closer, and her body obeyed the unspoken command, arching into him. Her arms slipped around his neck. She no longer felt warmth but heat—his, hers.

Her breasts flattened against his chest, a hard ridge of male arousal pressed against her stomach. Her body reacted in strange ways, her nipples hardening to an ache, places low and inside softening and melting to liquid.

Fear ripped through the pleasure and left it in shreds.

She had no chance to panic. He lifted his head, his hands gone from her before she could drop her arms to her side.

"Too much?" His voice was still Trey's but deepened by emotion, his eyes darker and hooded.

Beyond speech, she nodded.

He turned and picked up William's nightshirt. "You'd better show me where I'm supposed to spend my night safely out of harm's way."

After showing Trey to the guest bedroom and leaving him there, still wordlessly, Deborah hurried to her own room. Instead of reaching for the light in the wall sconce, she crossed to her bed in the dark and sat there, fully clothed, her fingers pressed across her lips.

"How alone?" he said, putting down some tin contraption with a handle he'd been examining.

"Just you or you and Norah."

"All right."

Minutes later, Deborah faced her cousins over Miriam's kitchen table.

"Miriam took Ginny to her dressmaker," Norah said, putting the coffee pot back on the stove. "We're supposed to stop by there when we're ready to start home, so you don't have to worry about being interrupted."

Deborah looked around the familiar room, sparkling clean, with new flowered wallpaper in reds and yellows, and wished things were different with her youngest sister.

"I would like to ask your advice—help—with what to do about Trey, Mr. Van Cleve," she said.

"Let's not stutter-step," Caleb said, taking a cup of coffee from Norah, "Trey it is. What do you want me to do to him?"

"Nothing! I don't want you to do anything to him. I want you to help him."

"Help him what?"

"Stay alive. His sister is trying to kill him, and he won't do anything to stop her because she's his sister, and I want you to make her stop."

Caleb leaned back in his chair, dark eyes wide with disbelief. "You want me to kill his sister?"

"No, of course not, but I want.... Isn't there some other way to make her stop?" she said in a small voice.

"You better tell me the whole story."

She did. She told them everything, back to the time when Trey had described his sister as like Lady MacBeth before the murder and admitted Alice wanted him dead.

"So you don't know it's the sister," Caleb said when she finished. "You have a strong suspicion, but you don't have evidence."

"He said...."

"What he said, joking with a stranger, isn't evidence. His father is twisted enough to kill his own son if there was money in it, and his mother is a very strange woman. The sister's husband has all the same reasons she does, and there may be others. I'll talk to him."

Caleb was on his feet and headed out the door before Deborah registered what he was going to do. "No! You can't do that. You can't tell him I told you." She jumped up and started after him, but the door shut in her face.

"Make him listen. Make him stop," she implored Norah.

Norah stirred sugar into a fresh cup of coffee, unmoved. "You asked for help. He's going to help. You can't expect to tell him how to help when you don't have the slightest idea what to do yourself."

Deborah sat back down, unsure whether to be angry and at whom to be angry. "This is why I didn't ask him before. I knew he'd just go off like that without listening."

"He did listen. He just isn't going to take orders from someone who doesn't know a thing about what to do or how to do it. Trust him."

"Trust him? When the first thing he's going to do is talk to Trey?"

"How else are they going to resolve things? Calm down and stop fussing. We've been married almost twenty years, and it's never done me a bit of good, and it won't do you any good now. Tell me what's going on instead. Judith says you've been dragging Trey home and pulling his clothes off in her kitchen."

Deborah drew herself up very straight. "Judith is having you on. He was hurt because he came looking for me, and he wouldn't have done it except for Judith being ridiculous, and she ran off and wouldn't clean and bandage the wound, and I had to do it. I had to put in stitches."

Norah's dark brows did exactly the same annoying wiggle Judith's often did when the subject was Trey Van Cleve.

"That must have been an interesting evening." She rose, piled cookies from a tin box on a plate, and brought it to the table.

"If Miriam knew I was here, drinking her coffee and eating her cookies, she'd have a fit," Deborah said, helping herself to one of the cookies.

"I don't know. I've heard about your quarrel from everyone in the family except Miriam, and she's been very quiet when I've seen her. If she's as unhappy as she looks, she may be rethinking some of her positions. She spends too much time trying to impress some of the worst snobs in town, and I don't think Joseph likes it any more than you do."

They munched Miriam's cookies and drank her coffee companionably for a few moments until Deborah blurted, "He kissed me."

"Did he?" Norah didn't looked as surprised as Deborah thought she should. "I'd wager he's good at it, isn't he? He has the look of a man who would know how to kiss very satisfactorily."

Satisfactorily? "You can tell how a man kisses by the way he looks?"

"Of course not, but we're getting to know him a little now, aren't we? He spent that night with us. Are you telling me I'm wrong?"

"No, you're not wrong. At least he's better than the other two I know about."

"Two?"

"Hiram Johnson cornered me in the barn last spring. He held me by the arms, and the barn wall was behind me. I struggled and tried to get away, but he just...." Even telling it, her breath came in fast spurts. "I kicked him and that finally got through to him and he let me go. I told him if he ever did it again, I'd tell Caleb."

Norah's blue eyes had narrowed and her expression turned grim hearing the tale. Now she relaxed. "So that's why he went from tripping over your skirt hem to staying so far away Emma has to take him by the arm and drag him over to you. You should have told someone. Jason and Eli would have turned him inside out."

"I just wanted him to leave me alone, and since then he has. I can't imagine that he thought doing that was going to change my mind about him."

"Some men are remarkably arrogant that way. You said two. Who was the other?"

Deborah waved a hand. "Oh, years ago. Roy Kates. He didn't force me. He surprised me, and it was more like bumping his mouth on mine than a kiss. One of my front teeth even cut my lip a little. I slapped him, and he never tried it again either."

"Hmm. Do you know you've kissed more men than I have? I've only kissed husbands, and I've only had two of those. So Trey is the best of a poor lot?"

Deborah hesitated, examining her cousin's face with the laugh lines radiating from the corners of her eyes and mouth, and remembering all the years of understanding and love.

"He kisses as well as he shoots," she said slowly. "He asked me to marry him, you know, but he's changed his mind now."

"He asked you to marry him, you said yes, *and he changed his mind?*"

"I said no, but then when I asked him later, he said he had reconsidered and he didn't want me any more." Deborah squirmed on the chair a little then added the rest. "He said he didn't want to marry me unless I couldn't live without him."

"And what exactly does he think it means that you're running around hiring men to keep him safe and stitching him up in your sister's kitchen?"

"I think he knows how I feel, but he knows about me too. He figured it out from things I said and other people said, and when he asked me about it, I got so upset...." Even hinting at a subject she'd refused to say a word about all her life, even to Norah, who had always known, Deborah shuddered and whispered. "He knows."

"I'm sorry," Norah said, "but if things are the way I think between you, he needs to know."

"I think he believes if I admit how I feel, it will fix me, but nothing will fix me, will it?"

"I don't think people ever get fixed," Norah said thoughtfully. "Almost all of us are broken in some way, so we patch up the broken places and work around them. You can't believe with a family like his, Trey doesn't have some patched places himself."

Deborah had never considered it. He seemed perfect, handsome, whole. She thought of the scars she'd seen. She had a large family that loved her. Trey had one man, no relation by blood, he regarded as a brother—*he was dying and I was dead from the waist down.*

"I suppose you're right, but he deserves a wife like Judith, doesn't he? Someone who likes... things I don't."

"You didn't like this kiss?"

"Well, yes, but then.... It was too much, and he could tell, and he stopped."

"Too much?"

"I started to feel dizzy, and some places were—doing strange things."

"Oh, sweetheart, that's supposed to happen. If things—progress to their natural conclusion, that all makes it better."

"I don't want things to progress."

"Kiss him a few more times, and let his hands wander. I think you'll change your mind."

Deborah gaped at Norah, unable to believe what she just heard.

"Don't look at me like that," Norah said impatiently. "I'm not recommending you throw caution to the wind and risk no marriage and a child, but there's no reason not to enjoy some more of the kissing you know he's good at and try out a little of what else he's probably good at."

Deborah bit into a cookie with a snap to keep from saying anything. Respectable, married mothers of three, one of them a girl old enough to be in normal school, should not be handing out that kind of advice. Then again, kissing him another time or two couldn't hurt anything, could it?

TREY LOOKED UP at the sound of the bell and watched Cal Sutton stroll into the office as if he owned it. Surely Deborah wouldn't have her cousin paying visits over a kiss. She had seemed a willing participant in the whole experiment right till the end, and he'd stopped as soon as he sensed her slight withdrawal.

Oh, hell. "Are you here to shoot me?"

"I hear someone else is working his way up to that. Accidents, pipe, knife. Unless he's afraid of loud noises, it will be a gun next time."

So Deborah had sent him sure enough, and no one would send Cal Sutton away with a few laughing words and a month's pay for a working man. "So she sent you to watch over me?"

"That's what she wants, but I haven't got the time or the inclination. Nobody can keep anyone else safe, but we might catch him next time he tries."

Sutton leaned against the counter, looking down at Trey where he sat at the desk. Trey fetched another chair from the back room, positioned it on the other side of the desk, and gestured.

"With all the company I've been getting, I think I need to find another chair to keep here permanently." He reached into the bottom drawer and pulled out the whiskey and glasses he'd been keeping there since Jamie's last visit. "Too early for you?"

"I never figured what time of day had to do with it."

Trey poured. "You said 'catch him'. Deborah didn't convince you it's my sister?"

"Not particularly, but a woman could hire it done as easy as a man, and since you didn't recognize him, he's hired help. But if we catch him, I bet we can get a name out of him."

Trey would bet the same. "There's an old fellow who works at the ranch, Herman Gruner. He was there when I was a boy, so you may know him."

Sutton just nodded.

"He's too stove up to stay on a horse for long these days, so he takes care of the stock that's kept up around the home place, does odd jobs, anything to earn his keep and get to stay on. I've talked him into getting me some information."

Trey pulled his notes from the inside pocket of his jacket. "My sister and her husband have a home in Kansas City. For that matter my parents live there half the year these days too, but this year, when Alice found out she was expecting another child, they all dug in at the ranch. She lost her first at two months old to a fever, and they think the ranch is safer."

Sutton took a swallow of whiskey. "They must have been delighted when you came limping home after the government quarantined everyone who had been in Cuba for fear of the fevers."

Trey tipped his glass at Sutton, acknowledging the truth of that statement. "Alice was in favor of throwing me out on the spot. My father showed a preference for a live son over a possible grandson, which made Alice even more furious, and my mother had no opinion. My sympathies were with Alice. I should have left then, but I didn't have the energy."

The bargain with God that had brought Trey home was staying between the two of them where it belonged. Maybe he'd tell Deborah about it someday if.... Well, if.

Trey took a sip of his drink and went on. "The thing is Alice hasn't been off the ranch since I came home. According to Herman, she's guarding that baby like a lioness and still hasn't been to town. So if Alice hired someone, he has to work on the ranch, and I'd recognize anyone who works there. You can say she got one of the hands to do the hiring for her, but I don't think she's foolish enough to leave herself vulnerable like that."

"Someone on the ranch cut those reins."

"Yes, and that's one thing Alice could have done without help."

23

HER OWN MUDDLED feelings about the kiss haunted Deborah. Trey's attitude infuriated her. Except for a single wink over breakfast the next morning at Judith's, he went back to avoiding her and behaved as if nothing had happened.

Which made it easier for her to do the thing she had avoided so far—ask Caleb for help. Caleb and Norah lived far enough from Hubbell that their trips to town were two-day affairs, a day on the road to town, supper and an overnight stay with family, a morning buying supplies and a second day traveling home.

The morning after a family supper made awkward by Miriam's aloof presence, Deborah poked her head in the *Herald*'s office only long enough to tell Trey and Mr. Richmond she had someone to see and promise to sit at the desk in the afternoon. After that, she hurried to the general store, arriving only moments after it opened, but still after Caleb and Norah. Jacey had stayed home to take care of the farm this trip, and Ginny was thankfully nowhere in sight.

"I need to talk to you alone," she whispered to Caleb.

"What about her husband?"

"Vernon Forbes. He travels back and forth on business constantly, so he's more likely, but there's nothing telltale in his movements. He was at the ranch when the reins were cut and when the wagon almost ran me down, out of town for the pipe attack, and I don't know yet about this last time."

"What about your mother?"

"My mother? She has nothing to do with this. Why would my mother want me dead?"

"Let's see. She's angry because you ran off for ten years. She likes your sister better and wants her happy. After being married to your father for years, she hates all men, and you're a man. Having a son come home on crutches embarrasses her. You want more? Give me a minute, I can think of more."

"Don't bother. You're wrong, and you can forget about my mother."

"Your mother is not a forgettable woman."

There was no compliment in the words. Trey glared at Sutton. "You had better forget about her or stop drinking my whiskey and get out of here."

Sutton took another swallow. "Deborah mentioned a brother."

"A broth.... Oh, yes, Vernon's brother, Daniel. I suppose he could want to help his brother, or even think if everything goes to Vernon and Alice's son, it would benefit the whole Forbes family. You understand there's absolutely no chance my father is going to leave anything to my sister, Alice. If she never had a son, he'd leave it to a business partner sooner than a woman. The way he sees it, taking care of Alice is Vernon's job."

"Your sister and mother ought to get together and kill him. Even if there's no money in it, they could do it just for the pleasure."

"You are capable of a very ugly turn of thought."

"And for someone who's been lucky four times, you are capable of turning a dangerously blind eye. Got that from your mother, did you? Along with pure mule-headed stubbornness from your father? It's easy to see why Deborah thinks you're a fine fellow."

Trey considered smashing the whiskey bottle over Sutton's head, decided against it, and refilled their glasses instead. "You have room to talk."

"Not an inch. Have you considered Herman Gruner?"

"Of course not. He's just an old man who'd rather eke out a living cleaning out stables instead of cleaning up vomit in some saloon."

"And what happens to his living if you inherit?"

Trey opened his mouth to give the easy answer, then considered. "It goes away. I'd sell everything, the ranch piece by piece to people like you. Raising cattle on the dry lands to the west is one thing, wasting rich farmland with good water on cow pasture is another."

"So Herman has cause, or he may be in love with your mother," Sutton said, holding up a hand before Trey could leap to an indignant defense, "or your sister."

"He can't be that stupid. My father is no older than you, and he's healthy. There's no reason for anyone to worry about what's going to happen when he dies when it's twenty, thirty years away."

"Accidents happen. Someone's trying to see you never reach thirty. Maybe after you, they'll decide your father's been around long enough, not that he hasn't."

"It's crazy, all of it."

"It is, but crazy people don't always look crazy. I didn't know the regular hands on the ranch well, but Herman never struck me as a man I'd want at my back in a tight spot. He had a mean streak with a horse."

"He did? I never saw that." Trey thought about Irene, a gentle little mare, corralled with a bunch of horses half again her size, of Herman's attempts to hurry the boss's son on his way before he found out what Lenny was up to with the puppies. He didn't like where those thoughts led. "I suppose he wouldn't let me see that side of him."

"Not unless he saw some of the same in you."

"He'd have to hide it from my father too then. Much as you don't like him, and I don't admire him, my father has no use for meanness for its own sake. He wouldn't stand for someone abusing livestock or even the ranch dogs for that matter, and he wouldn't stand for one of his hands shirking or giving me a hard time. I knew he'd back me on firing Lenny, even when I was walking out."

"Lenny?"

"The hand I took the puppies from. I had to whack him across the legs with the cane, and if he were still in town, he'd top my list, but he took a train west a few days after he got here and had one leg in a cast when he did it. I can't see how he'd have the money to pay someone else to come after me or why he'd want to. He's one who would come after me himself."

"Probably so, and I guess you're thinking of a trap."

"I am."

"Can't be both bait and hunter."

"No, I was waiting until Jamie Lenahan got back to town."

"When is he due back?"

"Next week. I think his brother-in-law will help, so will Peter, Peter Richmond."

"Good. The more, the better our chances. Right now I need to get Norah and Ginny home and explain to my boy I'll be gone a few days, but next week I can spend a few days hunting." Sutton drained his glass, rose, and started for the door.

"Caleb. Don't tell Deborah."

"You tell your woman what you want to. I tell mine anything that concerns her. And you call me Cal. Caleb is for Norah and the girls."

"Cal Sutton is the man who had my mother so frightened she packed me and my sister up and took us to Tennessee for months. He walked into our house with a gun and hung bodies in front of the windows. I hated Cal Sutton most of my life. I think I could be friends with Caleb."

Sutton stared off as if seeing a different time and place. "I always felt bad about you and your sister, but war is war." He focused back on Trey. "If you have trouble with Cal, wrap your mouth around Mr. Sutton until you marry her. After that at least you'll be family."

Trey waited until Sutton was out of sight, trickled a little more whiskey in his glass, and hefted it in the air. "My woman," he said and gave in to laughter.

24

TREY MOVED FROM the new First Street Hotel to the old Hubbell Hotel located only three blocks from the office. The building had been renovated since the days it was shunned as a filthy last resort plagued by blood-sucking insects, but it still suffered in comparison with Jamie's old room.

Instead of fresh blue paint, blotchy gray coated the walls. No pleasant scent of floor wax floated through the air here. Cigar smoke dominated, but the underlying scent was of unwashed men.

Accommodations in Alaska would be worse, Trey reminded himself. He walked to the office morning and evening, sticking so close to the buildings no sharpshooter could get an angle on him from a rooftop on his side of the street. He set out at times when the streets were busy and blended in when he could.

For the first time he saw an advantage to his father's short stature. His own head stuck all too far above most of the people on the street.

Restless and pacing through the office, he accomplished little in spite of being at the desk every day. Deborah noticed, of course. After much internal debate, he told her the truth.

"You're going to let someone shoot at you so Caleb can shoot him?" she said, eyes wide with horror.

"No, we're going to let someone *try* to shoot me, or I suppose attack some other way. It's only a three-block field. Jamie will be back any day. He and Nolan will help. Peter's going to help. We're not going to kill anybody. The idea is to catch him and find out who hired him."

"Trey, please, please. If anything happens to you.... I can live without you, but I don't want to. Changing your name isn't so terrible. I did it. Judith and Miriam too, even though Miriam was too little to care. When we came to live with Uncle Jason and Aunt Emma, it just happened. No one ever said our name again. Judith and Miriam wrote it when they married, to be sure it was legal, but no one ever says—my father's name was Whales. Abel Whales."

Her face had paled, the big dark eyes glistened with unshed tears. He wanted to give in, wanted to give her anything and everything he could. If only in his years of drifting he hadn't known men who always faded away when trouble came. He'd seen what running did to a man, and he suspected what losing her family would do to a woman—his woman.

"You want me to change my name so you don't have to be Mrs. Van Cleve," he teased, unable to keep from reaching out, catching the bead of a tear with his thumb. She came to him, fit in against him as if she'd done it a hundred times before. He folded her in his arms, whispered with his lips against her temple. "Nothing will happen to me. We'll be careful. This fellow isn't a very good assassin, you know."

"Your luck can't last forever."

"Luck? You are supposed to tremble with admiration for my fighting skills."

She tipped her head up at him. "You shouldn't have to fight to stay alive."

Words weren't reassuring her, and she was relaxed in his arms. Her scent was light and fresh, like the spring breezes that would sweep out the last traces of winter in April and May. She had to feel the effect she was having on him, but he felt no resistance or withdrawal. Giving way to temptation, he closed his mouth over hers, unable to be as careful or gentle as the first time, wanting to possess and devour.

She kissed him back, yielded to the pressure of his tongue along her lips. Her arms wound around his neck and tightened as if she'd never let go. She followed his lead, made a soft sound in her throat when he coaxed her tongue far enough to him to suck....

The bell on the door jingled. "Ahem." Jamie's voice was full of laughter. "Why don't you do that closer to the window so everyone passing by can see better."

Trey's willing woman disappeared. Arms flailing, feet pedaling, she twisted away, a lovely pink suffusing her face as he watched. "I need to go to the mill this morning anyway. William says they've installed new equipment that will move sacks without the men having to do so much lifting."

"You're not going to the mill by yourself," Trey said. "That's a story for me to cover."

"You can't go. The equipment won't be new any more by the time you can go."

"I don't care. Get your brother-in-law to describe it to you in detail tonight over supper, but stay away from the mill unless he takes you there and brings you back."

The pink on her cheeks had brightened to red. "Fine. Just fine. I'll go see the Mayor. As if I haven't heard enough about paving streets and sewage disposal to last a lifetime."

She nodded at Jamie, grabbed her coat from its peg, and zipped out the door with it half on.

"If you'd spent more time toying with ladies in the past, you'd have learned better than to give orders like that," Jamie said. "Gets their dander up every time."

Trey turned to Jamie, who looked like an advertisement for a successful businessman in a knee-length tailored gray coat, a black derby tilted at a jaunty angle on his dark hair.

"We were doing fine until you showed up. If you could see so well through the window, you could have had the decency to go have a cup of coffee somewhere and come back later."

"That's a fine greeting. Would you prefer Mrs. Tindell to be the one seeing such a performance through your window? I've saved you from yourself."

"Save me like that one more time, and you won't receive a wedding invitation."

"Do you heathens send wedding invitations to the best man?"

"I haven't a clue." With Deborah no longer in sight to keep his total focus, Trey noticed the vehicle parked outside in the street. "Is that one of them? Criminy, it is just a horseless carriage, isn't it? It looks just like my buggy, but without shafts."

"It's superior to your buggy in every way. That is a Columbia Runabout and can be yours for a mere nine hundred and fifty dollars. Come take a look."

"And how much did it cost you?"

"Seven fifty," Jamie said with a grin, "but we had to pay the railroad to get it here. Don't forget that."

Trey followed Jamie outside, giving no more than a passing thought to what kind of target he'd make in the street. He was tired of worrying about it. If Jamie wasn't exaggerating, this contraption could move at speeds up to fifteen miles an hour. A man who had fumbled killing with a pipe and knife probably couldn't hit a moving target with a gun.

He'd hear about the trip and the new vehicles, take his first automobile ride, and fill Jamie in on the plan to catch the would-be killer. By the time Deborah returned, she might be amenable to another kiss or two, this time safely out of sight in the back room.

DEBORAH PUSHED OPEN the heavy wooden door and left the thick air of the flour mill behind. How did men work all day in that atmosphere? William's office was bearable, but down where the grain was ground, the sacks filled? She had thought the sound of the press churning out the *Herald* in the back room once a week too noisy. Now she knew—the presses and the machines on the farm barely whispered.

Turning up her collar against the bitter March wind, she looked around for a place to sit and wait for William. He had been as unhappy as Trey that she'd come here alone and insisted she wait until he could give her a ride home. In truth she was happy to wait. In spite of her lovely new Christmas boots, walking back and forth over most of the town day after day was taking a toll on her feet.

Here in front of the massive stone building, the sounds of machinery, men shouting, and wagons coming and going sounded faint. Unable to find anything else, she sat on the low brick wall that separated the yard from the visitors' drive. Her bottom would get cold, but she didn't want to go back inside. Now that her notebook and mind were crammed with details that would make an excellent story, she wanted to think.

There had to be a way to make Trey give up this dangerous plan. There had to be a way to make him leave Hubbell. Agreeing to marry him had been an abject failure. She admitted to herself the thought of living without him was unbearable, but so was the thought of living with him knowing he was unhappy because she was—as she was.

The door opened, and William hurried down the walk without a coat. "I'm sorry, but I need to deal with a situation that's arisen. Come back inside and warm up. I won't be long."

Deborah rose, unwilling to return inside, but not eager to walk a mile across town either. Movement out on the road caught her eye. She watched in wonder as a buggy with no horse rolled up the drive toward them.

"Truly a horseless carriage," she said to William in delight.

"Is that Van Cleve's Irish friend?"

Deborah pretended not to hear any disapproval in the question. "It is."

The vehicle stopped in front of them, and Jamie Lenahan jumped down. After Deborah made introductions, he said, "Trey asked if I'd demonstrate a Columbia Runabout to his best reporter by giving her a ride back to the office."

"Oh, I'd like that." She turned to William. "Thank you so much for showing me the mill and offering me a ride, but I'll go with Mr. Lenahan. Do go back inside, William. Judith will never forgive me if you contract pneumonia standing out here without a coat."

She couldn't tell if William's unhappy look had more to do with the cold turning his ears red and his lips blue or reluctance to leave her with Mr. Lenahan.

"Is this thing safe?" he asked, giving the vehicle a critical look.

"Safer than horses," Lenahan said. "I've driven one hundreds of miles now without a single mishap."

William continued to frown, but he helped Deborah to the automobile's seat, gave Lenahan one more stern look, and returned inside.

"Trey didn't really send you, did he?" Deborah said as the door closed behind William.

"Of course not. I have spent my adult years studying the workings of the female mind, but Trey is an innocent. It would never occur to him that after he told you not to come here, that's the first thing you did."

"I don't know why not. It's not like he listened to me when I begged him to give up this stupid plan he has to act as human bait and rely on you and your brother-in-law to keep him alive."

"And your killer cousin, don't forget him."

"Caleb is probably the only one who possibly could keep anyone safe. What kind of shot are you?"

"Decent enough to hit a man at the distance we're expecting, nothing like Trey or your cousin."

He started the automobile moving, and Deborah held on as she never had in a buggy. "Oh, without the horse in front I feel as if I'm going to fall forward on my head."

Lenahan laughed. "Give it a minute, you'll get used to it. You're less likely to fall, because an automobile isn't going to spook over a dog running in the street, or bolt over a loud noise."

They glided along for a few minutes, and gradually she relaxed. "I expected it to be loud, but it's so quiet. What is that whirring sound beneath us?"

"It has a chain, like a bicycle. We visited companies that are manufacturing steam powered machines and machines with gasoline powered engines, but these electric vehicles seemed most practical. The steam engines take too long to get going and if the pressure gets too high, boom! And where would you buy gasoline in Hubbell? We have a coal-powered electric generator of our own now. We'll charge batteries for customers until the town electrifies."

Deborah didn't know what gasoline was, much less where to get it, and had no understanding of charging batteries, but she loved the Runabout.

She waved at acquaintances and friends alike as she and Lenahan rolled past the surprised faces. "Oh, I do like this. Do we have to go straight to the office?"

He turned toward the east side of town. "We can go at least twenty more miles before this little wonder will need a charge, but after a turn around town, I'd better take you home. If you go straight to the office and Trey sees that floury look, you'll have to 'fess up."

Deborah looked down and saw the dusting of white on the shoulders of her dark blue coat. She tried to brush it off and only succeeded in creating a smear.

"It gets into everything," Lenahan said. "You'll find it on your hat and in your hair."

"He'll be able to tell when I write the story that I've been there. I'll tell him before then, but not today."

They passed horse corrals. The animals watched with curiosity but no fear that Deborah could see. Did they worry about being replaced and no longer considered worth keeping by the humans who provided hay and grain? What a foolish, fanciful thought.

"I owe you an apology," she said to Lenahan. "I'm sorry I was so rude when I asked for your help. I thought you were taking advantage of him. I thought you were just someone he employed when he was ill after the war. I didn't realize how terribly he was hurt and what you did for each other and that you're more like brothers."

"No apology needed. You were right. I did take advantage. I presumed on friendship and asked for money for something he didn't believe in because I knew he could afford it."

"He believes in you. You helped each other through bad times someone like me can't understand. I'm glad the automobiles are a success for you, and I understand why that is now. This is wonderful. I'd love to have one for going back and forth all over town. It would be so much easier to find somewhere to leave this than a horse and buggy. Could I learn to drive one?"

"You could. I've seen ladies driving them back East." He hesitated a moment, then said, "I owe you an apology too. I thought you were wrong for him, and I tried to put him off you. It's what we quarreled about. I shouldn't have done it, and I was wrong to boot."

The joy went out of the automobile ride. "You weren't wrong," she said. "I wish you had succeeded. I love him, but I'll never be able to make him happy. He should have someone better."

Lenahan glanced sideways at her, surprise on his face. "I don't think 'should have' comes into it. It's you he wants, and he's a stubborn man. It would take you years to make him take no for an answer."

She smiled at that but didn't say anything.

"When I first met him, he offered to pay for medicine for the fever, something other than plain quinine the Army was giving men like me. I almost turned down the chance. Pride came into it, but I was afraid too, afraid it wouldn't work. How foolish was that? I was dying before, and if it didn't work, I'd still be dying, no worse off at all."

Lenahan drew up in front of Judith's house and helped Deborah down. She hurried inside, glad to be out of the cold, and watched through a front window as the Runabout disappeared down the street. Which was worse, she wondered, fear of dying, or fear of living?

JAMIE BROUGHT TWO more men into the plan, making a total of six watching the three blocks between the Hubbell Hotel and the *Herald's* office—Jamie, Nolan, Peter, Caleb, Shanahan, and Maguire. They positioned themselves in the cold, predawn hours, two in alleys, four on roofs.

Trey made the walk from hotel to office, not totally abandoning his previous caution, but leaving himself open as he crossed the two intersections, the back of his neck tingling with every step.

For three mornings, nothing happened. Trey couldn't even commiserate with the blue-lipped men going to such lengths for him as they warmed up over breakfast out of sight at the Daltons' house.

On the fourth morning, Trey approached the first intersection as he had every day, shoulders tight, cane clenched tightly in his fist. A single shot rang out. He dove to the ground and rolled, kept rolling until he reached the walk. Jamie shouted. Caleb cursed. Men and women on the street ran.

On his feet again, Trey saw his small army all on the ground, converging around something in the alley between the bank and an office building.

Caleb had been the one positioned on the roof of the two-story bank building.

"It's where I'd set up," he had said. "Of course this fellow doesn't seem to be any good at killing. He may sit in an alley."

Trey had swallowed hard at the words. He knew all too well how very good Caleb was at killing. "We need him alive."

"We need you alive too. Deborah's not a forgiving sort."

Now Trey joined the others around the body. Dead, the man who had looked so large wielding a pipe looked smaller, flat. "So you had to shoot him after all?"

"I shot over his head and told him to stand, and he took off running. Damn fool tried to jump the alley. It must be fifteen feet. Even so I expected him to be alive down here. Dying, but alive long enough for a few questions."

"He broke his neck," Jamie said. "Look at the angle. Someone will have heard that shot and run for the police. They'll be here any minute. Tell them he jumped."

Jamie and Nolan jogged down the alley and disappeared, Shanahan and Maguire at their heels. "I'll wait for you at the office," Peter said, also hurrying away.

"You need to go too," Trey said to Caleb. "I'll deal with the police."

"In a minute." Caleb knelt by the body and began searching through pockets. "I'd like to know who he was."

But not a single scrap of paper hinted at the man's identity. The only thing in any pocket was a small wad of cash. "Fifty dollars," Caleb said, pocketing it. "No wonder he wasn't much good, he came too cheap."

Trey considered arguing over disposal of the cash and gave it up as futile. Without an identity and family to claim it, that money was going into someone's pocket. It might as well be Caleb's.

"Too bad he was suicidal," Caleb said. "At least the target will be off your back for a few days until somebody takes his place. Get rid of the police, and you can buy us all breakfast at the café. Maybe somebody has an idea what to do next. I sure don't."

Trey watched Caleb disappear down the alley like the Irishmen before him. As if on cue, two policemen appeared, still blocks away, but striding toward the bank fast. Trey leaned back against the bank building and waited.

25

TREY HAD ADMITTED that Deborah's story about the mill—and her story was really about the mill and the men who worked there, not just about the new machinery—was excellent. He had also walked around for days after she confessed to walking there alone muttering about sneaky women.

She would have known even without that broad hint, however, that when William insisted on walking her to the office each morning and Peter insisted on walking her home, Trey was behind their sudden concern. He wanted to make sure she didn't interfere with his insane plan to trap the killer. The only surprise was that he hadn't arranged with Judith and William to lock her in her room.

How he could think she'd sneak into the middle of his trap, she couldn't imagine. She wasn't the kind of woman who did things like that. On the fourth morning, she set out with William, thinking the extra danger would be over soon. Caleb was already showing signs of restlessness. He wouldn't stay away from Norah and the farm much longer.

As they walked, she became aware of excited buzzing among the people they passed. Her heart started beating faster and took flight when she heard the words, "Shot him dead."

William had a firm grip on her arm. "Let's return home and wait. We'll hear what happened soon enough."

Deborah twisted and struggled but couldn't break his hold. Finally, she stopped fighting. "If you don't let go of me right now, I'm going to hit you and start screaming," she said coldly.

"Deborah, please."

"Right. Now."

He let go. She ran until she reached the hotel, ran along the path she knew Trey had taken, and found where it had happened by the crowd gathering around. Pushing through the line of spectators, she saw him, leaning against a building. Alive. Whole.

She would kill him herself. Wring his neck. Smash him to smithereens. Close now, she launched at him, wrapped her arms around his neck and kissed him hard. Only her skirt stopped her from wrapping legs around him too. Forced to stop for breath, she shook his shoulders. "You. You. I heard *shot*. I heard *dead*. How could you? How could you?"

Behind her a whistle sounded, then a scattering of applause. She let go and stepped back, cheeks burning.

"I'm sorry," William said, stopping beside them, panting, leaning over with his hands on his thighs. "I couldn't hold her and couldn't catch her."

"I should never have asked you to try," Trey said.

He had an absolutely idiotic grin on his face. As if they weren't standing next to a dead body. As if the police weren't there with suspicious faces. As if she hadn't just made a spectacle of them both. Uncle Eli had looked like that once—after several drinks to celebrate the birth of his first son.

Trey waved at the goggle-eyed bystanders. "Read all about it in this week's paper. Miss Deborah Ann Whales Sutton and Webster Alexander Van Cleve, III."

Oh. That explained it.

Deborah didn't say another word until they were back in the *Herald's* office. "I never said I'd marry you."

"Do I have to get down on one knee and make a fool of myself asking so you can say yes properly? If I do, I probably won't be able to get up again without your help."

"I won't say yes."

"You asked me not long ago."

"That was different. You haven't met my condition, and you said no, so I withdrew the offer."

"You never met my condition either, although I've decided 'don't want to live without me' is an acceptable alternative to 'can't live without me'."

"That's very generous of you, but no."

"What if I drag you off to a cave like some Viking and keep you there until you say yes."

"Vikings had ships not caves, and you'd end up doubled over panting like William because you couldn't catch me."

She couldn't help but smile at the memory. Trey smiled back. They both started laughing and ended up in each other's arms. This kiss was the best so far. The very best.

"Next week?" he whispered against her mouth.

"Oh, Trey, you have no idea. You need to marry someone like Judith, someone who can make you happy. I can't be a wife. I can't."

"Because of something that happened when you were seven years old?"

She stiffened and tried to pull away. "Don't...."

He kept his arms around her. "Sweetheart, at the risk of damaging my own cause, I have to point out I have my own scars. Let's take a chance on each other anyway."

She closed her eyes and burrowed against his neck. "Your scars are just marks on the skin."

"No, they're not. I'm past the point of waking up every morning afraid to try moving for fear it won't work, but I still have nightmares about how I'll be in ten years, or twenty, or thirty. Marry me, and there's no telling how soon you'll have a useless lump of a husband in a wheelchair."

"That's not true. You're better all the time. You say you'll never be able to run again, but you will. You probably could right now."

"Ask any stove-up cowhand what happens to old injuries as the years pass. Nothing ever gets better, and you should know if we never have children the fault will be mine. The part of me needed for that was the last to show life again. In fact it never twitched until the first time I saw you."

She smothered something between a laugh and a sob off against his shoulder. "Now I know you really are a liar."

"No, God's truth. The day I saw you in the ice cream parlor was the first stirring. I almost flew over to the first empty table, half because I was giddy with relief and half because I needed to hide."

"Then it was the sight of Judith."

"Judith was waving her spoon at Jamie. Watching a woman admire another man does not inspire lust."

"Miriam."

"Miriam is a mere child, and she's plain compared to you."

"If we all did our hair the same and dressed the same, you couldn't tell us apart from across a large room."

"Oh, yes, I could. Blindfolded, I could pick you out. Something would just pull me to you."

"Flatterer. Liar."

"Say yes. Let's take a chance on each other. On us."

She gave in. "Yes," she whispered against his cheek. "Yes," again into his kiss.

THE ONLY WAY to marry Deborah in one week would indeed be to carry her off like a Viking. Judith had plans. As soon as Deborah's aunts got word, they joined in, as did Norah.

Trey made his own plans. He wanted to build a life in Hubbell, finish turning the paper into something the town and even the county found of value, watch Jamie's business grow, and keep Deborah close to the comfort of her family. For that matter, he didn't mind marrying a whole family himself.

Still, if another killer showed up, they'd pull up stakes. Not Alaska or even Montana. Somewhere warmer, although not the oven of Arizona. California maybe. He said nothing to Deborah, found a house not far from the office and made plans—and plans.

At least Deborah didn't try to make him worry about hats and dresses and flowers that weren't available this early in the year. She came up with concerns a man could handle.

"If we get married, do I have to stay home and dust furniture?" Deborah stopped typing and looked up to where he was writing a story by hand on the counter.

"What do you mean 'if'? You said yes."

"All right, when. After."

"Of course not. We can get someone to come in once or twice a week for that."

"Just doing laundry takes a whole day."

He waved a hand in the air. "That's what laundries are for."

"We need another desk."

"And chair. I'll talk to someone."

The door crashed open so hard the only sound from the bell was a metallic rattle. Trey reached for the pistol he had taken to carrying, then let his hand fall away. "Father."

Webster Van Cleve slapped a copy of the *Herald* on the counter. "If you want to see your sister's son with everything that should be yours, you just go ahead and do it."

Trey stared at his father's angry face. "I told you a hundred times I don't want any of it. You never listened to a word, and now you're telling me all I had to do was marry a Sutton? If I'd known that, I'd have married at sixteen."

His father flushed an ugly red. "You damned fool. Once it was yours, if you wanted to run every business like a charity, you could. You'd lose most of it in your lifetime, but you could do any damn thing you want."

"What I want is no part of any of it. Sign the papers, and we'll publish notice in the paper. Trey Van Cleve, disinherited at last."

His father pointed a finger at him. "You'll publish no such thing. I'll tell your mother and sister my own way. Don't ever set foot on the ranch again. Stay away from your mother and sister. You're worse than an embarrassment, you're a blood traitor."

Trey felt Deborah's hand on his back, saw his father's focus switch, and his chest swell as he drew more breath.

"Say it, and I'll knock you right through the front window," Trey hissed. "Father or no, say it, and I'll knock every tooth in your mouth down your throat."

Another glare, and his father turned and walked out, this time slamming the door so hard the glass cracked and the bell fell to the floor with a clang. Deborah pressed her fore-head against Trey's shoulder. "How did you ever grow up to be you?"

Trey rested his cheek against her hair, breathed deep of her scent. "The tutor he hired when I was five was big on morals and ethics. Father never paid much attention to us at that age, so he didn't realize what was happening until I was eleven. He kicked the poor man off the ranch the day he found out. And there's my mother's family. They're good people, and we lived with them for months once. Visited for a couple of weeks most years."

They leaned against each other wordlessly for a few moments until Deborah said, "Do you think this means you're safe now?"

"I hope so. It would be just like the old son of a gun to make that scene and then wait to see if I come to heel before doing anything. Let's not worry about it today."

Trey led her to the back room. "Peter, go get a cup of coffee."

Peter looked up from the linotype machine with resigna-tion. "Again?"

"Again."

"This wedding can't come fast enough," Peter muttered as he left.

Amen to that, Trey thought.

26

As a girl Deborah had loved pretty clothes as much as her sisters. That changed when she first noticed men and boys following her with their eyes. Plain clothes of heavy materials made slightly too large had been one of her many ways of hiding.

Dressing to fit in at the social events she attended for the paper had begun to bring back her former pleasure in pretty things. Her wedding dress completed the transformation. Every fitting had been a pleasure. Looking at the frothy creation of creamy lace and silk in the full length mirror in Judith's bedroom, Deborah almost forgot her nerves.

"You look lovely," Aunt Em said, fussing over the drape of lace across the bodice.

"Beautiful," Judith said, whirling in her own spring green silk. "Exquisite. He'll pass out at the front of the church when he sees you, and we'll have to run and fetch water to throw on him to get him up again."

Deborah's stomach lurched. "Thank you, dear sister. I always count on you to calm my anxieties."

"What anxieties?" Judith started to hug her, backed off before Aunt Em pulled her away to save the lace, and settled for hands on both of Deborah's cheeks. "He loves you. You love him, and tomorrow you'll be off on a wonderful wedding trip."

"And Mr. Richmond will be putting out the paper alone again. Trey thinks circulation will fall by half before we return."

"He was joking. You know he was joking. Stop looking for things to worry about. You even have a perfect spring day. It rained the day William and I got married."

Deborah had to think back. Her strongest memory was of the way Judith had lit up the church and the hall where they held the reception with her joy. "I do remember. I remember Uncle Jason and Uncle Eli holding an oilskin over you like a canopy so your hat and dress didn't get wet on the way to the church."

"And that was in June. I wonder why everyone thinks June is the best month to marry. April is obviously better, fresh spring air, warm, perfect wedding weather."

April weather was also notoriously fickle, but Deborah didn't say so.

"There are flowers in June," Aunt Em said. "Brides don't have to carry bouquets made of artificial flowers with wire stems."

"Do you really think it's all right that we decided on the church here in town?" Deborah asked. "Have Caleb and Norah said anything about having to come to town and stay overnight? I know it's harder on all of you."

"If you ask that one more time, I swear I'm going to pinch you," Aunt Em said. "We'd be happy to get on the train and travel anywhere we had to for this, and you know it. I never thought I'd see this day, and now here we are, and I still have trouble—Van Cleve—and he's such a nice young man, who would ever believe it?"

"It was an accident," Deborah said. "His father hired the wrong tutor."

Her aunt gave her a questioning look, but Judith burst out laughing. "You mean the right one."

A tap sounded on the door, and Judith went to answer it, still chuckling.

Miriam. "May I come in?" she asked.

"Of course you can," Deborah said.

"You look so beautiful. That dress is...." Miriam made a helpless gesture with one hand indicating she had no words.

"It is, isn't it?" Deborah said, unable to keep her own delight in the dress out of her voice.

"I hoped I could speak with you a moment before we left for the church."

Judith grabbed Aunt Em by the arm and pulled her toward the door. "Minutes, only minutes, and if you're not downstairs and ready to leave for the church on time, I'm sending William and Uncle Jason to pick you up and carry you to the buggy. You do not want that. It would crush the lace."

Deborah regarded her youngest sister thoughtfully. "You look very beautiful yourself, Miriam. You always do." In truth Miriam had often looked better. Dark circles shadowed her eyes.

"I came to apologize, to tell you.... Joseph and I quarreled before Christmas. He thinks I.... Well, we've resolved that for the most part, but it made me say things to you I never should have, and I want you to know I'm sorry for that and even more for turning you away. No matter what I think of what you're doing, you're still my sister, and I love you, and I'm sorry." Her face twisted as she fought tears.

Deborah forgot about the lace and hugged Miriam tight. "Oh, Miriam, lots of families have one odd stick. Laugh me off to your fancy friends."

"I can't. I hate it when your name comes up and they look as if they smelled something bad, or say things."

"They're quick enough to want me there writing about their social events for the paper." At least they had been ever since Trey had set Mrs. Snopes straight.

"I know. That makes it worse somehow."

"If you can't laugh, then look martyred and try for sympathy."

"Now you sound like Judith."

"That's the nicest thing you ever said to me."

They smiled at each other, Miriam's smile a little watery.

"I didn't want you to think I was sitting in the church wishing you anything but the best today. I want you to be happy. I really do."

Deborah hugged her again. "I never doubted that for a minute. Now you need to wash your face, and I need to go downstairs before everyone gets nervous for fear I've run off to hide."

One last glance in the mirror and a little fluffing of lace, and Deborah was ready. All she needed to do was remember to breathe.

"You've got this place fixed up as good as new," Jamie said.

Engrossed in his third attempt to make his tie look like something other than a used lariat tied by a man without thumbs, Trey concentrated on his own image in the mirror.

"I didn't do anything but hire painters. Deborah did the rest."

The house was farther from the office than he would have liked, but a rundown bargain. In truth, he'd had carpenters and plasterers working around the clock these last weeks, but the soft blues and greens Deborah had chosen for the rooms already made the house seem like home, even without much furniture.

The kitchen was the only room Trey had expressed an opinion over. Yellow with blue trim. From the look she gave him, Deborah knew exactly why he wanted that combination. She hadn't said anything, but she'd picked the perfect shades of each color.

"I'd do that for you, but I never tied anything that wasn't on my own neck," Jamie said.

A knock sounded on the front door.

"Oh, damn," Trey said, yanking out his latest effort. "Get that, will you? Make whoever it is go away."

He half listened to voices from downstairs, footsteps approaching.

"Mr. Lenahan says you need help with your tie."

Trey whirled at the familiar voice. Cool as ever, his mother took the limp piece of cloth from him. "Do you have an iron? Or another tie?"

Wordlessly, he handed her the next tie he had planned to ruin.

"I checked them both for weapons," Jamie said, walking back into the room, shooing Alice ahead of him.

"He did not," Alice said indignantly, "and it's a good thing." She glared over her shoulder.

Unperturbed, Jamie leaned against the door frame and folded his arms over his chest.

Trey lifted his chin as his mother worked on his tie, feeling ten years old and ridiculously pleased over it. "I didn't expect to see you today. I was afraid you wouldn't even get the invitation."

"Your father and I have had a discussion," his mother said. "You are not welcome at the ranch, but who I visit when I am in town is my own decision."

Trey almost choked, and it had nothing to do with the tie. His mother had never opposed his father in his memory, and she didn't come to Hubbell except to take the train to another destination.

Finished with the tie, she gave him a little pat on the chest. "Tell me you aren't marrying this woman just to plague your father."

"I'm marrying her because I love her. I was half in love with her before I knew who she was."

Another pat. "Good. I want you to be happy. It's all I ever wanted for either of you."

She looked exquisite, dressed for the wedding in peach silk with a matching hat. The gloves she had removed to work on his tie matched as well.

The temptation proved too great. He pulled her into a bear hug, picked her up and whirled her in a circle.

"My goodness." Straightening her dress, she retrieved her gloves. "I believe your sister would like to talk to you alone. If Mr. Lenahan would be so kind as to show me out."

Trey eyed his sister. "You look good, Alice. It's good to see you."

She did look good. The simple lines of her yellow dress suited her sturdy frame, and a frothy hat without much brim added height.

"Herman told Mother someone tried to kill you. You can't believe I had anything to do with it."

"No, I don't."

"I was so angry I hardly remember everything I said. You just waltzed back into our lives after nine years. Nine years!"

"Hardly waltzed."

"But I never would do anything to hurt you. You must know that."

"You were pretty convincing, but in the end, yes, I do know that. Let's just forget it all. It was an emotional time, and at least your children will have what you want. Where is my nephew? Do I get to see him?"

"Vernon has him at the hotel. Mother and I will be the only ones at the church, but we'll bring Web to the reception long enough for you to meet him."

"Web. I hope he wears it better than I did."

"That wouldn't be hard." She looked away, smoothed the fingers of her gloves. "You know Father hasn't signed anything yet. I wouldn't even know he had a new will drawn and ready except Mother told me. I think he's hoping you won't go through with it."

"Not a chance. Deborah may panic and run off, but that's his only hope."

"I don't understand you. How can you not want the ranch, not want something?"

"I don't understand you either. He's going to live another forty years. By that time you'll have grandchildren and should be past caring. Make your own lives, you and Vernon."

"That's what Vernon says too. We'll be going home soon."

"Good." He didn't pick her up and whirl her around, but he gave her a hug and kiss on the cheek. "I'm glad you came and glad we talked."

"If you really love her, you don't care who's here and who isn't."

Trey shrugged into his jacket and followed her out of the room. "You're right, but I care about you, and I'm glad you're here."

DEBORAH DROPPED HER bouquet again.

Judith picked it up, frowning at the stiff, artificial flowers. "We should have settled for the sickly hothouse carnations. I thought I wrapped the wires well enough they wouldn't bother your hands."

"They're fine. I can't feel the wires." Deborah's icy hands couldn't feel anything, which was why she kept dropping the bouquet.

"I think the matron of honor has to dance at least once with the best man," Judith said. "I hope Mr. Lenahan knows that. I hope he's a good dancer."

"Judith."

"What Judith? Don't look at me like that. You listen to me. Keeping a husband on his toes should be part of every wife's strategy. I have no intention of ever letting William become complacent. And life is much more fun this way."

Would the piano never start? They stood on the steps of the church, waiting. Uncle Jason looked as calm as ever. Judith bounced on her toes.

Deborah examined the grass that ran around the side of the church to the alley behind.

"Oh, no, you don't."

"Ouch!" Judith's hat brim bumped hers so hard Deborah recoiled, feeling the pull on hat pins and hair pins alike.

"I'm sorry," Judith said, right in Deborah's face, "but you are not going to run off, not even if Uncle Jason and I have to sit on you and ruin that dress."

"I'm not running anywhere," Deborah said, giving the beckoning escape route one last look.

The piano music started. Finally. Uncle Jason swung the door open.

"The Methodists have an organ," Judith muttered as she disappeared inside.

"If you're going to run, now is the time," Uncle Jason said, smiling.

Deborah took his arm. "No more running." Maybe she even meant it.

Although not tightly packed, guests filled every pew, and every one of them was turned, looking back at her. Her knees wobbled. Only the solid support of Uncle Jason's arm made walking possible.

Aunt Em, Judith, and Norah had each assured Deborah that once she saw Trey waiting at the front of the church, once she met his eyes, she would see nothing else. How could she look past that sea of faces and find him?

Open windows on each side of the building let warm, sweet spring air circulate. Dragging in a breath of that air, Deborah stared at the windows. A shadow crossed one. Again. As if.... Distinct this time. Only a few inches, but long and narrow.

"The window," Deborah gasped, jerking Uncle Jason to a halt and pointing. Too afraid to say more, she let go of his arm and ran. Outside, across the grass that had beckoned earlier, into the narrow space between buildings. The man who had not been quite careful enough about the shadow of his gun barrel ran too, away from her, with a stiff, awkward gait.

Deborah caught him easily, crashed into his back, and fell to the ground on top of him. He tried to push her away, hit at her with the rifle. The blow landed on her shoulder and only increased her fury. She smashed him in the face with the bouquet in her hand. Artificial flowers fell from their wires. She struck again and again in a frenzy. "You think—kill Trey—I'll kill you!"

When hands tried to pull her away, she fought them just as hard, until Trey's voice broke through her fury. Trey's hands restored her reason. She wrapped herself around him, panting and shaking. "He was.... He was...."

"Sshh. I know. I know. It's all right now. They've got him. They've got him." He shook her gently. "Forget about him. What about you? Are you all right?"

She kept her face buried against his neck. "I'm fine. My dress is ruined, isn't it?"

"Looks good to me."

Which was a lie. He couldn't possibly know what it looked like with her pressed tight against him. She raised her head long enough to take in the scene around them. Her uncles had Herman Gruner on his feet, hands tied behind his back. Bloody red stripes covered his face. Gruner's rifle dangled from Caleb's hand.

Wedding guests had spilled out of the church and crowded into the narrow alley. Trey's mother pushed through them.

"Did you know she was here?" Deborah whispered to Trey.

"I did. She and Alice came to visit me earlier."

Mrs. Van Cleve walked right up to Gruner. "Herman?" she said as if unable to believe her eyes.

He refused to look at her. "Killing him's the only way," he mumbled. "The only way to make it all like it used to be."

Trey had said his mother never showed emotion, but she looked both astonished and angry now. "You told me someone tried to.... You? You tried to kill my son?"

Gruner's head jerked back from Mrs. Van Cleve's slap.

A short, dark-haired woman who must be Trey's sister put an arm around her mother and pulled her away, after calling Gruner a name Deborah didn't think ladies ever spoke out loud.

Everyone was looking at Trey—and her. Deborah had no urge to let go of him, but she finally did. For a second, the same sappy look she'd seen on his face in the alley next to the dead body flashed across his face.

He touched her cheek. "Next time you throw yourself in my arms, you have to be laughing."

"I didn't throw...." Maybe she had. Laughing?

"What do you want to do?" he said. "Tell all these people to come back in an hour? Tomorrow? Next week?"

"No! I don't want to spend another sleepless night worrying about what I'm doing to you. Let's get married. Right now."

Trey looked at the Sutton men. "Dealing with the police will take hours. Can you stash him somewhere?"

"I believe the church has a basement," Uncle Jason said. "Don't start until we get back."

He and Eli ignored Gruner's struggles and dragged him away.

Aunt Em fussed, smoothing lace wherever she could reach. "Deborah, honey, if you would just stand straight, we need to see what we can do about your dress—and hat—and hair."

Deborah stood still while every female in sight fussed over her grass stains and torn lace. None of it mattered to her any longer. Trey waited, and they walked to the altar arm in arm.

THE WEDDING FLEW by in a blur. Deborah had vague impressions of Uncle Jason joining her at the front of the church, giving her away. Of saying the words the pastor led her to say, of a ring sliding on her finger. As predicted, the memory that stayed with her was of Trey's eyes, his voice, his kiss.

The pleasant fog surrounding her disappeared in the squat old building the Hubbell town police used as their head-quarters. Trey didn't want her there. The police did.

"I'm sorry, sir," the chief of police said, "but if Mrs. Van Cleve is the only one who saw Mr. Gruner point the rifle at you, she needs to tell us about it."

"He confessed. There's no reason she can't join her family at the wedding reception." Trey paused then added, "Our families."

Deborah laid a hand on his arm. "I want to be here. I want to tell what happened, and then I want to hear what Mr. Gruner has to say for himself."

"Now, that's not possible," the chief said. "We can't have a woman—ordinary citizens—sitting in while we question a suspect."

Trey switched sides like lightning. He leaned back in his chair and folded his arms. "Why not? My wife is the one who captured Herman. If she wants to hear what he has to say, why shouldn't she? And if you want to hear what she has to say...."

The chief's eyes were small in his heavy face and grew smaller as he stared at them. "If that's a threat, I could just release him."

"Of course you could," Trey agreed. "I'll write up the whole incident in the paper exactly as it happened. We'll only have to postpone our wedding trip a day or two. By the time the next edition comes out, I'll be able to report that you released Herman and now he's missing, presumed dead, and the Hubbell police have no idea which Sutton or Van Cleve to point a finger at."

The two men eyed each other while Deborah looked around the dark, dirty room. She didn't want to stay here one minute longer than necessary.

Judith would treat the police chief to a saucy smile, bat her eyelashes, and have him giving her anything she wanted in no time at all. Miriam would do delicate female distress to perfection and achieve the same result. Deborah knew if she tried either of those things every man in the room, including Trey, would roll on the filthy wood floor laughing.

"Please, I know it's irregular, but could you just leave a door cracked so we could listen if we promise not to interfere? Someone has been trying to kill Mr. Van...."

Trey stopped glaring at the police chief and shot her a hard look. Reality set in. "My husband," Deborah said, testing the words out and finding them to her liking. "Someone has been trying to kill my husband for months, and it would be reassuring to know that Mr. Gruner is responsible for it all."

After all, Trey had reported the earlier attacks to the police, even though he'd downplayed them and attributed them to a would be robber and belligerent drunk at the time.

"You think old Herman attacked you with a pipe—or a knife?" the chief asked now.

"No," Trey said. "If he was involved, he paid someone else, probably that fellow who missed his jump and broke his neck falling off the bank building a while back."

The chief made a sound of disbelief. "Where would Herman Gruner get money to pay anyone? He's been doing odd jobs at the V Bar C for no more than found for years."

"I'm embarrassed to admit he got at least part of it from me. I've been paying him to keep me informed about the comings and goings of everyone at the ranch. It serves me right to know what he did with that money, and he probably had savings. He earned a top hand's wages for a lot of years before the fall that crippled him. He has no family, and he's never been much of a spender."

"Did you and the missus hear this confession of his?"

The missus. Deborah smiled. It had a nice ring to it really.

"Yes. So did at least half a dozen others," Trey said.

Deborah told what she had seen and done as succinctly as possible, ignoring the incredulous looks on the other men's faces and the self-satisfied expression on Trey's.

"You beat him with your wedding bouquet?"

"It was all I had, and they weren't real flowers."

"She used my cane to beat the man who stabbed me too," Trey said, sounding so smug she wanted to pinch him. "She's very protective."

The chief closed his eyes for a moment, but couldn't hide his amusement. "All right. Let's see what he has to say."

The chief offered no chairs but allowed Trey and Deborah to stand out of sight near the cell when he and one of his men questioned Herman Gruner. Deborah fished her handkerchief out from her sleeve and buried her nose in it. The cells smelled worse than an outhouse in mid-summer.

"Why don't you wait for me outside?" Trey said in her ear. "The chief is right. This is no place for a lady. Your ears are going to be as offended as your nose."

"I don't care. I want to hear this. He can't use any words you don't use over the linotype."

Sounds of chairs scraping and the chief's voice telling Gruner how much trouble he was in and what he was accused of sounded clearly enough.

"Why did you tell the chief I beat the man with the knife? I only hit him once, and you know it," Deborah whispered. "And now you were stabbed? You insisted it was nothing but a scratch even when you were dripping blood, but now you were stabbed?"

"Editorial license. It makes a better story. Let's listen."

Except there was nothing to listen to. Nothing except increasingly frustrated questions from the chief. Gruner didn't say a word, grunt, or cough.

Finally the chief gave up the attempt and joined them in the hall. "I'll talk to everyone who heard what he said, and after that it's up to the prosecutor. I don't know what he'll do."

"I can get him to talk," Trey said, and walked around the chief into Gruner's sight. Deborah hurried after him.

"My father and I may not like each other, but I guess you know he'll never let you set foot back on the ranch," Trey said to Gruner.

Gruner's eyes went wide. He'd obviously not considered that. "You arrogant bastard, come crawling back after all them years, then strutting around giving orders. Your father's the best man I ever knew. Kept me on all that time I was laid up and found me work after, didn't he?"

"He did," Trey agreed. "He's a saint."

Gruner spit at him. "Better than you'll ever be. You drove him half mad and your mother and sister to tears. You think out in the bunkhouse we didn't all know what you were doing to them good people, and what you'd do if you got your hands on the V Bar C? Driving some fancy little pony, afraid to throw a leg over a real horse, sniffing around the Suttons. You think any of us has any respect for the likes of you?"

"Being an arrogant bastard, I never thought about it. I suppose you're the one who cut the reins and loosened the wheel on the buggy."

"Damn right, and it almost worked."

"It did, and you came close to crushing me like a bug with the wagon after that. How did you beat me to town?"

"I got on a horse and rode, like a man."

"Either you've been lying about your condition for years, or that put you in bed for days."

Hot fury chased away the cold anger, and Gruner's face reddened to match the stripes of the wire marks. "I never lied. I had to stay in town for days all right. Mr. Van Cleve was decent too. Said I had the time coming. Not like you, firing Lenny Hart over dogs. Dogs."

"So after that you had to pay someone else to do your killing for you. He wasn't very good at it, you know. Cal Sutton figures you were too cheap to hire anybody worth his salt."

"Sutton. That bastard!" Gruner launched himself off the cot he was sitting on at Trey, who just stepped back from the bars. The chief and his sergeant wrestled Gruner back to the bed, but Trey didn't make it any easier. "Of course you aren't very good at it either. After all, Deborah Sutton beat you to a fare thee well."

"You traitor! I should have shot you sooner. I should have shot her when she come running at me."

After that everything degenerated into a cursing, shouting babble. Trey took Deborah's arm and led her outside into the clean early evening air. "He's right. He could have shot you," he said, pulling her close.

"No, he couldn't. He was already trying to run away and had his back to me when I first saw him."

"Promise me you won't do anything like that ever again."

"I promise I won't ever do anything like that again unless someone tries to kill you again."

"Aah, Deborah." He pushed her hat brim out of the way and leaned his forehead against hers. When approaching footsteps sounded, Trey brushed his lips over hers before straightening.

"I guess you don't have to worry about him from here on," the chief said. "If he won't plead guilty in court, we'll just bring you in and have you wave a red flag at him again."

"Is he insane?" Deborah asked.

"No more than most we get in here," the chief said. "At his age he'll never be a free man again. We'll keep him until he goes to court and then it will be prison. You go on to your party now and forget about him. And best wishes for—a quieter future."

"I forgot about the reception," Deborah admitted as they walked toward the town hall.

"Me too, but we'd better go eat wedding cake and do whatever else is expected or they'll never forgive us."

"Yes, they would. Let's run away."

"Later. We'll escape together later."

27

"Is it later yet?" Deborah said. "We could slip out the back door before anyone noticed."

Trey looked down at the woman in his arms—his woman, his wife. A smile curved her lips, but the worry was there, deep in her dark eyes. His own nerves ratcheted up a notch. His wife, who hit men with knives and threw herself at men with rifles, was afraid, and only one thing was going to take away the fear—if anything could.

At least she didn't want to stay at the reception as long as possible and put off being alone with her new husband. Maybe that proved her courage. Maybe she believed in getting unpleasant things over with as fast as possible. Whatever her motive, her desire to leave immediately and without a fuss coincided with his own.

Dancing couples filled the floor of the town hall. The reception had been in progress long enough no one seemed to be paying particular attention to the bride and groom. As they circled again, Trey maneuvered to the outer edge of the dancing couples, opened the back door with no hesitation, swung Deborah through, and followed her.

"Being married to a sneaky woman is going to corrupt me, isn't it?"

"Do you think anyone saw us?"

"Everyone, but after the day we had, they're willing to let us get away with it. No newly married couple should have to spend the first hours of their marriage with the police. Your family can throw things at us tomorrow at the railroad station, although I don't expect my mother and sister to brave a crowd of Suttons again that soon."

"Did you know they were coming?"

"No. They surprised me at the house before the ceremony. Really surprised me."

"Does it mean they'll visit us? We won't have to go to the ranch, will we?"

Trey guided her toward the garden where they'd first met, aware of the anxiety in her question. "No, remember I'm forbidden to set foot on the ranch. Mother may visit us once or twice a year when she's in town on her way somewhere else. Alice even less often. She and Vernon live in Kansas City when they're not hiding out with a new baby."

"Little Web really is adorable. How old were you when you made them stop calling you that?"

"Five. I just stopped answering to it until they gave up."

"Maybe this Web will be like you and make his own life."

"Maybe he'll find an easier way."

"Your father...."

"Don't worry about him. We'll stay estranged, as they call it, until he's doddering. At that point if he gets maudlin and wants to see me, I'll probably give in, and we'll have one last raging quarrel, but you'll never have to see him. Let's pretend he lives in China."

He stopped between the two benches they had used a year ago. By the light of the half moon shining from a cloudless sky, Deborah's features were shadowed—beautiful, beloved, and easily distinguished. He cupped her face in his hands and whispered against her lips. "If we were this close that night, we could have seen each other."

"I'm glad we weren't," she whispered back. "I would have run and never known you."

He kissed her, a soft promise of more to come. "No more running?"

"No more running."

They left the garden and headed for home. Her hand was cold in his, perhaps nerves, perhaps the cooling April night. Trey shrugged out of his jacket and draped it around her shoulders.

"Now you'll be cold," she said.

"Being near you has this mysterious warming effect. I'm fine."

She turned her head away, but kept a comfortable hold on his arm.

Their house came into sight, soft gray paint pale in the night. Instead of opening the wood gate, Trey led the way between houses to the alley.

"Where are we going?"

"I have something to show you."

What had been a one-horse barn sat behind the house. Trey fumbled with the kerosene lantern he knew hung by the door, wishing the barn had gas lights like the house, and heard Deborah gasp when the wick caught and light reflected

from the glossy dark green paint of a new Columbia Runabout.

"Jamie convinced me you'd like one of these for a wedding
present better than jewelry."

"Oh. Oh." She walked to the vehicle slowly, pulled off a
glove and ran her hand over the leather fender, touched the
dashboard. "It's really ours?"

"Yours. I have Irene."

"Oh, but for town. Trey, this is…. It's beautiful."

"You have to be careful, and you have to let Jamie teach
you how to drive it."

"Only if you do too. After all, I can't go back to the mill
alone, can I?"

"I hope not, but I have a feeling you're still going to sneak
off on me now and then."

She hugged him around the neck and kissed him. A good
kiss, one without any reserve he could detect.

"What did you mean when you said the next time I did
this, I had to laugh?"

"After the shooting contest, I saw Norah rush into Caleb's
arms. He kissed her right there in front of the crowd, and she
kissed him back, and she laughed. I watched them, and I
thought, that's what I want. I want a wife who loves me like
that."

Her arms were still around his neck, his around her waist,
holding her close.

"Twice now you've thrown yourself in my arms and kissed
me. I want it to happen without you being frightened into it.
I want you to be laughing."

He had another kiss in mind, but she pulled away.

"We have to go inside. I have something to show you too."

Disappointed, he followed her into the house. A long narrow box lay on the only table in their parlor, and his spirits rose.

"This wasn't here when I left for the church today," Trey said, staring at it.

"No. Uncle Eli brought it here after you left."

"Tell me that's not Caleb's Big Fifty."

"No, of course not. Open it."

The rifle in the box was indeed a Sharps .50-90, if not Caleb's, its twin.

"Mannie Ascher bought it, thinking it would help him beat Caleb, but it didn't. He tries something new every year as if the right gun will make him better. When I inquired about buying this for you, he said if he could help beat Caleb that way, he'd give it to me. He let me pay in the end but probably only about half what it's worth."

Trey lifted the rifle out of the box and ran a hand over the barrel then the stock with reverence. "Do I have to win for you to kiss and laugh?"

She tipped her head to one side as if considering. "Another draw will do."

"Does Caleb know?"

"No, and you have to stop calling him that. He won't let anyone but Norah and the three of us call him that."

"He's making an exception for me. Since I'm family now, he says."

"He really likes you."

"I'm very likable."

"Yes, you are."

"Lovable even."

"Yes."

The tension flooded back into her face, fear into her eyes.

"Let's go upstairs," Trey said, placing the rifle back in the box.

She nodded and led the way, looking small and vulnerable inside her repaired lacy dress.

Trey watched her, his own desire muted by fear he wouldn't find a way to love her that would stop her fear, much less bring her pleasure. She'd come to enjoy kissing. That made at least a starting place.

"Can the light be on?"

Her request was the opposite of what he expected, yet hadn't he once thought she needed to leave the dark and come into the light? He lit the lamp in the sconce beside the bed, enough light to see by, a single golden glow. "Enough?"

"Yes, thank you." Her voice was high and thin, her breathing ragged.

He began pulling pins from her hair. It fell down her back in a silky dark cloud, taking his breath away. He swallowed hard, forced a matter of fact tone. "I'm not going to hurt you, you know."

"I know."

As big a lie as she'd ever told by the look of things. "I have some liquor downstairs. Suppose I bring you a glass of brandy. It will help you relax."

She shook her head violently. Good old Aunt Em's influence there, he'd bet.

"What else?"

"Talk to me," she whispered. "Your voice. I'll know it's you, and your voice makes me feel safe."

He slid his fingers into the silk of her hair by her temples, stroked her brows with his thumbs. "Aah, but I can't talk when I kiss you, and I want to kiss you. Shall I see if I can kiss and hum?"

One corner of her mouth curled, and that was enough. He kissed her, feathered kisses over her face and neck, until shining eyes and parted lips invited a slow, deep kiss, exploration.

Between kisses he talked. Talked of how much he loved her, how beautiful he found her and each part of her, his thoughts that first time he'd seen her at the ice cream parlor, before he knew she was his mystery woman.

She relaxed and kissed him back. This was going to be all right. All the lust for her he'd first denied and then hidden surged hot in his blood until he ached so fiercely he wondered if he could get his trousers and drawers off without exploding.

Beginning to unfasten the dozens of small hooks hidden under a seam of her dress turned her into a marble statue.

"Would you rather do this yourself?" he asked. "Get into a gown in another room?"

"No." More a breath than a word.

Unsure if he should continue, unable not to, he murmured more soothing words he no longer heard or understood himself. Petticoat, corset cover, corset, drawers, the layers that protected her seemed endless.

He kissed, caressed, whispered. She neither resisted nor responded.

Throwing covers aside, he eased her onto the bed, traced gentle circles on the soft skin behind her knee as he removed one stocking, the other. Her legs were long and slim, exactly like the ones he had dreamed of having wrapped around him.

Touching her now, kissing the arch of a foot, achieving that dream seemed farther away than ever. Except. Her bowed head lifted. She touched his mouth, traced his lower lip with a look of wonder.

The chemise could stay. So could his shirt. It wouldn't hide everything, but maybe enough to temper her fear. Yanking off the rest of his own clothes as rapidly as possible, Trey forgot to talk, too afraid the signs of her arousal would disappear at the sight of his own.

She didn't watch, turned her head away before he finished. Biting back a curse, he slid down on the bed beside her, silent again, as he pressed his head to her breasts and was still, aroused, frustrated, half afraid to go on.

"Please talk some more." Her voice was still barely a whisper.

Aah, yes. That talking thing. Her first sound of pleasure came when he cupped a breast, rubbed the nipple to a hard peak through the thin fabric of her chemise. Leaving even so fragile a barrier was too much. He slid the straps from her shoulders, pushed the cloth to her waist. Her breasts were as he'd envisioned, perfect in size, tipped with rose brown nipples.

She touched him again when he kissed the rounded white surface, her hand knotting in his hair. She didn't try to pull him away, but her fingers tightened as he sucked one nipple, licked, kissed, fanned his breath over wet skin.

Afraid to kiss lower, he stroked a hand along her ribs, circled her navel with a fingertip, caressed her inner thighs until they parted slightly. She was wet. Not drenched but wet, yet she pulled away from his exploring fingers.

Unsure what else to do, he lowered his body over hers, nudged her legs apart, and pushed his aching cock partway inside. She'd asked for light, but now her eyes were closed, her hands fisted at her sides.

Sensation overwhelmed uncertainty. He thrust deeper, withdrew, stroked slowly.

Talk. Talk. He couldn't talk. Yes, he could, damn it. "Sshh, sshh, it's just me, just me, and I love you, am loving you."

He moved faster, not wanting to frighten more but not wanting to prolong. He finished quickly, the bursting pleasure of physical release giving no other kind of pleasure.

Rolling off onto his back beside her, he wondered what he'd just done. Her eyes remained closed. No tears, no sign of flight.

He wished he had stashed some of that liquor here in the bedroom. His mouth was dry. He could really use a drink.

Her hand moved slowly toward him, touched his wrist, moved to his hand and took hold. He closed his own eyes for a moment, relief washing through him.

SHE LOVED HIM, yet she had still expected pain, that feeling of strangling, the frantic need for a breath that wouldn't come. She had expected wrongness, the sense of being less, her feelings and desires of no consequence.

When he had begun removing her clothes, memory had frozen everything inside. Then the difference of what he was doing had melted the ice away, melted *her*. She had expected taking. He had given.

When her hand touched his, he laced his fingers through hers, his thumb rubbing gently on the side of her hand.

"I was afraid."

"I know."

"A blind man would know, I suppose."

"Mm hm."

"I didn't expect.... I think I could like that."

"Could? What would have to happen for you to like it?"

"Maybe if you sang." She turned her head, looked into indignant green eyes, and smiled.

He smiled back. "All that talking was the most I could manage. You need a stronger husband."

"I'm keeping the one I have."

He hooked the covers from the end of the bed with a foot and pulled them up. "I like looking at you, but you're getting goose bumps."

They lay companionably side by side for a while before she closed her eyes again.

"Everyone knew Mama was dying except Judith and me, I think. She lost babies after Judith, so we thought it would be like that. She'd be in bed a few days and then fine, and we were so excited about Miriam. A baby sister."

She concentrated on the warmth of his hand, the occasional stroke of his thumb.

"The first time—the first time he touched me that way was before she died. He said since I was the oldest I would have to take over Mama's duties until he married again. I didn't want to. I struggled and fought, and he held my throat, and he said if I wouldn't then Judith would have to. So I stopped fighting."

She was afraid Trey would say something, try to touch more than her hand, but he stayed quiet beside her, listening, the way he had always listened.

"Mama saw something. She must have. She wrote a letter, and Caleb came for us. Papa went to the door with the shotgun. He always did that. When Caleb said who he was and that he'd come for us, Papa reached for the shotgun and brought it around, and it boomed so loud, I almost didn't hear the pistol shots. Papa fell back inside the doorway. He didn't move, and there was blood, and Caleb stood there looking at me, still holding the pistol. I couldn't move, and he didn't either, and then Norah came. She came running."

Deborah opened her eyes, staring at the ceiling without really seeing.

"I felt guilty because I knew it was my fault. Caleb came and killed Papa because of me. And I felt guilty because I didn't feel glad the way Judith did. Papa was always strict, stern. Everything was better with Uncle Jason and Aunt Emma, and I was happy that it wouldn't happen ever again, but...."

She stopped, unable to say the devastating words.

"But he was your father."

She turned her head, amazed that he understood. "Yes. No one ever understood that. No one ever said his name, our real name, again."

"You said it. You told me."

"Yes. It's the first time I ever said it since then too. Because you.... Because you always seemed to know, to understand."

"There's a reason I understand," Trey said. "You just see my father as bad. The first time you ever heard of him, you heard about the greed and the hired killers, but when I was a boy he was my hero. He ran the ranch. Everyone deferred to him. I see Caleb with Jacey and Ginny, and I realize he wasn't much of a father to us in some ways, but he was *there*. The one who made everything happen."

She raised his hand and kissed the knuckles, keeping their arms against her stomach instead of between them.

"I was sixteen when he decided to teach me how to run what I'd inherit. He couldn't do that without letting me see the truth, and he never understood why it bothered me. And the truth is he cheated. He stole. He took advantage of anyone vulnerable. He paid other men to kill for him. For two years I made excuses. I tried to be like my mother and see only what I wanted to, and I almost succeeded, until one day in Chicago, he and his partners started talking about a deal they wanted with me sitting right there."

He stopped, didn't seem inclined to go on. Kissing his hand again didn't spur him on, so Deborah did the same for him as he had done for her. She waited.

"They wanted to buy an entire city block, tear down the derelict buildings there and put up office buildings. The derelict buildings were tenements, and one owner refused to sell, at least for what Father and his partners wanted to pay. They sat there and discussed the best way to burn that building and whether to have their hired arsonist set fire to the whole block or just the one building. People lived in those shabby apartments."

She turned on her side and pressed her hand flat in the center of his chest, wishing she knew better what might comfort. Him? Her? Both of them.

"I tried to talk to him, but he couldn't believe I saw anything other than the profit he could make. For him there's no right or wrong, only a calculation of the chance of getting caught. I knew I should tell someone what they planned, but all I did was write an anonymous letter to the police. They probably threw it away the day it arrived. I should have gone in person. I should have been willing to swear to what I heard. But I didn't, because he's my father. So those buildings burned, and an old man died. That man died because I couldn't stand the thought of my father in prison. When we got back to the ranch, I took every dollar of cash I could find on the place, packed a bag, and walked out. I didn't intend to ever come back."

Deborah studied the side of his face, assessing, touched his cheek, and he pulled her into his arms. "We'd better hope sins of the father is just an old wives' tale," he said.

"I have to. My grandfather, my mother's father, was terrible too."

"My mother's family are good people. They took me in back then, helped me find jobs so I could go to school. We'll spend a few days with them in Tennessee. You'll like them."

"Caleb says Uncle Jason is a saint."

"One saint in the family only counterbalances Caleb. You need more."

"You like him."

"To my chagrin, I do."

Hearing his voice while lying in his arms was even better than his voice alone. She breathed in his scent, ran her fingers along his collar bone through the opening at the neck of his shirt, felt the rise and fall of his breathing.

Her skin felt—alive—like a separate thing that needed touching, especially her breasts. Well, except maybe her stomach even more so, and then down lower where everything still felt—stirred up—as if having him back inside might fix that achy throb.

A small spot in the hollow of his throat pulsed. She touched it with her tongue. He tasted ever so slightly salty. The flutter of his pulse grew stronger and quicker, so did his breathing.

"You do realize you're stoking fires here, don't you?"

"If you'll take the shirt off, you don't have to sing."

He sat up, whipped the shirt off over his head, and dropped it over the side of the bed. She wiggled out of her wadded up chemise and did the same. The feel of his skin against hers along her entire length was even better than she'd imagined. She explored his chest and belly with a tentative hand.

"Can I talk a little less this time?"

"Mm hm."

He kissed her, at first slow and deep, then soft and light, brushing kisses over her face, down her throat. She kissed back, touched and caressed. She laughed when she elicited a growl trying to do to his nipples what he did to hers, moaned when he demonstrated the proper way to nibble there.

Laughter dissolved into something fierce and serious when he kissed lower. She lost the ability to do more than cling to him. His exploring fingers frightened her again, and she pulled away. This time he persisted, soothed, murmured of love and need.

She trusted him, she did. Trembling, she held still for his touch, expecting he would explore the entrance to her body. Instead he stroked a place above, and sensation shot through her like a streak of light. Again. Again. Red stars exploded behind her eyelids, the world fell apart, and she shattered with a cry.

"Sshh. Sshh." His weight. Thick hot heat filling the hollow place. She tried to catch his rhythm, meet him, curved her arms around his back as if she could pull him deeper. Sensation shivered through her again, less this time, a lovely shadow of before.

He stilled, made a deep sound in his throat. Heat on heat deep inside. She smiled to herself and tightened her arms, wanting to keep him.

"Here." He rolled, taking her with him.

"Is that how it's supposed to be?" she whispered.

"On good days."

"That felt—almost holy."

"Mm."

His eyelids were at half mast, his voice slow. She wanted to cuddle down and sleep too.

"I'll get the light," she whispered.

"Mm. You need the light."

Deborah sat up and looked at her sleeping husband. After a moment, she pulled the cover higher over his scarred shoulder, bent down, and kissed his cheek.

"You are the light," she said and reached to turn off the gas lamp.

Afterword

DEBORAH STARED IN disbelief at the two old men sitting behind the chair Judith had saved for her. So much for any plans to stay far away from the old gossips this year.

Mr. Ascher's grin told her their presence wasn't an accident. "I hope the rifle Mannie sold you wasn't too much for your husband and he figured out how to use it. I bet on him this year."

"Shouldn't you bet on your son?" Deborah asked frostily.

"I put a few dollars on Mannie to make him feel good, but my real money's on your husband, even if he does still carry that cane."

"His fancy stick?" Deborah said, trying for ice this time. She waved the plain wood cane Trey had left with her back and forth for emphasis.

Ascher's grin faded. As it should. If either one of these old codgers said one nasty word about Trey, she was going to grab their scrawny necks and....

"Well, I bet on Sutton," Mr. Lawson said, oblivious. "Experience counts. Where'd you put your money, Miz Van Cleve?"

"I don't bet." Deborah turned her back on the old men and took her seat.

Judith leaned close. "If you spent any longer out on the field wishing Trey luck, they'd have charged you an entry fee."

She did that annoying thing with her eyebrows, and Deborah ignored her. "Miriam really isn't here?" she asked, searching all the Sutton faces filling the front row of the audience for Hubbell's first Fourth of July shooting contest of the Twentieth Century.

"No, and she's not being snooty again. She's so sick every morning she'll be lucky to crawl out of bed and clean up in time for the fireworks tonight. I was the same for months with Emmy. I told her to expect a girl."

Deborah resisted the urge to place a telltale hand over her stomach. Her monthly flow was two weeks late now, and she felt vaguely queasy in the mornings. If she never got as sick as Miriam, did that mean a boy? She wasn't telling anyone, not even Trey, until more time passed, she saw the doctor, and could be sure.

"You look like a cat with a canary feather stuck on his chin," Judith said. "Do you know something about this contest I don't?"

Deborah shook her head and raised her voice a little as she answered. "No, if anyone thinks I can give them inside information for betting, they're wrong. I've watched Trey and Caleb practice together, and once they pass 700 yards, you might as well flip a coin to decide which one to bet on."

Behind her, Deborah heard unhappy muttering.

Judith squinted as she did the math. "Seven hundred.... Can they even see the target at that distance?"

"They're wondering about that too with these paper targets," Deborah said. "I guess we'll find out."

"We're going to be here all day."

"Not all day, but quite a while unless there's a surprise."

The Mayor had a bullhorn this year, but no one in the audience paid him any more attention than the contestants did as they waited on the field.

"If this thing is going over 700 yards, I hope Caleb won't let the Mayor prattle on too long," Judith said.

Knowing snickers sounded from behind them, and sure enough there was Caleb's white handkerchief waving around before he ran it over the barrel of his Sharps.

Deborah heard all sorts of whispers and murmurs behind her. A tap on the shoulder had her jerking away.

"Sorry, Miz Van Cleve," Mr. Lawson said, not looking sorry at all. "I just thought you should know, word's going around we got professional shooters down there. Your husband and your cousin know that?"

Professional shooters? What did that mean? Caleb and Trey had noticed the two strangers, everyone had. So they weren't just men from neighboring counties come to try their hand?

Much as she didn't want to join the old men in gossip, she couldn't help asking, "What do you mean professional?"

"That's how they make their living," Mr. Ascher said. "They travel around to fairs and contests. Sometimes they put on exhibitions and charge admission. I just heard that fellow in the duster used to be in Buffalo Bill's Wild West Show."

"But first prize is only fifty dollars. Even if they win most of the time, how could they make a living from contests like ours?"

"Betting," Mr. Lawson said with a frown. "If I'd a known about them before I put my money down, I would a kept it. I bet they're in cahoots, and they'll cheat."

Judith was listening too. "Cheating Caleb would be a very bad idea," she said with a frown. "Is it too late to warn them?"

Yes, it was too late. The men were raising their rifles. Deborah barely got her bits of cotton into her ears before the first volley came. Once again Lawson and Ascher had spoiled her pleasure in watching the contest.

She had expected the whole thing to boil down to competition between two well-matched men who liked each other. Now anxiety knotted her stomach.

TREY FELT GOOD, really good. Maybe it was arrogant, but he and Caleb had already agreed whichever one of them won this year would buy the family dinner at the First Street Hotel.

After that, he and Deborah would leave the Suttons to their own devices and stroll down to the town hall to watch the fireworks from one of the benches there. Side by side this year, with her in the curve of his arm. With luck, he could even talk her into....

A small clod of dirt landed on the front of his shirt. He had denim trousers and a blue cotton work shirt on this year, but still.... He brushed the dirt off and frowned at Caleb, who wasn't impressed.

"Stop daydreaming and pay attention or Jacey will beat you. The victor only gets the spoils if he wins."

Deborah would be equally generous, win or lose, and Caleb had to know it because Norah would be the same, but he was right. Jacey wasn't a threat to his father or to Trey yet, but he would be in a few years. Some of the other shooters were decent. Ascher got better every year, and whoever the strangers were, they wouldn't have entered if they didn't think they were better than average shots.

Trey settled down and focused.

Switching off and using his father's rifle to make his shot at each distance, Jacey made it past 450 yards and accepted Caleb and Trey's congratulatory hugs and slaps on the shoulder with shy head bobs before jogging off the field. Ascher didn't miss until 500 yards and was close to ecstatic.

The volunteers had foreseen this year's distance. They had an elaborate signal system set up with flags so that the men checking the targets and replacing them knew when it was safe to go on the field and could signal hits and misses without anyone having to run back and forth.

Trey and Caleb had expected to be alone on the field past 500 yards, but both the strangers were still with them. The short fellow in the fancy shirt with silky looking fringes hanging from his sleeves carried an 1885 Winchester single-shot and tended to let out loud barks of laughter at times Trey would have preferred quiet.

The redhead in the duster was worse, his breech-loading Remington pointed every which way between shots. Trey only knew of the long-range accuracy of those models by reputation, but he knew they gave one advantage. The Winchester and the Remington together would barely weigh as much as a Sharps Big Fifty.

Duster's position was to Caleb's left. Shorty was on Trey's right. Trey heard Caleb tell Duster to watch where he pointed his rifle, once, twice. The man was a fool. There wouldn't be a third warning. Trey tried not to imagine what Caleb would do next.

Closing in on 700 yards, the target was no more than a white dot in the distance, and Trey's pleasure in the contest and the summer day had evaporated into a grim determination to make Duster and Shorty wish they'd stayed home.

They passed 700 yards, and before taking his shot, Duster shrugged out of his coat and managed to shake it out so that it fluttered inches from Caleb's face just as he squeezed the trigger. On Trey's right, Shorty's bark of laughter sounded louder and longer than ever in perfect time with the gesture.

Trey had to wait, drag in several long calming breaths before taking his own shot. Caleb stood relaxed, and to Trey's surprise the men down the field signaled all four shots had gone true.

They all set up again, raised their rifles. Something was wrong. After each shot, Trey had been aware of Caleb reloading, his movements mirroring Trey's own. Not this time. Caleb hadn't reloaded.

Trey whipped his head around in time to see Caleb flip his rifle, seize the barrel in both hands, and club Duster's raised rifle into his jaw. The Remington would never be good for anything again. The man would be a long time healing. He fell as if poleaxed and lay still.

"I told you to stop waving things around," Caleb said, looking down at the unconscious man. "This fellow isn't going to make the next round," he called over to the gaping Mayor. "Better get someone to drag him out of the way."

"You aren't making the next round either!" Shorty yelled, all but jumping up and down. "You can't just kill a competitor. What's wrong with you? Are you crazy? Someone needs to get the police."

Leaving his rifle waist high but aimed straight ahead, finger on the trigger, Trey swung around toward Shorty. "He had two warnings. I'm giving you one. Shut up."

Shorty was smarter than Duster. He shut up.

Trey had cotton in his ears to dull the sound of the rifle fire enough to save his hearing, but not so much he couldn't hear at all. The muffling of sound had helped him tolerate the barking laughter although it still grated. He dug the cotton out now and listened to the Mayor and Caleb behind him. The Mayor sounded shaky, Caleb unconcerned.

"Mr. S-Sutton, I'm s-sorry," the Mayor stuttered, "but what you did. I do think he tried to cheat, no police—at least I'm not—but I can't, you know I c-can't...."

"That's all right," Caleb said. "I'd disqualify myself if you didn't, but next year, instead of telling us about the Declaration of Independence, how about you read some rules about behaving on the firing line. Say it's for everyone's safety. This fellow sure would have been safer behaving himself."

Trey decided Shorty had calmed down enough to be no threat and looked around in time to see Caleb nudge Duster with the toe of his boot. A loud moan proved the man was alive.

Two volunteers carried Duster away. Caleb showed no signs of leaving. He cradled the big buffalo gun across his chest and stood beside the Mayor unmoving except for a wink at Trey. "I'll just help the Mayor monitor the rest of this contest. He's upset."

Trey almost barked out a laugh as loud as Shorty's. He moved over to Caleb's former position, putting more distance between himself and the other man, raised his rifle, drew in a deep breath, let half of it out, and steadied his sights on the minute white dot in the distance.

Shorty was good. Even after the violence and threats, he was good enough he didn't miss until just short of 800 yards. The problem was Trey missed that shot too. His shoulder ached as viciously as it had last year in spite of the padded vest under his shirt that Deborah had designed for him. The Sharps felt as if it weighed sixty pounds instead of sixteen.

They set up again. Trey's concentration wavered. He remembered how alone he felt last year, thought about how different things were now. He pictured Deborah in the stands waiting for him, keeping a secret she thought was only hers. How would she react to his winning? To his losing?

The words Caleb had used to lift him out of the chair the final time last year came back to him. Did he want to go down on his belly? He regained focus. They were at the outer limit of the range he could be sure of without a tripod or other support, but the same must be true for Shorty.

The target was as much in his imagination as his sight. Even the muffled sounds around him faded. The world narrowed down to the long corridor of distance between him and the white square of paper, the weight of the rifle, the scent of gun smoke. Shorty's rifle spoke. Trey hesitated, took another breath, squeezed the trigger gently.

Flags fluttered. Caleb whooped and almost knocked Trey down with a whack on the shoulder. Trey whacked back and gave his own whoop, celebrating the end of it all as much as the victory. Ignoring Shorty, who looked too stunned to notice, Trey shook the Mayor's hand, thanked the volunteers.

Spectators streamed out of the viewing stand toward them, small in the distance. Trey matched Caleb stride for stride, eager to get back to Deborah. At first he searched in vain for her in the crowd. There. Her dress was pale green, a yellow ribbon fluttered behind her.

Clutching her raised skirt in one hand, holding her hat with the other, she sped toward him, more beautiful than any woman had a right to be.

Trey forgot everything else. The rifle slipped from his hand, and he began to run, awkward at first, then with the same ease he'd once thought gone forever.

He slowed and caught her before they crashed together, lifted her in the air, and kissed her. Right there, in front of family, friends, neighbors, and strangers, Deborah wrapped her arms around his neck and kissed him back. And when he raised his head, she kissed him again. And she laughed.

Author's Note

FOR THIS BOOK more than the previous romances, my first readers had questions about historical matters, so I'm going to enlarge on some of them here. First of all, as to "patent" medicines. Until the Pure Food and Drug Act was passed in the U.S. in 1906, anyone could concoct any recipe and sell it as a cure for anything.

These were "patent" medicines, which weren't patented at all. The name was a holdover from the good old days in England when the King put his seal of approval or patent on certain recipes. And you could buy anything in 1898–1900 America. The medicines almost all had a high alcohol content, but they also often contained narcotics and sometimes contained a dash of a poison like strychnine.

Vendors advertised their cure-alls in wonderful and inventive ways, and small papers like the *Hubbell Herald* relied heavily on advertising revenue from patent medicines. Some of these formulas worked, and some survive today in modified form: Absorbine, Bayer Aspirin, Luden's Cough Drops, Phillip's Milk of Magnesia, Vicks Vapo Rub. I've used all but one of those (the Absorbine on horses).

It's also true that quinine did not magically fix up all those who suffered from malarial fevers and that far more men who fought in the Spanish-American War were laid low by fever and disease than bullets. Patent medicines containing quinine and methylene blue did work for some of those men when pure quinine did not. In 1891 Paul Ehrlich proved that methylene blue, a dye he was using to stain slides, could kill malaria.

Were soldiers returning from the Spanish-American War really hospitalized and quarantined in tents in Montauk, New York? Yes, absolutely. Remember that Long Island in 1898 was not like Long Island today. The tent hospital, called Camp Wikoff, was situated on 5,000 acres leased by the government for that purpose. For more background and a photograph, see www.spanamwar.com/campwikoff.html.

Did you wonder about Trey's paralysis and recovery? Yes, complete (inability to move or feel) paraplegia can happen from such spinal trauma. And, yes, there have been cases of spontaneous recovery, rare, but it has happened, almost always within four months of the original injury.

Were there really police in 1899-1900 as opposed to the town marshals and sheriffs we're all used to? Oh, yes. Not only yes, but to my surprise I found that in 1873 Wichita, Kansas (when Wyatt Earp enforced the law there), what Wichita had was a police department. Wyatt was a policeman.

Electric cars were another surprise for me. In the early days of automobiles, electrics beat out both gasoline and steam. In 1900 New York City, the vast majority of taxi cabs were electric vehicles. Gasoline engines came into prominence after battery-powered ignition systems were developed and hand cranking was no longer necessary to start the cars (and

Henry Ford pioneered more affordable gasoline automobiles). Also, of course, the vehicles with gas engines could go much farther on a tank of gas than an electric could go on a charge, and in the end the gasoline vehicle could go much faster too.

The Columbia Runabouts I mention in *Into the Light* would have been the Ford Focuses of their day, small and economical. Even so, consider the price Jamie was charging ($950) versus the average American annual income of the day, which was about $450 or the equivalent of about $5,000 in 2004. Median annual income back then was $1,200 for male manual labor.

If you'd like to see some of those old vehicles, you can find wonderful old photographs online. I particularly liked the collection at www.earlyamericanautomobiles.com/1890b.htm although the Columbia shown there is not a Runabout.

When I first dreamed up this story, I thought Hubbell's annual Fourth of July shooting contest was my unique invention, born of a desire to use Trey's and Caleb's talents with a gun. Imagine my surprise when a little research showed me that in that time period shooting matches were popular spectator sports! Thousands came to watch the biggest matches, and distances started at 1,000 yards and went to as much as 3,000. Needless to say rules were more complicated, but I kept Hubbell's event smaller and simpler.

Oh, and lastly, if you would like to see a Sharps rifle "in action," rent *Quigly Down Under*. Not only does it feature a Sharps buffalo gun, you get Tom Selleck in one of the best "Western" movies ever.

I hope you enjoyed *Into the Light*.

Ellen O'Connell

Printed in Great Britain
by Amazon

64976628R00189